IRONBOTTOM SOUND

IRONBOTTOM SOUND

Lindsay Baly

Walker and Company
New York

Published in the United States of America in 1989
by the Walker Publishing Company, Inc.

Library of Congress Cataloging-in-Publication Data

Baly, Lindsay.
    Ironbottom sound / Lindsay Baly.
        p.   cm.
    Reprint. Originally published: Worcestershire, England : Malvern
Pub. Co., c1986.
    ISBN 0-8027-1063-8
    1. World War, 1939–1945—Fiction. 2. Guadalcanal Island (Solomon
Islands), Battle of, 1942–1943—Fiction. I. Title.
PR9619.3.B317I76   1989
823—dc19   88-25866
                                                                    CIP

Printed in the United States of America

10   9   8   7   6   5   4   3   2   1

IRONBOTTOM SOUND

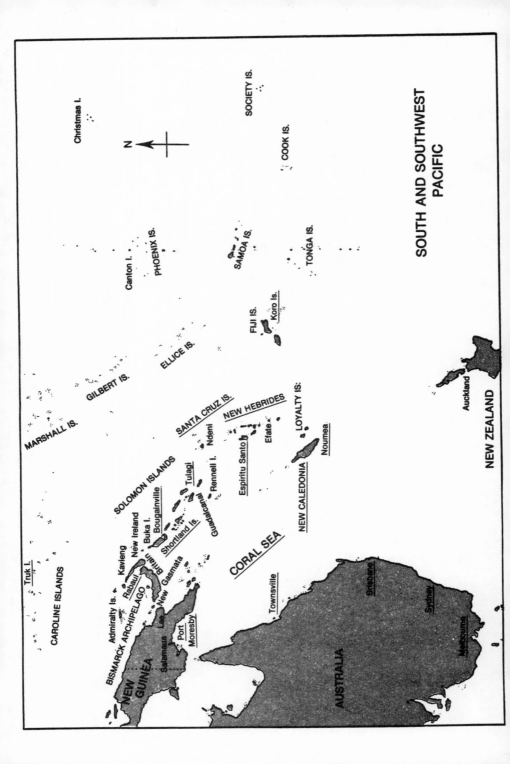

SOUTH AND SOUTHWEST PACIFIC

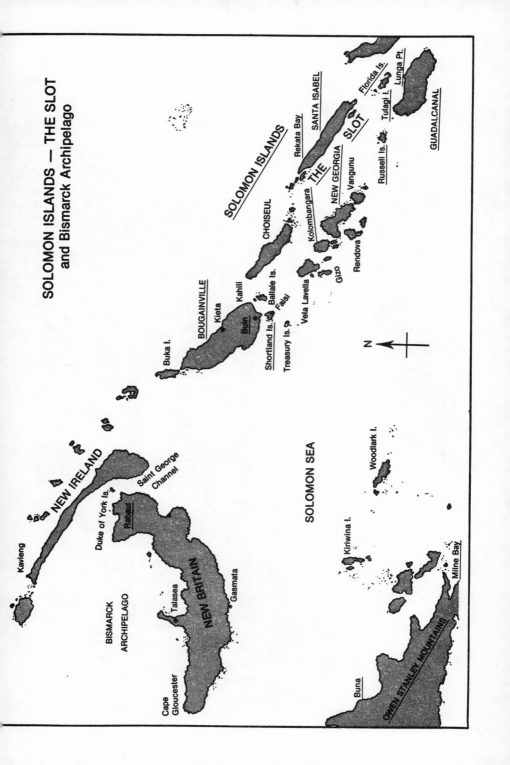

SOLOMON ISLANDS — THE SLOT
and Bismarck Archipelago

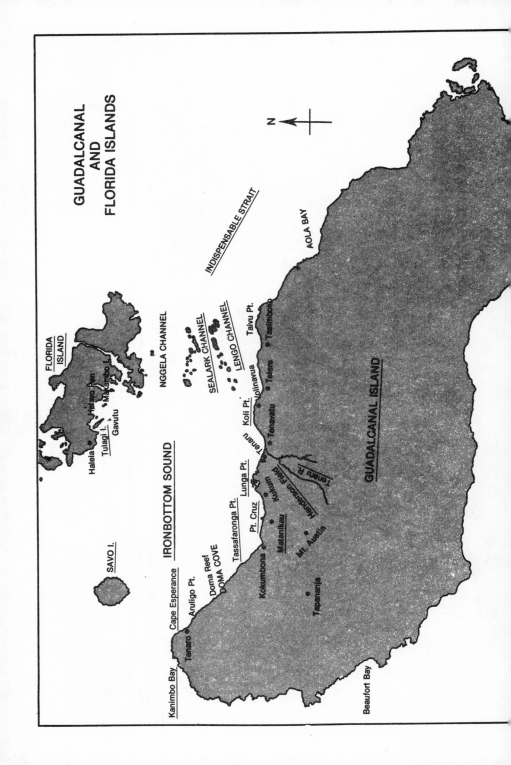

PREFACE

A critic has said that the trick in writing historical fiction is to reconstruct without distorting, yet distort without lying. I have tried to follow the critic's maxim. The literal truth of a story such as this would throw a jumble of imponderables together with the haphazard and outlandish and would not make for a smooth, or even credible, tale in fictional form.

For the sake of narrative, I have taken some liberties with the chronology of unimportant events, but the thrust of the story mirrors the times. In particular, I have reconstructed the naval battles of the Guadalcanal campaign as faithfully as I can. The unnamed Australian destroyer at the Battle of Savo Island did not exist, and neither did its nameless counterpart at the Battle of Surigao Strait, but otherwise, the parts played by individual Allied and Japanese ships are in accordance with previously published accounts. It is especially true of a battle that no two observers will interpret events in exactly the same way, but the book will succeed in an important respect if survivors from both combatant sides find here no errors of fact. As I have said in the text, the battles were originally known as the First Battle of Savo Island, Second Savo, Third Savo and so on. They were not given their geographical names until later.

Much of the book's historical content is based on Samuel Eliot Morison's *History of United States Naval Operations in World War II, Vol. 5, The Struggle for Guadalcanal.* (Little,

Brown and Company, Boston, U.S.A., in association with the Atlantic Monthly Press). As he completed the daunting task of recording this epic piece of his country's history, Morison wrote:

'Sometimes I dream of a great battle monument on Guadalcanal; a granite monolith on which the names of all who fell and of all the ships that rest in Ironbottom Sound may be carved. At other times I feel that the jagged cone of Savo Island, forever brooding over the blood-thickened waters of the Sound, is the best monument to the men and ships who here rolled back the enemy tide.'

Lindsay Baly
Kangaroo Ground
Victoria, Australia

Full fathom five thy father lies
Of his bones are coral made;
Those are pearls that were his eyes:
Nothing of him that doth fade,
But doth suffer a sea change
Into something rich and strange.

The Tempest, Act I, Scene II.

CHAPTER ONE

'Chickweed, this is Limbo *himself*. Get those Goddamn cans outa that clambake and formed up on me!'

The exasperated American voice on the tactical radio circuit cut through the confusion and noise on the bridge and the yeoman of signals threw back his head and laughed, an explosive cackle. These Yanks!

Looking round, I could understand 'Limbo', otherwise Commander, Task Force 61, Rear Admiral Richmond Kelly Turner, U.S.N., blowing his top. The destroyer screen had been badly scattered thanks to an accidental sequence of events that was nobody's fault.

It had started an hour ago. The destroyers had been refuelling from the main body when there was a red air alert caused by our own aircraft. A stray flight of Avengers from the aircraft carrier group away to the south of us came in from the wrong direction without identification. They had to be presumed hostile and our refuelling formation broke up. The destroyers raced for their former stations, but at the same time Turner himself ordered a major course change for the whole formation. The resulting confusion as the destroyers turned and raced away again was still ordered, but then U.S.S. *Monssen,* on the starboard wing, got a submarine echo. Sonar responses were suspect at high speed, but it proved to be catching and soon six ships in the screen were hull down on the horizon, chasing apparently non-existent submarines. The rest of us straggled out of formation, unable to close the gaps.

A British task force commander might have described the milling submarine hunters as 'whores at a christening', but I thought I liked 'at a clambake' better after all.

The yeoman had his telescope glued to the heavy cruiser *Australia* wherein the screen commander – 'Chickweed' of the voice circuit or Rear Admiral V.A.C. Crutchley, Royal Navy – resided. The yeoman read the signal flags as they came off the deck.

'Execute to follow,' he called in his deep bass voice. 'Form screen number 31 on axis 314 degrees.' We barely had time to flap through the signal book for the screening diagram and work out our new position when the yeoman shouted 'Stand by... execute!' Chickweed, no doubt smarting under his rebuke, was in a hurry.

I took the ship, dipping and soaring over the big Pacific swells as she built up speed, round the stern of the U.S. destroyer *Mugford* and handed over to young Lachlan, the second officer-of-the-watch.

'Don't overshoot,' I told him. 'Work it out, don't guess it. You have to lose 8 knots and end up in station. What distance away will you reduce speed?'

'Signal from *Australia*, sir.' The only time the yeoman ever used the word 'sir' was when he was reporting a signal. 'Buck up.'

My turn for a kick in the pants. I was tempted to signal back that I was doing revolutions for 28 knots, but thought better of it and climbed into my captain's chair. Martin Field, the first lieutenant, had been hovering in the background and saw his chance to get in a word.

'Can we secure action stations, sir? I could start dinner at 1130 and then we'll be ready for anything that happens this afternoon.' We were still at action stations from the false alarm air attack.

I said he could send one watch to dinner at a time. We were less than twenty-four hours steaming away from our objective and luckily so far undetected by the Japanese, though they must discover us soon, surely.

The engineer officer was at my other elbow and launched into a complicated account of an ailing fuel pump. Could he isolate the forward fuel tanks and get to work on it?

'How much fuel will we have without the forward tanks?'

'Sixty per cent, sir.' We had completed our refuelling.

'Can you still deliver full power, Chief?'

'Yes, sir.'

'Then go ahead.'

He scuttled away, relief flooding his anxious features. He was older, cross-grained – a worrier. He might be a weak link in a crisis.

'The leading steward wants to know if you'll have your dinner up here, sir.' Able Seaman McNab, my cabin hand.

'Yes. No, on second thoughts, I'll come down.' Decisions, great and small, were a commander's lot. 'McNab, why aren't you at your action station?'

I didn't hear what he replied, because Lachlan, who had been sighting through the Stuart's distance meter, reduced speed far too early.

'Jesus, Sub. You're miles too early. Put your revs back on. Give me that thing.'

I took a reading with the distance meter.

'You're still four cables away. Don't you know how to read it? What distance did you work out you will run on, reducing from 28 knots to flank speed?'

'Execute to follow,' bellowed the yeoman again. 'All ships turn together to 314 degrees.'

I took over the con, as the Americans called it, and eased the ship out to port. I was anticipating the turn, cutting the corner of it so that I would end up in station instead of being a good six hundred yards out. Had the turn been the other way, the error would have doubled and we would have been a fitting target for Chickweed's wrath.

'Stand by... execute!'

I dropped the revs to make 20 knots and steered the new course. The circular screen of destroyers was miraculously symmetrical about the fleet centre – the 'Whacky Mac', Admiral Turner's transport, U.S.S. *McCawley* and we were in our appointed place.

'There you are, in station,' I said to Lachlan. 'Be ready to start the zig-zag.' I returned to my chair.

Poor Lachlan. Aged twenty, disguised as a sub-lieutenant after four months' reserve officer's training, how could he be expected to cope with modern fleet work, the like of which would have turned Nelson's captains grey? But he'd learn. He would be a good officer.

This forenoon was typical of the last eleven we had spent on passage since the task force assembled four hundred miles south of Fiji. There were eight cruisers, three of them Australian, and sixteen destroyers, one, (my own), Australian, screening the main body of troop transports. Our air support, under Admiral Fletcher, were the famous carriers *Saratoga, Wasp* and *Enterprise*; they were keeping well to the south, under the protection of the battleship *North Carolina.*

I stretched in the chair and reached into the chart table for a grey manilla folder stamped Operation Watchtower in bold black type. For the hundredth time, I turned the pages.

'Amphibious assault landing of the 1st Division, U.S. Marine Corps... 7th August 1942... 3 miles east of Lunga Point, Guadalcanal... objective newly constructed enemy airstrip... bombardment... gunfire support... interdiction of enemy positions... denial of surface routes available to enemy sea-borne reinforcements...'

Perhaps because I knew it too well already, I was not concentrating. My thoughts drifted off on a familiar path.

I, (Lieutenant Commander Richard Hugh Urquart Fitzallen, Royal Navy), marvelled again at my transition to a new war and a new world. I had started the year on the cruel Murmansk convoy runs, as first lieutenant of a destroyer in a North Sea escort group, but barely three months ago, and all in one hit, I had been promoted, given marching orders for the Mediterranean and my first command, a new Hunt class destroyer. I set out for Malta bursting with pride and anticipation, but arriving at Gibraltar, learned that she had been lost with all hands, mined and sunk off the North African coast.

I grieved as if I had been on board the ship, its captain already. I hung round Gib disconsolate and increasingly depressed as the days went by and no new orders came for me. The captain of the dockyard was an old friend and mentor.

'Well, what do you want to do, Dickie?' he said. 'Why don't you propose something to them? It sometimes works.'

I had had enough of the Arctic for a while, I knew that. The Med would have suited me well enough, but all the small ship commands had just been filled. I would be lucky to get another first lieutenant's job if I stayed there.

The East Indies Fleet based in Ceylon was a possibility, but it had been inactive so far and I was reluctant to commit myself to two years of isolation and boredom there. There did not seem to be much else.

'What about the Pacific Theatre?' asked Captain Macintyre. 'What about Australia? Or New Zealand, or Canada?'

'Love it. But, sir, we have nothing out there.'

'I don't mean us. I mean exchange service with one of their navies.'

Some time ago, over a friendly drink, Captain Macintyre had discussed a confidential report he had written on me which made me feel very much damned with faint praise. He said I was 'not a high flier, but hard working and reliable.' I responded well to challenge, was an above-average ship handler – how he arrived at that I'll never know, for he only grudgingly let me handle his ship on two occasions – and 'should mature, given the new horizons he needs.' He also said something about being practical but lacking imagination. If he made any connection then with the new and limitless horizons of the Pacific Ocean and the great clashes to come there (and I have wondered if he did), I certainly did not. I dare say I lacked the imagination!

Instead, I daydreamed of sun... cricket... brown girls... and that famous beach in Sydney, what was its name? I also remembered two Australians who had been on my subs' courses at Greenwich; quite decent, down-to-earth types who had appealed to me.

The next day I drafted several different versions of a signal to the Admiralty, bringing home between the lines their offensive and callous indifference to my affairs. Then I tore them all up and wrote flatly that, as I had not yet received another appointment, I wished to be considered for exchange duty with the Royal Australian Navy.

Five days later I was on my way, a destroyer captain-designate again. I touched briefly at Navy Office in Melbourne, where it became deflatingly obvious that my good fortune rested not on my reputation but on a desperate shortage of experienced officers, for the Australians were trying to cope with a fourfold expansion of their small fleet. I went on to MacArthur's headquarters in Brisbane, a frontier town full of khaki uniforms and rowdy, crowded pubs and from there I flew by U.S. Navy Catalina to the New Hebrides, then on to Koro in the Fijis, where my new ship and the task force lay. The beaches and the sunburnt girls would have to wait.

By sunset that evening, the dark slopes of Guadalcanal Island were showing well above the horizon on our starboard hand and a smudge of land fine to port represented the high ground of New Georgia.

'Have a good look at it, Pilot,' I said to Lieutenant Marks, the navigating officer. 'The next time you see it in daylight, we'll be through that hole and on the other side – and very close.'

'That's good, sir. Don't like getting my golf clubs wet on long boat trips.'

We laughed, too loudly. There was a headiness in the air. Who would not exult in that headlong zest, the tightening of the stomach nerves and sharpening of the faculties before action?

'Well, get a fix before the light goes and get the first lieutenant up here. I want a final run through the orders.'

I looked round at the formation. The crackling TBS – The Talk Between Ships radio circuit – was momentarily quiet and the breeze had died away. The swell had flattened out in the lee of the land and we purred and ploughed over molten water, almost steady. The bow waves of the escorts stood out sharply in the dusk: to starboard, the destroyers *Patterson, Helm, Blue*, to port, *Jarvis, Bagley, Buchanan*. The rest stretched round in a huge ring. Astern of us there was an inner ring of cruisers: *Astoria, San Juan, Canberra, Australia, Chicago, Hobart, Quincy* and *Vincennes*.

Further astern, inside the double protective ring, the squat black transports lurched along in their box formation.

I watched Toby Marks take a bearing of the setting sun, to check the gyro compass. The familiar routine was reassuring and I felt that the day's spectacular end was being savoured on every bridge. Perhaps it was an omen for tomorrow.

With the sun gone, it was unlikely now that we would be spotted from the air, and, unless we ran into submarines that night, we should arrive undetected. I slept well.

At first light next morning, the ships slipped ghost-like up to the island on a flat sea that merged into a flat grey sky. We lay hove to off Beach Red, north east of Lunga Point, startlingly close to the island, waiting to open fire at preselected targets. I scanned the shoreline anxiously but there was neither sight nor sound of the enemy. It was going like clockwork.

'The Guadalcanal Fire Support Group Commander will direct the bombardment at assigned targets... commencing fire on orders of the Task Force Commander... '

Time to break up the grey conspiracy and give the show away. Now.

'Commence firing,' drawled the voice on TBS as if its owner was stifling a yawn.

The first cat's paw of wind stirred the early morning

vapours and a fish jumped. Then the moment that reversed the order of things passed and that still, remote world vanished forever.

Guadalcanal had begun.

Time 0614. I turned and nodded my permission, with half a wince in anticipation of the blast. A and B mountings fired. An explosion and a blast of air and noise; I'd never get used to it. It felt like being hit on the chest with a log of wood. I also felt a premonition, a panicky moment of regret.

'They're slow. Get them cracking,' I chided Hughes, the gunnery officer. Some other ships had fired their second salvo.

We stepped up the rate. Now dive bombers and fighters from the carriers screamed overhead, strafing the beach. It was warming up. But there were no signs of any Japanese.

By 0700 I thought we were wasting ammunition. By 0800 I was sure. The firing slowed to a deliberate sledge-hammer rhythm.

'Are we on the start line, Pilot?'

'Yes, sir.' Five thousand yards off the beach, the destroyers marked the line of departure for the landing craft.

'Keep her there now.' They were due to move off at 0840. The liaison aircraft made low flying passes at the shore, dropping smoke markers at either end of Beach Red. Right on schedule the landing craft began to straggle past. We checked fire. The nearest one butted into the small chop thirty yards away, a square-nosed, unhandy-looking barge showing no sign of life within. But as we watched a helmeted head appeared over the gunwhale and a man sprawled over it, vomiting.

'Get down! Get that man down!' we heard clearly.

'Lootenant, he's seasick... ' The rest was lost, but the figure disappeared.

'Poor bastards,' rumbled Yeoman Treloar.

They passed on and now we had another job, to lay down a barrage on the beach itself to a depth of 200 yards, ceasing fire when the landing craft were 1,300 yards offshore. We fired and duly ceased. There were no Japanese there.

Then there was a merciful rest from gunfire while we stood by, awaiting fire support calls from the invaders. The assault landing gained momentum, but we had not yet fired a shot in real anger. We heard occasional rifle fire from the jungle as the sweating leathernecks pushed up the slopes from the beach and we assumed they had caught some fleeing Japanese, at last. The Wildcat and Dauntless squadrons from the carriers patrolling south of Guadalcanal swooped and roared overhead and American ships cut the water on their appointed tasks, unopposed. It was a scene of strenuous organized activity, a triumphant day for the Americans. The tension eased.

But eighteen miles north across the sound lay Tulagi Harbour on Florida Island, where the second prong of the assault had apparently run into opposition. We could hear more concentrated rumbles of high explosive from this direction and see aircraft diving into thin columns of black smoke. There must be frightful scenes of death over there, the tearing apart of trunks and limbs and squealing, pig-struck agony.

'Cup of tea, sir?'

'No thanks!' No imagination, indeed!

Our bombardment liaison officer did not call for fire support until 1000. There was a quick, businesslike exchange on the radio, the passing of grid references, then A mounting trained round and fired a ranging salvo. The spotter called for a range correction of 200 yards and then four salvoes; they got smoothly away and we waited.

'Oh, that's a crackerjack! Right on the barrel,' gabbled an excited American voice. 'Scattered 'em all down the hill. Okay, Easy Fox, thanks. Stand by. Out.'

What had we hit? Japanese tanks? Weapon pits? A counter attack? We never knew. I looked up at the fire control tower where the gunnery officer, taking a turn as bombardment control officer, was hanging out of the hatch with his headphones off and gave him an expansive thumbs up. That was more like it.

The day wore on. All around us cruisers and destroyers moved back and forth on their patrols, bombarding intermittently. Easy Fox's turn came again in short bursts during the afternoon and one half hour spell after dark, when we fired 150 rounds. From a bright blue and gold morning, the weather turned overcast and sharp, fitful rain squalls blew across the water. The air became soggy and oppressive and between squalls the sea was still and sullen, like a sheet of steel.

The main island reared above the ship and black arms of land lay all along the horizon. It was a rough approximation of a fiord. But, wide as the English Channel, it could be just as unruly, I guessed; there was no snug harbour charm about it. On the contrary, one felt exposed, though to nothing visible or tangible. There was just a sombre unease that tugged at the spirit. The Admiralty Manual of Navigation, a work not noted for soaring flights of fancy, nevertheless concedes that one of the portents of a tropical revolving storm is 'an indefinable feeling that all is not well.' It was apt, though this steamy seascape was well clear of the latitudes where such storms occurred.

The sun set and we still had not seen any Japanese aircraft. At night, the surface patrols extended to guard the sea approaches to the landing areas against Japanese raiders and reinforcements. The natural barrier of Savo Island, a round lump of land five miles across, sat roughly midway between Guadalcanal and Florida and divided the approach routes into three: by sea the enemy had to come either north about Savo, or south about, or from the east, through the Sealark or Lengo Channels.

Our ships covered these routes accordingly, and in the less confined water, captains were freer of the constant attention to ship-handling and navigation. But the periodic calls for gunfire support continued and it was a long, weary night. For men at action stations below decks, the atmosphere was foul and stifling.

I snatched cat naps in my chair and occasionally sent Toby Marks,who was officer-of-the-watch in action, down to the bridge plotting room, to get off his feet. At these times, the first lieutenant would come up from the plot for a breather and we would chat desultorily. In the bridge plotting room, which the Americans with their flair for nomenclature would later christen the 'Combat Information Center,' Field kept track of

22

both the strategic and tactical situations, but he was having a dull time; by first light next morning his plotting table was still bare of any significant enemy reports and he appeared to be concerned about it.

'What did you expect?' I asked. 'An enemy force could hardly slip through our air searches, Martin.' All possible approaches were covered by both carrier and land-based aircraft, including B17s from New Caledonia and Catalinas from Espiritu Santo.

'Yes, but they should have reacted by now,' he said. 'They have had nearly twenty-four hours and if they are going to resist the landings at all, they should have shown their hand. They should be steaming full bore down The Slot.'

'If they were Germans, I'd agree. But these are Asiatics, and their staff work and thinking are pretty suspect. They are probably in a flat spin.'

Like many people with experience of the war in Europe, I had suspected that the Pacific was a pretty ramshackle show and the Japanese were inferior strategists. The landing confirmed it. It was also said that the Japs were myopic and therefore poor seamen and airmen as well.

'You weren't at the Coral Sea, sir,' Martin Field reminded me. 'This airstrip they have been building is the key to this whole campaign. With it, they could attack the American bases at Espiritu and Noumea and without it, they themselves are threatened in the Shortlands and at Rabaul. They are going to fight for it, I'll guarantee.'

'I've no doubt.' I didn't need staff lectures from Field. The argument was becoming a trifle unseemly; one's second-in-command had responsibilities nearer to hand. 'But you let Admiral Turner worry about that, and just go round the ship. Let me know how the ship's company is getting on.'

'I've just been round. They're okay but tired, sir.'

The 'sir' was a bit grudging; an edge had crept into the exchange. We too were tired.

'Well, they can think themselves lucky they're not marines,' I said.

By about mid-morning on the 8th the troops were well

established on shore and holding a perimeter around the airstrip. The landing barges still streamed to the beach, but they were now carrying supplies, ammunition and non-combat equipment. The Tulagi side was quieter. We had returned to our beach patrol but the bombardment targets and the calls for supporting fire were less frequent. From Noumea, the Commander South Pacific signalled that 'the results so far achieved make every officer and man in the South Pacific proud of the task forces.'

'There, I think the show's about over,' I said to Martin Field, showing him the signal. 'ComSoPac seems happy. An absolute pushover. Now, Martin, I'm not ruling out the possibility of enemy retaliation of course, but the job's done and we can reduce action stations in daylight. Send one gun's crew away at a time and send the hands to dinner by watches. They've been closed up without sleep for long enough.'

He stood irresolute, as if he was about to argue again.

'Well, come on,' I snapped.

'Aye aye, sir.'

But no sooner had the men fallen out than there was a red air alert. Blast! Japanese bombers had little chance of getting through the fighter coverage in strength, but at last they were trying and I could see by Field's manner that he thought he'd won his point. In my exhausted state, I resented the man.

We waited for the Japanese Naval Air Fleet, searching the hot blue sky.

'Aircraft, bearing green 45 angle of sight 15, flying from left to right.'

Here they came. They were only strays, for the combat air patrols had in fact beaten off the main attacks, but they were determined, flinging themselves about desperately in a hail of anti-aircraft fire.

'Open fire.'

The twin 4-inch guns aft and the close-range weapons erupted with a vicious, ceaseless thudding. The gunners, strapped into the 20mm Oerlikons by their shoulders, waltzed gracefully round the mountings, their bare arms and chests jerking with the recoil, steel helmets awry, as they traversed

24

the guns with their feet, 'hose-piping' red tracer onto the targets. Two bat-winged Vals were coming out of the sun in a shallow dive through a maze of tracer and black, expanding AA bursts, curving down for the centre of the massed ships. There was a flash of sun on silver as the planes levelled out and turned steeply at masthead height over the cruiser *Astoria*. Then we lost them as they slipped behind *Chicago*, a few feet off the water. Marvellous flying like that through a fleet; the ships had to check their fire for fear of hitting each other. Here they were again, turning and jinking, flames fluttering along the edges of their wings from their own fire. But their bombs were gone and they were flying to destruction for the sake of emptying their machine guns. Stupid, obscene, mad!

And now they were coming straight for us with those pin-prick wings twinkling and the bullets stitching a straight white seam on the sea, just ahead of the bows. The drumfire pom-poms and Oerlikons arced skywards and the gunners sank to their haunches as the noise rose to a crescendo – then suddenly stopped as the planes were overhead. Too much wasted ammunition lay on the seabeds around the world, fired at retreating aircraft.

Martin Field was pointing wordlessly off the starboard bow and I caught the glint of sun on silver again, low down as they wheeled for the return pass. I ordered 'Starboard 30' to put the ship straight at them as the broadcast barked:

'Green 20... angle of sight zero... coming towards... close range... ENGAGE!' on a rising, urgent note and the barrels swung round and started the hellish hammering fire again as the planes lanced across the ship, before she had even turned, racing shadows under great, shining shapes with the bold red roundel in relief on those queer dihedral wings, a mocking bulls-eye.

The second one skimmed the forecastle and for a moment my eyes met those of the pilot through his black goggles, his Rising Sun headband swathed round the helmet like a blood-stained bandage. He had his hand raised in derisive salute. Involuntarily, I nearly raised mine. Mad or not, it took guts to run that gauntlet. But he was streaming dark smoke from a hit. They would not make a third pass.

They zig-zagged through the fleet and the storm of fire again and, together still, cartwheeled into the sea on the far side. One lazy-looking white splash rose against a green backdrop of land, then was obscured by a passing ship. The smoke drifted away and unnatural quiet prevailed.

I let the breeze blow under my tin hat, mopped my streaming face and lit a cigarette.

'Well, that was real nice shooting. Thanks for the show,' said TBS, apparently to no one.

'It wasn't my idea,' an equally anonymous voice said shortly.

Well. So this was the enemy. Not bad, not bad.

'Any hits?' I asked Field.

'Yes sir, we can claim that second one all right. There was smoke pouring out – '

'I could see that. I mean on us, for God's sake!'

He returned after a decent interval with the news that we had taken a few harmless nicks in the deck plates and a larger rent on the port side, too big for machine guns. It was a stray round from another ship.

The Japanese had left the transport *George F. Elliott* on fire and the destroyer *Jarvis* badly damaged by a torpedo hit. There were more attacks that afternoon, but they did no further damage except to exact a toll in intense concentration and effort from all hands. By the time we could relax again on our night patrols, sleep was becoming an urgent operational necessity.

I was no stranger to exhaustion. In my Murmansk convoy days I had experienced the creeping edge of paralysis from lack of sleep, interminable bad weather and Arctic cold, ten or twelve days at a time, before which body and mind retreated involuntarily. It is a vicious circle. The worse the weather is, the less sleep you get and the worse the food; and the more debilitated you become, the harder the cold grips, wearing the stoutest physique and most buoyant spirit down to the point of inertia, depression and mental muddle – to the point of making mistakes.

But we were now only at the start of the cycle and we were also at the other extreme of climate, a leaden, draining heat that sapped the vitality of the fittest Europeans on the best of days. God knows, I felt that advancing edge now as I tried to write my night orders in the stuffy chart house, crossing out words, dropping beads of sweat on the page. I slumped over the chart desk in frustration and distress.

Well, this wouldn't do. I took the little note book up to the bridge – a new note book, for what captain would deign to write in his predecessor's? – and handed it deliberately, without speaking, to Tom Hughes, the officer-of-the-watch. The gesture was meant to bolster confidence, command.

'Thank you, sir,' he said and ducked under the canvas flap of the chart shelter with it.

I eyed his broad haunches in grubby khaki pants with approval. Hughes kept a good underway watch – which augured well for the sleep I craved.

It was a black, oppressive night and the low overcast seemed to press down from the sky. From time to time, heavy rain squalls were building up over the land and blowing seaward, obscuring vision. As usual, between squalls all was still and breathless; the sea was docile and there were no stars, no moon. It was claustrophobic weather. I caught a characteristic whiff of rotting vegetation from the green hot-house shore, where fleshy tangles of rank, over-ripe growth, decomposed and stank on the forest floor. I exhaled in disgust and turned back to the ship with relief.

I checked the ship's head, the revolutions counter, the position of consorts and the dozen and one other things, conscious or unconscious, of a captain's ritual, which confirmed all was well.

We patrolled north-west, south-east on a line between Savo Island and Lunga Point, at a comfortable 12 knots, reversing course every hour. I was the starboard wing escort, with *Bagley* in the lead and *Patterson* on the port wing. Astern of *Bagley* steamed *Australia, Canberra* and *Chicago* in line ahead. To the north-east, out of sight, the cruisers *Quincy, Vincennes* and *Astoria*, with attendant destroyers, made up a separate force working round a simple box patrol at 10 knots.

27

It was as safe and as quiet as could be expected. I could leave my bridge with a clear conscience.

A routine report to the bridge – 'Quartermaster relieved, Able Seaman Edwardson-the-wheel-course-328-both-engines-'alf-a-'ead-revolutions-116', a muffled mouthful that I must have heard ten thousand times, in other ships, on other seas – spouted up the voice pipe with a nasal Australian twang, giving me a comforting sense of time and continuity.

'Tom, where's the northern patrol? Let's see them on the chart.'

'Er, they're not plotted, sir. They started their patrol around dark and I haven't sighted them. We don't know what their starting point was; could be point AA here, or BB or in the middle. If we knew the starting point, I could run them on by D.R. but...'

We bent over the chart together and I tapped the pencilled 10-mile square on it nervously with the points of the dividers.

'I don't like that. We ought to know. We did last night. You keep your eyes open for them and get a couple of cross-bearings. Let me know.' We had no radar.

'We could ask them for their position, sir, couldn't we? I've already been trying to sight them, but it's no go so far.'

He was probably right on both counts. But as a new boy I jibbed at asking other ships for information I should have known anyway. Even though it was hardly my fault, I could picture the smirks and frowns on other bridges.

'No. No, do as I said, Tom. You ought to pick them up. Well, good night.'

'Good night, sir.'

It was a more mature Hughes who said that, not the ebullient young man of a few days ago. The red light in the chart shelter threw faces into strange relief, rather like a photographic negative, but it showed hollows, deep lines and puffy, discoloured pouches in his face. It seemed we were all turning into zombies.

I went slowly down the ladder to my sea cabin and, fully clothed, dropped on the bunk. But I only slept fitfully.

An hour later I was called by the first lieutenant.

'We've had an enemy sighting report, sir.'

He thrust a pink signal pad under my nose. I read that at 1026 that morning an aircraft had sighted 'three cruisers, three destroyers, two seaplane tenders or gunboats, course 120 degrees, speed 15 knots,' off Bougainville, at the northern approaches to The Slot.

'Yuh, okay, what... ?' There had been similar reports of enemy movements in that vicinity and around Rabaul. That was Japanese country. It seemed a natural place for such a formation to be.

'The flag assessment is that they are making for Rekata Bay. I'm sorry sir, but I'm not satisfied with it. Will you come and look at the plot?'

I stumbled after him into the bridge plotting room where he had marked the contact on the plotting table. I rubbed my face and concentrated.

'What is it?'

'The time of that sighting was 1026 this morning. Why didn't we get it until now? I queried the *Australia* on this; they got it at 1839 and of course queried the same thing. It appears that this bloody Hudson pilot from Milne Bay saw the ships, didn't break radio silence to report them, continued on patrol for another *two hours*... and then flew back to Milne Bay and had his tea! He reported six hours late. That Hudson squadron's Australian, incidentally.'

'Well, that just puts the ships there, now, where you've plotted them. They're not off the quarterdeck.'

'No, but my point is, what reliance can you put on a lunatic like that? Seaplane tenders or *gunboats*, for God's sake! The last gunboat sank in the Yangtse River in 1930. Some of these sprog pilots couldn't tell a battleship from a hole in the ground. And, 15 knots! Are they supposed to be on a summer cruise, or something? I'll bet there isn't a Japanese warship within a thousand miles that's doing less than 25 knots, with what's been going on here.'

'Obviously, 15 knots is the best speed of the seaplane

tenders,' I said. 'They're not fast. Probably converted merchantmen.'

'If they *are* seaplane tenders.'

'What are you trying to say?'

He took a breath.

'I am suggesting that there is a *possibility* – you can't put it any stronger – that this force is larger than reported; for example that the 'seaplane tenders' are cruisers. And they are going faster than reported. I also suggest that this whole shower is *not* going to Rekata Bay, but coming down The Slot and, allowing them a speed of advance of... say 23 knots.' With a pair of dividers he stepped off the distance rapidly on the chart, 'they should arrive here some time during the middle watch, tonight.'

I looked at him closely. If he thought this would impress me... he'd been brooding on our little contretemps and his imagination had run away with him.

'Suppose I agree with you; what then?'

'Well, I think we should tell the flagship.'

'Certainly not!' I exploded. The man was crazy. But he had called my bluff, not the other way round. He was genuine. More quietly I continued:

'I don't agree with you. This signal's hard intelligence and all that stuff's just imagination. But more to the point, the staff doesn't, either. Don't you know what an admiral's staff is, man? They have a dozen officers a damn sight more experienced than you, or me, for that matter, who do nothing else all day but worry about these things. Don't you think your possibility, and many others, has occurred to them and been ruled out, for God knows what information they have that you don't have... ' I broke off, exasperated.

'Look here,' I continued. 'Rekata Bay is, what, 150 miles away and as good a place as any for a seaplane base. What could be more probable than that they will mount more air attacks from there tomorrow? Hence the seaplane tenders. Torpedo bombers. And if they were going to take us on with surface ships, they'd have more sense than to send three cruisers. It would be suicide.'

Just then a signalman entered the plotting room with a message from Admiral Crutchley. It said that he was departing from his station in *Australia* to confer with Admiral Turner on board *McCawley*, which was at anchor off Lunga Point. Tactical command of the southern force would devolve on Captain Bode of U.S.S. *Chicago*, until Crutchley returned.

I passed the signal to Martin Field and he said, 'Oh, my God!'

'Now, what the hell's wrong with that?'

'He's mad! Taking an eight inch cruiser out of the force at this time!'

I had had enough.

'Don't you listen?' I countered angrily. 'I have told you my views and they are final. So are Admiral Crutchley's; how do you expect him to get there, in the seaboat, under oars? It's twenty miles away! Stop playing Admiral of the Fleet and get down to your own job which is to present this ship to me as a going concern and to understudy me in command.'

His body sagged in defeat and he put out one thin hand weakly for support. Even through my anger, I was shocked at the state he was in: so white and drawn, with hollow, black-ringed eyes. He was a tall, stringy, good-looking fellow, somewhat reserved, but he had seemed strong and steady enough. Now he looked almost ill. Certainly his imagination was feverish.

'I'm the ship's operations officer in battle, sir,' he said in a low voice. 'The response is too half-hearted. I have to say that.'

As I looked at him, I wondered just for a second if he could be right. Oh, no, no, it couldn't hold water. The staff had ruled it out.

'I think you'd better get your head down, Number One. You look as if you need a salt tablet. You have no business criticizing the conduct of a senior officer, especially on such shaky grounds,' I said and left him.

31

CHAPTER TWO

I was awakened by a sharp explosion; the whole ship seemed to jump sideways and bits of granulated cork showered down on me from the deckhead. Torpedoed! I sprang for the ladder but before my feet hit the bridge grating a tongue of flame spewed out forty feet to port from the ship's side below the bridge and there was another ear-splitting explosion. B mounting was firing, both guns!

'CEASE FIRE, CEASE FIRE!' I yelled and jammed my thumb on the check fire bell. I saw Lachlan beside me, pressing the action alarm button. The two bells rang out discordantly through the ship.

'Who opened fire?'

'I am firing at a Japanese cruiser, sir.' It was Field. He was pointing over the port side into the pitch black night. I snatched binoculars but could see nothing and Field, frantic with frustration, cried: 'Now I've lost the bloody thing. It was out there, going like the clappers... ' The implication that my intervention was the cause of this catastrophe was not lost on me. His angular frame whirled away from me, binoculars sweeping a wide arc.

'If you fired on friendly ships, I'll court martial you,' I said grimly and dived at the chart. 'Where is the northern patrol? If they are on their southern leg, they could be on that bearing.'

'I don't know. I haven't seen them all watch. All I know is *Patterson* came up on TBS and said: "Warning, warning, strange ships entering harbour." Then I saw this Jap cruiser. B gun's in local control so the layer and trainer must have seen it too or they wouldn't have fired. It all happened in ten seconds; I didn't have time to call you.'

'You make time. I left orders to search for those ships and you're telling me no one's sighted them? Is everybody blind?'

No reply. But at least the pandemonium on the bridge had subsided.

It *had* to be a friendly ship or black was white, the sun would not rise, two admirals were fools and knaves and I was a criminal.

'Look!' shrieked the starboard look-out, forgetting all he had been taught. Then he added: 'Green 130.'

Three brilliant flares hung over Lunga Point bathing the shoreline in silver light and silhouetting *Canberra* and *Chicago*. Starshell?

'They're aircraft flares,' said Field. 'That's that thing that's been droning round for hours with navigation lights on. It's a Jap! A marker plane! They're amazing!'

Then all round *Canberra*, tall pillars of white water rose in seeming slow motion, hung as if frozen and gracefully subsided. I had seen these before; she was straddled by shell fire. From further astern there was a bellowing explosion and tongues of red flame.

'That's *Chicago*,' cried Field. 'Eight inch broadside. Thank Christ somebody's seen them.'

'Just hold everything! Something damned dangerous is going on here, but we're not going to make it worse... '

I searched out over the port side and then I saw a stab of orange flame again, but this time it was just forward of the beam.

'Get a bearing,' I shouted, but Lachlan was already bent over the pelorus, taking it. Good.

'Bearing 345, sir. Red 75,' he called.

33

'Alarm surface port, bearing red 75. Load, load, load,' boomed Field over the armament broadcast.

I turned on him in fury, but just then the *Canberra* was hit. There was an angry red flash and part of her super-structure seemed to subside like a landslide on a cliff face. Immediately she was hit again, on the forepart, a tremendous crash that heaved up the forecastle deck and dozens of flaming planks spun crazily upwards, like so many matches spilled from a box. She was smothered in splashes. She swung to starboard and slowed and then there was a third hit in the engine spaces, a great geyser of steam shot up and dark and white smoke mingled over her, screening red fires. Then she was lost to sight behind the smoke.

'Oh, my God.' It *had* happened, it must have – and yet there was no proof, I would not accept it until there was.

'Whoever they are, they've got to be stopped. Full speed. Steer 045. Stand by torpedo tubes; bridge control. Tell the chief I want everything he's got. We'll get clear of this bloody mess and search.' I heard the clang of telegraphs repeating 'Full Ahead' and the rising whine of the turbines and I felt the screws bite deep and drag the ship's stern down as she moved off.

I took up the armament broadcast microphone myself.

'Do you hear there? This is the captain speaking,' I said. 'We are under attack by unidentified forces, presumed enemy. Wake up, settle down and get straight into action. Stand by.'

From the same direction as before, on the port beam, a searchlight flashed on. It groped towards us and away, found a target which from that distance seemed to be *Chicago* and switched off. A second later there was the orange flash of a broadside, fired from perhaps three miles away. This was no friendly ship. I was convinced.

'Target, a cruiser, bearing red 80. Open fire,' I screeched into the microphone.

Oh no! Oh no!

'I've got her. Get down to the plot,' I said to Field and shoved him aside at the binnacle.

If the Japanese ship was heading about north-east, as

seemed likely, we were on a good parallel course for a torpedo attack. Meanwhile, we could engage with gunfire.

I saw the back of our other sub-lieutenant, Hathaway just disappearing into the director control tower hatch. Oh, God, the gun crews were not closed up yet, we would be too late.

'Watch out for torpedo tracks. Weave,' I said, registering a flabbergasted Toby Marks beside me still struggling into his shirt, and sprinted for the control tower. I clung on to the outside of the hatch in the 30-odd knot wind of our passage in an agony of impatience while Hathaway talked into his headphones.

'Can you see anything?' I shouted.

'No, sir. We'll have to use starshell. X gun's ready.'

'Right, get going.' I half fell down the vertical director ladder, just as he ordered:

'Starshell fire spread!'

X gun cracked out three rounds in good time, but now I had lost my orientation on the bridge.

'What can you see, Pilot?' I gasped.

'*Canberra's* burning like a haystack back there sir, but apart from that, nothing. I can't see the target. There's nothing on TBS; there was a bit of gabble but I couldn't make anything out of it.'

'Where is the northern patrol?' I cried in anguish. 'We *must* be getting close to them.'

Marks muttered that he'd give his head for a radar set; only the newest American ships were fitted with this magic eye and the best equipped radar ship, *San Juan*, was patrolling off the Sealark Channel, far to the east, with *Hobart*.

The first starshell burst dead over the unmistakable pagoda-like superstructure of a *Kako* class heavy cruiser at 6,000 yards. It showed a beam-on silhouette, a black shape surging forward with immense power and dreadful menace. The starshell should have burst to the right, but this was a fortunate saving error. I took up the fire control phone to hear Hathaway saying:

'Inclination 100 right... Range 062, deflection 4 left.'

35

'Clock tuned, deflection set!' From the transmitting station down below. At last.

'Spread line... *shoot*! From two stars right, starshell go on.'

The fire gong rang, there was a maddening three-second delay and our first 6-gun, 4.7 inch broadside was in the air, followed immediately by another starshell round. That was under way; now I could concentrate on the torpedo attack. I put the phone down but as I did so it was nearly snatched out of my hand by a bleary, cross-looking Tom Hughes, dragged from sleep. How long had he been there? I had forgotten all about him and I had been doing his job instead of my own. And why that ridiculous dash to the director? The phone I had just put down would have done just as well.

'Did you sight the northern patrol or didn't you?' I barked at him.

'No sir, I did not,' he shot back.

'Oh, Christ. This is it, Tom, it's bad. Good shooting,' I said and added 'Port Five,' down the voice pipe.

'Port Five. Five of port wheel on, sir.'

The ship started to swing in, rapidly at this speed. I could have fired torpedoes from where we were, but if I could get to 4,000 or 3,000 yards, I couldn't miss. But although we were going perhaps 10 knots faster than the Japanese cruiser, we were on converging courses and therefore keeping about steady relative to each other. The more I swung in, the more bearing I would lose and I risked slipping hopelessly astern if I was not careful.

'Midships.'

'Midships. Wheel's a-midships sir.'

The turn slowed up. Another starshell plopped over the cruiser and I saw our shell splashes rise around her; there should be hits in that. But God, she was close! 3,800 yards. If she shifted target to us, as soon she must... I gritted my teeth. In the next second, the searchlight flashed on and swept lazily across us.

We felt like bugs pinned on a board under that light; we

wanted to squirm off the pin but had nowhere to go. I saw instant tableaux of guns' crews in motion; the very flash of our own broadside paled feebly in its glare, faces twisted in desperation on the bridge and the seething white cascade of wake distorted into a live thing, seeming to charge after us, about to swallow us up from behind. The light paused at the bridge, travelled insolently forward, swept aft, dwelt on the after part, and switched off. There were audible gasps of relief.

Now I hugged the shuddering binnacle to keep myself upright watching the target, instead of cowering for cover. I forced myself to read the target bearing: 265, 267, 270... we were losing bearing pretty fast. Range? 3,400. It would have to do.

'Steady.'

'Steady. Course 342 sir.'

'Starboard ten.'

'Starboard ten. Ten of starboard wheel on.'

'Steer 010.'

It was the wrong way to turn for shell splashes but I had to fire torpedoes now or never.

'Check fire.'

'Check firing! Check check check check... ' The check fire bells jangled and the guns stopped. A steady platform was needed for torpedoes.

'Set course. Bridge control. Fire on your sight,' I called to the torpedo officer, crouched over his sight on the port look-out sponson.

A deluge of dirty white water swamped the bridge, drenching everyone on it and out of the corner of my eye I saw another tall column collapsing to starboard. Straddled, first pop, but we were not hit. Somehow the terror lessened once the fall of shot could be seen.

What was happening on the torpedo sight? He should have given me thirty seconds to go. He had his hand on the sight, his body bent forward.

'How long to go? Torpedo control! You'll miss it, you

37

bloody fool, what are you doing?'

Nothing happened. We passed the firing angle and no sleek warheads were streaking for the target. I stared in disbelief, from the black water to the control position.

A phone squealed and Lachlan answered it.

'It's the tubes, sir. They got no orders to prime! The torpedo gunner's mate says the fucking firing pistols aren't even shipped!'

I was speechless.

'But who – but I said – *why the hell not*?'

There was a loud explosion aft with an enormous sheet of flame, somewhere about the mainmast and more grey and white water cascaded all over us. Straddled again and hit this time. Was her back broken? I gave a wheel order and we swung rapidly through north east, heeling hard in the turn; she was still answering the wheel at least.

'Hard-a-starboard!' I roared. 'Torpedo officer!' Through a red mist of rage I could see him, still hunched over his sight. He hadn't moved. 'Mr. Morley!' I thundered. Lachlan scrambled over to him.

'Sir,' quavered Lachlan. 'He's dead. He... has no head.'

Oh, my Christ. Morley. No head?

'He's just standing there! Blood all down his front and he's... bits everywhere, I trod in it. It's all over me!'

He started scraping and scuffing his shoes frantically on the grating in a grotesque, shuffling dance.

'That will do, Sub!' I was ready to hit him.

He stood still.

'Sub, pull yourself together. If you don't want to go the same way, fight back. Do you know anything about torpedo control? Can you work that sight?'

'Sorry. Yes, sir, I can.' He was recovered now and reaching out for responsibility

'Then get on the starboard sight and get the tubes ready. I am going to starboard and will fire to starboard this time.'

We drove hard round with full wheel on and those torpedoes got away straight and true. But, dear God, how could a 35 knot torpedo catch a 26 knot ship, end on and going away?

Suddenly it was quiet and we were alone. We could see no targets. It was now 0148 and I had been on the bridge for five minutes. We blundered blindly on northwards, searching and scanning ahead and to port where we could sense the malevolent presence so strongly that I caught myself sniffing the wind for it. The firing had stopped astern and except for the desolate echoes of exploding ammunition on board the ruined *Canberra*, the night was still again. A big rain squall had built up on the slopes of Savo and was heading east, across our bows.

The chief reported that the shell aft had burst about the potato locker of all things. It had peeled the deckhead of my day quarters back like a sardine tin lid, twisted the mainmast, demolished the wireless aerials it carried and started a fire in the cabin flat. One man of X gun's crew was badly wounded by a fragment and three more had suffered flash burns; they fought bare-chested for we had not yet learned from the Americans the necessity of protective clothing. There was no damage at the waterline or to essential equipment. We had been lucky.

There was a brief interval while I tried to piece things together with Marks. It was clear that a Japanese force had come south about Savo Island, decimated the southern patrol and was now presumably still headed north east, probably with the objective of getting through to the transports anchored off Tulagi, where the still burning transport *George F. Elliott* would serve as a beacon to guide them in. But where was *Chicago*? Why had we no information or orders? For that matter, where was *Australia*?

We thought that *Chicago* must be either disabled or headed

out of action, south of Savo, and that *Patterson* and *Bagley* were probably still with her; after all, we were all supposed to be escorting the southern force. The yeoman produced a signal from Admiral Crutchley to say that when the conference finished at midnight, *Australia* would not rejoin the formation but would patrol independently off Lunga, so that settled that. She would be there now and would not have the faintest idea of what had happened. What of the enemy?

'Plot, bridge,' I called down the voice pipe. 'Sitrep. What do you make of it?'

'There's no information coming in at all, sir,' said Field. 'But I would guess that the two enemy ships we saw were at the head of their column in line ahead, and the one we attacked was the second in line. That gives them a good interval between ships, say 1200 yards. And it would put us still abreast of some part of their formation; I am assuming they have at least five ships. You remember that signal?' There was still tartness in the voice.

Poor chap! What unspeakable things I had done to him. Betrayal, murder, worse!

'I shall never forget it,' I said humbly.

'We lost ground during our turn but we are going 10 or 12 knots faster and would have made a bit of it up again since.'

There were still a hundred questions. Why hadn't *Blue*, the picket destroyer stationed west of Savo and practically in the path of the Japanese, seen them? Where were they now? Could they even have doubled back towards the fat, unprotected transports off Lunga Point? And where, oh where, in their ten-mile box, was the northern patrol?

'Bridge, plot,' called Field, with a new note of urgency. 'I know it's bloody crazy – this time it is, but we could be the only ship in the area with even that much grasp of the situation. Oughtn't we to broadcast what we know? Warn the others?'

It was true that in the beginning, through pure instinct, I had turned to a roughly parallel course to the enemy and we had been in touch with his column. We did have information on his disposition, course and speed, but it was getting old now

40

and the truth was, I didn't know where they were, any more than anyone else. Suppose they had even split their force, one part heading for Lunga and the other part for Tulagi? If I broadcast anything, it would have to be questions, not answers and I would just add to the confusion. And what was going to happen next? Some new development demanding instant textbook solutions, miracles of clear thinking, split-second coups, out of chaos?

But now the rain squall was on us, driven by a whipping little north-west wind and reducing visibility to less than one hundred yards. With my vision restricted, I watched the ship cutting through the weather steadily, silently – and much too fast, but what was the point of reducing speed? She threw off the rain carelessly in streamers and sprays of spume, the one dependable thing in the universe. She, at least, would not let me down.

I stared through the rain and forced myself to think. The northern patrol, if it was still even in the area, should have been alerted by the gunfire to the south; but they could have mistaken it for a ship-to-shore bombardment, or even artillery fire on shore. This would have been consistent with the pattern of the last couple of days. But what had happened? Where had they gone?

Oh, to hell with it. Martin Field had suggested that and Martin Field *knew*. I would never disregard his advice again. I took up the TBS handset.

'Small Boys, Small Boys, this is Buckboard,' I began, but I was too late.

'Bridge, port look-out! There's a blue light, dead ahead.'

There was. It flickered off, obscured by rain, came on, went off again and then glowed steadily, perhaps seventy yards away.

'What the blazes is that? Phosphorescence?'

'I don't know sir, I've never seen anything like it,' said Marks. 'It must be some atmospheric or electrical thing. But we'd better give it a miss, I don't like the look of it.'

'Port fifteen. Neither do I.'

Did the bloody spectres and hobgoblins have to assault us

41

too? But it had more substance than that. It *was* a light, a steady, deep blue light. I'd never seen or heard of one at sea before. What did it mean? A fishing float? No, it was moving, before a dismal-looking triangle of pelting rain.

A triangle. And there was something about the *way* it moved in the binoculars and height above water... I had seen lights like this before... yes, by God, *but they were white...*

'Hard-a-port!' I screamed. 'That's a shaded stern light. It's a Japanese ship!'

The flesh of our backs crawled as we turned away, though through my gut-dissolving fear a vestige of reason told me that we were as safe here as anywhere else, for the Japanese could not depress their turrets sufficiently at that range to hit us and would have to fire high. Then I caught a chilling glimpse of the after section of a heavy cruiser thrashing along at over 20 knots, the gun barrels of its after turrets questing to port like the feelers of some monstrous insect. And as X and Y mountings commenced a ragged fire, the rain immediately obscured the target and they had to check.

X gun shifted to starshell, but the first spread were all duds. We were blind and groping again.

I jumped at Hughes. *'Now* what's wrong?'

He was speaking rapidly into his phone, his face hidden under a tin hat dripping rivers of rain.

'It's a bad batch I think, sir, I'm trying to – '

'I *know.* Get rid of it! Miss twenty rounds and start again! Get the things going!'

The tin hat jerked up and his face blazed with anger. No one browbeat Tom Hughes easily. But he just said, 'Aye aye sir,' in a reasoning tone he might have used with a fractious child.

That's what I got for stamping my foot, humiliation. As if they weren't doing all they could. A bad show, to lose control of myself like that.

But we were still careering westwards. I planned to open the range sufficiently for a torpedo attack to starboard; we were in a disadvantageous firing position, on the target's port

42

quarter, but we must strike while we could.

'Pilot,' I said. 'Time a run of 1200 yards on this course. I want to turn as soon as possible but not inside it.'

'We could fire now, sir,' piped Lachlan. 'The after tubes are ready.'

'Oh, bloody hell, Sub,' I exploded again in vexation. 'Torpedoes won't arm under 600.' Poor Lachlan shrank over his sight.

'Turn!' called Marks.

'Starboard twenty. Fire on your sight! Can you see it?'

But it was still no use, no use at all. Two feeble starshell burst away off the target and the rest were still duds. We couldn't see it. Once again, we passed the firing angle and nothing happened. I felt balked and angry. Another starshell round fired in vain.

'What'll I steady on, sir?' From Marks.

'Keep after it! Close the enemy again! Steer north-east.' I wanted nothing more in life than to hound that thing down and ram it. We speared through the night, but in vain. The ship stayed hidden.

Time, 0150. Could it be only two minutes since our first torpedo attack to the south? Unbelievable, it seemed more like two hours since we began the attack.

I wondered why the Japanese cruiser had not returned our fire, such as it was. I was thankful for that, but it was curious... unless she was after bigger game.

Suddenly the rain cleared and the yeoman called out:

'There are ships, fine on the starboard bow.'

No one on board had a better pair of eyes than Yeoman Treloar, but he conned me on to the objects and by using the old technique of moving my eyes quickly, back and forth, high and low, I could just make them out in peripheral vision. There were two – no, three... in line ahead. Going very slowly. A north-west heading. Cruiser types patrolling.

They could not be Japanese. They could be no one else but *Astoria*, *Quincy* and *Vincennes*. The northern patrol. The bigger game.

Four people went for the TBS handset at once and Marks' elbow caught me painfully in the throat as he snatched it up. But before he could speak, it spoke; a rather aggrieved mid-western voice delivered the one and only intelligible message we heard on the circuit all that night.

'Small Boys, this is Speedwell, Speedwell. You are illuminating me. Douse your light. Douse your light.'

It was *Vincennes*, at the head of the column and she was lit like a Christmas tree by the searchlight of the Japanese ship we had so nearly run down, now on our starboard bow. *Vincennes* thought it was one of us.

Marks was shouting something in reply but I doubt if they even heard it for the carnage had commenced. It was the battle south of Savo all over again, but infinitely worse. Those three cruisers were shot to pieces before our eyes.

I saw with horror that two more searchlights now swept the cruisers from the port hand; there were Japanese on both sides of them. The enemy column had indeed split, but in a way we could never have imagined. They would now have the northern force sandwiched in a cross-fire. They were uncannily skilful, superb night fighters. And they had no radar. So much for 'myopia'!

Under the pitiless lights, the Americans seemed just as unprepared as we had been earlier; they were ambling along on their sleepy 10 knot patrol, with turrets trained fore and aft. Perhaps on this hideous night they had looked from their bridges and wondered about the shot and shell and flares to the south – surely they must have – but they were not yet alert.

The searchlights went off, the orange flashes spurted out of the night from starboard and rippled down the line from port and the broadsides burst upon them in a fusillade of white columns of water. The stabs of flame from the Japanese guns on either side seemed like footlights, while in centre stage, fountain after white fountain rose regularly against a black velvet backdrop of sky, in a spellbinding, wraith-like ballet of insane slow motion. But suddenly there were some lights, clear points of green and white light in the foreground, in a cluster.

'Recognition lights,' growled Yeoman Treloar. 'Setting's correct – they're ours. I'd say the middle ship: *Quincy.*'

Oh, Jesus, no! 'Tell them to switch off!' It seemed a dozen voices shouted. Oh, the poor blind fools!

But there were targets now and I had work to do – and there was that cruiser, farther away than I had thought, but dead ahead, flicking its bulky silhouette on and off with every flash of its own guns. I lined up on it and urged my ship forward with fierce, obliterating curses. Our forward guns opened up, mere pop-guns in this league, but I nursed the thought of my four remaining torpedoes and the moment when we would release them and swing away, then wait for them to strike with those sweet, leaping paroxysms. We would rip that ship's guts out and this time there would be no mistake.

'THAT ONE, STAND BY... ' I bellowed over the wind kicking spray at Lachlan. But that shifted my attention to the general scene and it had transformed itself again; our friendly ships had been hit. *Quincy*, with her ill-starred lights, suffered a near miss that set the aircraft on her catapult into leaping yellow fire. It was quickly smothered, but by that time she was hit again; a deep red flare burst from her, then dimmed, then grew again through thick black smoke. And now *Vincennes* ahead of her was throwing off spurts of bright flame. I guessed it was ready-use ammunition going up on her upper deck in small fire-storms. There would be people running this way and that through them, trying to pitch ammunition overboard, alive one second, burnt to death the next by igniting charges in their very arms. And now the high explosive hits were steadily mounting on all three ships in bursts of dull red, imposed on lighter-coloured fuel fires that rose and fell in intensity, but never died. The sky behind them leapt and flickered as if from bolts of lightning. What need of searchlights now? The burning Americans lit themselves – and chasing this target, we were diverging too far from them. By the time our attack was over, it could be too late. I knew what I must do.

'Tell the engine room to make smoke,' I said and altered

course back to port, parallel to our own ships. Please God I'd have another chance at that Jap cruiser later, but meanwhile, we were steaming at 35 knots, three times their speed and if I could overhaul them, our smoke might shield them from the enemy. There was not a second to lose.

We shifted target towards the gun flashes to port as they came nearer and raced for the stricken ships. But the Americans were fighting back: *Quincy* was launching 6-gun 8 inch broadsides to starboard already. And something new appeared: a glorious burst of red, on our starboard bow. It was a hit on my own target, the Japanese cruiser! We waited for the next one that would crush her with tons of obliterating steel, the full broadside that would smash them to pulp and shrivel them to ashes. But it did not come. *Quincy* was too far gone. Yet that one stray hit did something: it was visible proof of striking back against frightful odds, and for the first time that night, a thin cheer arose on my bridge. We were all losing our cowed confusion; defiance and determination were taking hold.

When I had first identified the American ships, there had been a murmur of excitement and relief on the bridge. None of us had ever been so glad to see anything, but not everyone had realised the peril of their comrades-in-arms. To the bridge messengers, the signalmen on the flag deck and the strained look-outs, they meant but one thing: we were among friends again. And now these friends were being slaughtered. Hope of deliverance from the nightmare was snatched away.

A new mood of dogged anger was growing throughout the ship, the same battle rage that had seized me.

The gunners pumped out the rounds like clockwork men and in between firing I could hear B mounting's crew, the closest, shouting their reports and orders at the top of their lungs. The unoccupied hands on the bridge, signalmen, messengers, the boatswain's mate, no longer hung back at the rear but lined the side, for all the world as if they were at a football match. Calmer now, with the die cast and the commitment made, I felt some detachment, yet as never before my own sixth-sense nervous feelers went out to every corner of the ship and all the people in her.

46

'Got ya, you bastard!' someone roared and there was a ringing cheer. It must have been a hit of our own, our first for many minutes.

'Another one! Christ, look at that Yank!'

It was *Astoria*, broken, burning, stripped. The cruisers had fallen out of line and each one limped and listed in its agony.

Both Marks and Treloar started forward uncertainly to clear the onlookers off the bridge.

'No. No, let them go,' I said and they drew back, aware that there was something new.

I called down to the plot.

'Martin, you won't do much good down there any more. Come up.' I was not going to let us die with bad blood between us. Now was the time.

The implication of my words was clear. When he came up, I said:

'I thought you'd want to see it.'

'Yes. Thanks. I do.' He smiled.

'You were right, Martin. I take full blame. I'll see that your name is cleared and the whole story comes out – '

'No one's to blame, sir. I don't think anyone would have believed me.' What a grand, loyal fellow he was. I grabbed his hand and shook it, saying 'Somehow we'll get out of this.'

He stood back from me with that smile again, looking more like the man I'd known days ago.

He said, 'I'll go and see the wounded.' He didn't have time, but how better could he die than on such an errand?

I looked around. Where was Lachlan? On his torpedo sight, of course. I couldn't pull him off it, but he turned his head back inboard and looked at me.

I waved and smiled at him as his mother probably did not so long ago, seeing him off to school.

'Keep it up, Sub, you're doing well,' I mouthed and he raised his hand and turned away.

47

Morley. Somebody had laid him down and dragged him clear. I couldn't see the body.

Tom Hughes was too busy to interrupt and there wasn't time for any more. Sparks shooting from the funnels, black smoke rolling astern, spray flying and men cheering, we sped into the inferno.

'Torpedoes port,' sang Marks.

I had been weaving continuously and we were in a turn to starboard; I put full wheel on and then there was nothing to do but wait. Unless I put the starboard engine astern... no, it couldn't make any difference. The white streaks bounded over the water and we seemed to be well clear ahead but there was one fish heading straight for the stern. The long flush deck of the after part spun towards it. The barrackers were suddenly hushed. Then in a moment of silence I heard:

'B gun won't bear!' from the captain of the mounting as the ship's structure masked his fire, followed by the irreverent 'B gun don't care,' from some irrepressible hard case. It could have been a practice firing.

'Missed! Beauty Skipper! Get into 'em!' yelled the watchers and one added 'Sir,' lest they be thought impertinent. All the officers looked at me askance, but I shook my head. I needed the support.

I reversed the turn and we began a dance with the shell splashes; a broadside fell short and I turned towards, the next fell over but I stayed turned towards. When the third fell over, the Japanese would correct and I would turn away.

It was working. We were only a mile short of the rear American cruiser, now turning out of control to port and I felt we were winding back the odds against pulling the whole stupendous thing off. I seized a moment to dash into the chart shelter, to try to check our position; it might be a long time before I could do that again.

There was a dull, pile-driving explosion of great force and the whole ship staggered. My first thought was of a bad accident I'd seen in a gunnery practice, years ago. I sprang back to the compass platform.

'What's that? Explosion in the breech?'

Tom Hughes was ducking under a deluge. 'An explosion in the breech doesn't do that,' he shouted. 'We've been hit, underwater.'

Warm salt water hit us like shrapnel. There was steam in it, too, and acrid smoke that set us coughing and gagging. As soon as it cleared, I stood on my chair to gain a better view ahead.

The forecastle deck had buckled and sprung and the bow waves came up askew, more to one side than the other. We had lost both anchors, and pieces of anchor cable had evidently gone flailing off into the night. It seemed she was holed, right forward. How long now?

Martin Field's voice called: 'You spare hands there: go forward and join up with the damage control parties.' He'd made it back, thank God. I needed him. And that was the end of the watchers; they rushed the ladder as one man, struggling to be first.

'She's got quite a pull to starboard, sir,' called the coxswain from the wheelhouse. 'She's carrying about 10 degrees of port wheel.'

'Thank you, Coxswain.' What else could I say? 'Engineer officer to the bridge!' I blurted on the broadcast. Where the devil was he? How long could we crab along like this? The ship had started a coarse, fluttering vibration, quite distinct from the regular beat of the screws. It was slower, more violent. Instead of the trim forefoot, she now thrust a jagged hole into the churning water; that explosion would have been wickedly tamped below the surface and the pressure on the bulkhead would be enormous.

The chief appeared, white-faced and breathless, his overalls covered in black grime.

'You'll have to reduce speed, sir, the collision bulkhead won't hold. I'm not risking men down there, shoring it up – '

49

'I can't reduce speed. Confound it, report the damage!'

'The forefoot's blown right off but I can't tell how big it is.'

'Is the forepeak bulkhead intact?'

'Yes but –'

'Then we've got a chance. It's got to hold. Don't shore it up, shore up the next one.' He should have known that, he should be doing it already.

He was grey with fear. He opened his mouth as if to curse me for a madman, but scuttled off. The chief would have to go, he just wasn't up to it. I'd have to get rid of him, if we survived. I guessed we had lost 8 or 10 knots from the damage anyway and while there was still a chance of catching the crippled cruisers, I would not reduce speed.

It was, more than ever, a race against time. The cruisers were scattered, but our broad ribbon of black smoke astern would still cover them. *Astoria* was so close, so beautifully, horribly, close! But she was listing 20 degrees and there were some plates on the port side that were red hot. A forward turret was still firing but its eruptions paled to a glimmer beside the red hell of more shell hits from the stately fountains that hung and clung about her. Parts of the ship remained recognisable but other parts were demolished or hidden in steam and smoke. Through the glasses, I fancied I could see the small black shapes of human beings struggling with equipment. They seemed so weak and leaden-footed; it was agonising to watch.

But those same fountains were rising thickly around us again. They had changed colour, back to a streaky dark; there must be dye in them. I had given up trying to dodge them in the interest of speed and now charged straight on. As things stood now, if we tried to save what was left of the cruisers, we could not save ourselves. The odds were too high. Every lynx-eyed control officer in every Japanese control tower would fasten on us, this preposterous sprat daring to disrupt the smooth Imperial plan of annihilation.

Suddenly, out of nowhere, another ship appeared, apparently undamaged, travelling fast, making south across our bows. Desperately we fixed binoculars on it.

'Yeoman?'

'Destroyer. That'd be the northern patrol's port escort – *Helm* or *Wilson*.'

'You're sure? It's not Japanese?'

'It's American. It's *Wilson*.'

'Is it? *Is it?* Challenge them. Then call them up, say: 'I am laying smoke for your consorts. What are you doing?'

'Clark! Give us the pin-point Aldis with the red filter. Quick!'

But the Aldis lamp was still clacking out its message when B mounting was wiped out in a gust of destruction that felled a dozen men. Some of them, and pieces of gun, flew up past the bridge, outlined in searing light. The ship quaked with shock. Then a rending star-shaped detonation overhead rooted the control tower out like a rotten tooth and laid it over on one side, a pile of junk. Two bodies dropped from it: Thud. Thud. Like shoes being cast off one by one. One was young Hathaway, whole but dead, and the other unknown, legless, screaming. We ran to him with a stretcher and I left them bundling his thrashing body down the ladder, wrapped in a signal flag.

Phones shrilled and voice pipes called on the bridge. Reports of disasters and predicaments came pouring in:

The forepeak bulkhead is giving way.

Evacuate A magazine.

Flood it?

Less buoyancy but more safety – yes.

But if the forepeak goes and the deck above floods too? Still yes.

The low power circuits have failed.

No instruments, no phones except the sound-powered ones, no gyro compass.

Steer by magnetic. Main armament in local control.

Darky Nolan's pinned under a bit of B gun shield. He's shocking, but we can't shift it. There's six of us down here and we've tried everything, but we can't shift the fucking thing!

Get the oxy-acetylene cutter and rig sheerlegs.

All clear of A magazine.

Clear the transmitting station too, it's useless anyway.

Kirkwood, the legless chap, has died.

Has Hathaway been moved?

Yes, the body's gone. Hathaway? I scarcely knew him.

Some plates buckled and rivets popped on the next collision bulkhead when B mounting went up. Oh, Christ.

Field ran down to B gun deck to rig the sheer legs and the inventory of disaster petered out. In a self-conscious pretence that none of this was as bad as it sounded, I sat down in my chair.

And after all, our guns were still firing, our smoke was still streaming out, our progress was not much impeded. But of course, we still couldn't make it. Or would we? Oughtn't I to turn back now, while I still could? I had no right to squander any more lives on this errand of purgatory. But we were so damned close, *we still might pull it off.*

Marks was looking at me quizzically and I knew he was reading my mind.

'Well, Pilot?'

'Don't get me wrong, sir, but this is our last chance to turn back. I thought I'd just mention that. From now on... ' He shrugged. 'Anything could happen.'

'Yes, I know. What do you say?'

'Sir, I think we ought to bail out.'

There was nothing in it but the toss of a coin.

'No, we don't,' I said.

Marks was now looking at me accusingly.

'What would you say if you were on board there?' I pointed towards the three cruisers. 'Suppose you *saw* us turn and run. A few scratches and we ditch them when the going gets tough. How would it look? How would you feel?'

He followed my gaze and said gloomily. 'I suppose I couldn't live with it.'

'I'm sure you couldn't. Let's get some sort of fix on this chart, then, and send down for word on what's happening at B gun.' There was another reason, to go on. If we ran, I would be letting Martin Field down a second time.

I gave orders to get rid of our remaining torpedoes – for we could soon be dead in the water and unable to spread them. We did it with the minimum of fuss this time, firing to port at the gun flashes, at about 5,000 yards.

We did not know if our torpedoes hit anything for we did not last out their run. The Japanese had at last decided to put us out of action and co-ordinated shellfire fell on us like rain. The ship rocked and shook under the impact. I saw the mainmast fall and trail its tip into the sea and I felt the coxswain struggling with the wheel. Then through the blackness of our own smoke a great red balloon burst up, a gigantic, reverberating gout of explosion that tossed the ship up and down like a ball, and with a blast that blighted everything in sight. Only one thing could produce that convulsion: an exploding magazine.

I picked myself off the deck and staggered to one side of the bridge but cannoned into Hughes coming the other way, shouting something I could not hear. Communication was impossible. It dawned on me that we had come to an abrupt and horrifying halt. I looked about for the reason and saw licking flames where some engine room plates had been. And the ship was settling by the stern, tilting back 10 degrees already. That forepeak bulkhead had held up, after all.

Another salvo hit us. The ship whipped back and forth as if it was made of bamboo. I clung to some structure with both arms as dismembered bodies and the sheer legs from B gun deck soared fifty feet in the air past my eyes. I had an incongruous moment of bitter fury that sheer legs, a clumsy contraption of lashed spars and blocks and tackles left over from the days of sail, was all we had to lift wreckage off bodies. Somebody ran up and shouted that the engine-room

53

was flooded, the boiler rooms were being evacuated and the engineer officer was dead. It would be merciless, but short now.

The third broadside struck on the port side. The ship was merely drifting now and absorbed it without those painful leaps and shudders, as if she was too tired to react. But she listed sharply and immediately to port, which meant waterline holes in the hull.

Then one last unlucky projectile, a seeming stray, must have clipped something overhead, for it burst in a blinding flash above the bridge. I felt the ship drop inexplicably and smoothly away beneath me – then realised that it was I who had been catapulted upwards. I remember falling across the grating, breaking its slats. Then there was a long black silence.

I heard a faint buzzing noise, a deep, intermittent drone that seemed familiar. A bee, or a wasp? I put out a hand and touched something soft, a grey and pinkish mound that seemed to quiver slightly. Brains, or guts! I squirmed away from it and sat up. Smoke swirled around the bridge, but through the gaps I could see only twisted metal ruins like melted chocolate bars. It was finished. But I could see no people. There were sounds like pistol shots nearby. What on earth were they?

I felt myself carefully all over. That grating had broken my fall; I seemed to be whole apart from grazing and bruising.

The low droning noise was back and I went towards it, bumping awkwardly on my backside across the sloping deck. It grew into human speech, as if someone was reading aloud – and I knew that voice, it was Treloar's.

I found him lying on his face near the flag deck. I put my ear to his lips and heard in disbelief:

'... the fruit of thy womb, Jesus. Hail Mary, full of grace, blessed art thou among women and blessed be the fruit of thy womb, Jesus.'

That this flinty iconoclast should acknowledge a god at all, let alone pray, even in this extremity, seemed amazing.

'Yeoman! We're not in church, we're on a sinking ship. And I need your help. What's the matter with you?'

He opened the one eye I could see.

'I'm a Catholic and this is private.' I was too taken aback to react. 'Just squaring off the charge sheet with the next skipper,' he said drily. 'Been a bad bastard. I've got no guts.'

'Nonsense. Where are you hit?' I could see no marks or blood on him. 'Come on, man, I'll get you up.'

'No! I've lost my guts. Over there, on the grating.' Oh, my God. 'There's nowhere to go anyhow, even if you could shift me.'

I stared at him.

'Done some terrible things. You wouldn't want to know. Not in the navy, I played my cards right there. Only one thing though, I never got that message through to the *Wilson*; lost her when we got hit. First time ever.'

'That's all right. That's all right,' I mumbled.

'Well, you better get going. You know, I never call anyone "sir" unless they earn it, it comes too hard with me. But I think you're one. Good luck, sir.'

I could only grip his shoulder for a few moments.

I stood up and called through the smoke: 'Hello, is there anyone there on the bridge?' But there was no answer.

I touched a black body, huddled as if in untidy sleep. The head was recognisable but there was just scorched, tarry meat below it. He was lying in vestiges of smoking clothing whimpering and moaning.

'Hoople?' I dropped to my knees. 'Hoople, isn't it? Boatswain's mate?'

'No, sir, it's me, Birch. I'm going to die, I'm going to die.' His face twisted and he tried to stretch the pitiful body. 'Oooh, don't do that!' he screamed.

55

Only messdeck obscenities rose to my lips. I thought frantically, I'm as useless at first aid as a cuntful of cold water. Did you throw water on them? I tore off my shirt and laid it over him, catching my breath at the terrible purple flesh and the smell of burnt hair. Then, rigid with shock and helplessness, I shouted something incoherent and went on.

The list was correcting itself and moving about was becoming easier. But she had settled more; there was very little time, I must be quick. Of course, Field would have gone up with B gun deck. But surely Marks, Hughes, some of the others stationed on the bridge had survived? Then I found a row of shining teeth in a thing like a – baked potato. A charred corpse. It had a pair of smouldering officer's shoulder straps and there was a blackened American issue cigarette lighter sitting on the rib cage where the shirt pocket had been. Marks had had a lighter like that. I went on and found body after body; signalmen, look-outs, boatswain's mates, scattered like chaff, some dismembered, some moaning, moving, still alive. There was nothing I could do. I could not become a one-man casualty clearing station. And Treloar was right, there was nowhere to go, anyhow.

'I'm sorry. I'm sorry,' I cried, and hurried on.

A fused tail-end of electric cable burnt me on the leg and the cartridges in the Very pistol locker ignited, churning round inside it with a shrill fizzing and showers of sparks. Now there was fire and it took rapid hold on that side of the bridge. Now I must go. The strange pistol shot noises intensified and I traced them to popping rivets on the transverse bulkhead. Something was close to giving way.

I forced my way to the front of the bridge and climbed over the wind dodger, feeling for a vertical steel ladder I knew was there. From here, I could see aft. There were some men gathered on the high part around the stump of the mainmast, which formed an island, still clear of the water. I waved and some waved back. I gestured to the side, towards the water and they acknowledged. They would take their own time.

Then A mounting fired. I saw the recoil; the left gun only. Good God, what now? I went down the ladder, past the slaughterhouse of B gun deck where the naked torso of poor

Darky Nolan still lay pinned under a mass of crumpled armour plate, then forward, trying not to step on the dead.

Leading Seaman Cuthbert, the captain of the mounting, crashed into me as he ran round the rear of the gun shield, apparently on his own.

'What are you doing?' I asked stupidly.

'Firing the gun,' he said. 'Open sights, sir. I can see a target.' He was wild-eyed, a little mad. His chest heaved from exertion.

'No, no, it's all over now. Abandon ship,' I said and went towards him with restraining hands, but too late to heed his warning shout, I stepped on a piece of deck that was no longer there and fell into the sea.

When I looked back, her poor blackened snout was cocked sharply upwards. She hung there for a time, then gave a sigh of escaping air and slipped below. Those oddly chosen words, 'Warning, warning, strange ships entering harbour,' were ringing in my ears.

CHAPTER THREE

After a time I grew calm, cocooned in silence in the warm, soupy water. I became numb in mind and body, making just enough effort to stay afloat. The buoyancy was relaxing. But this phase soon passed and my mind became active.

I was quite ready to drown; I thought it should be a lot more peaceful than being blown to bits. And I'd had enough of struggles and decisions to last me a lifetime.

Life! Half mine had been spent in preparation for taking this one gamble and it hadn't come off. So that made me a failure, or worse. Of course, if it had come off, if there had been one straw in the wind that had blown the other way, I'd have been a success, or better. I'd have been celebrated, held up as an example, promoted even.

But it wasn't all bad luck; there had been mistakes, of omission and commission, that could be held critical, damaging to my case. You don't wipe out a ship without accounting.

Now I couldn't stop my mind. It had taken charge. But I shall die. And they will hang my portrait beside Uncle Edgar's, flanked by generations of soldiers with the famous prize-fighter's nose and that will be the final account... two captains of ships who died in two wars. The traditions of a warrior family being served, the legend will say that I did not fail at all. The grandchild I will never have, if you see what I mean, will be shown my picture and told: 'That is your grandfather. He sacrificed himself and his ship at the Battle of Savo Island, trying to save others. He set a fine example. Be worthy of him.'

When they get the news, my father will run down from the War Office for the day and say things about honour and duty to my mother, who will save her tears until she can go for a walk on the Downs, her Kipling country. 'Kipling loved the Downs,' she used to say and somehow she got it all mixed up and brought us up on Kipling, this gentle woman whose retreat into books even reflected martial themes. We're all victims of the generations.

My brother Piers broke away, though; went into the Colonial Service. Wouldn't it be rum if he was Resident Commissioner here? It is a British possession... the British Solomon Islands Protectorate. Some corner of not even a foreign field. But there'd be a damned sight more justice in me dying for it than all these chaps from Nebraska and Wisconsin and New South Wales. God, what a place to die for! Stinking jungle. Useless.

It is getting cold. And there's oil fuel about, I'm in a patch now. Dangerous. It could catch fire. Move to a better 'ole.

Can't see a soul. Where are they all? A better question: how many are there? I wish I had been able to go round the ship at the end. It was a miserably undignified ending.

I wouldn't mind finding something to hang on to after all, can't keep on swimming for ever. Which means I don't want to die, doesn't it? To live, I'd need to find a raft, but then I'd have to ration the water, tend the wounds, pitch the bodies overboard, navigate the thing, lead the singing. I've no strength left for it. I'll probably resign, if I ever get out of this. Will they let you resign in wartime?

There is another Englishman here, Admiral Crutchley. I wonder what he's thinking now, with his fleet wiped out? Does he share my longing for the misty Scottish ports, cool places, with soft colours, somewhere you can understand? He's even worse off than me, poor chap; talk about disaster. We'll both have to take what's coming if there's any trouble, but I think he'll show loyalty downwards and that will be a great help. I only met him once. Called on him in the flagship when I took command. Bluff, red-bearded, he did not encourage confidences. He would have thought it out of place if I had referred to the fact that we were both R.N. Well, that's as it should be.

Or is it? Why can't we all be a little more human? It's the system. When I let the troops yell and cheer like that, wasn't I half rebelling against it? Why shouldn't they? It was good, it brought morale up from nothing. Never seen anything like it.

Poor old ship. They do come alive in a way, you know, your first, anyway. You think she's doing it just for you. So responsive, sweet as a nut, doing your bidding. And those tentacles I had out all over that ship. I just had to think of some compartment or place or area and I knew what was going on there; I could *see* it. They were like magnetic lines of force. I don't have them any more... because she's dead. Yes, she died. And it's not hard to believe she suffered pain and terror too, like the rest of us.

I can't hear firing now but I'm still pretty deaf. But the Japs would have gone. It was an appalling defeat. Why didn't *Blue* warn us? Why didn't I... no, *I am not going to think about that.*

Field's dead, Marks, Treloar, Morley, and McNab, probably... and poor old Chief. Cuthbert should have made it. Lachlan too; I never saw him after we fired the second lot of torpedoes. He could have been blown clear, I think the starboard look-out was. There's something wrong with our torpedo technique, the Japs are better. I think the American cruisers were torpedoed. When I get out of here I'll go to the torpedo school and...

But you're resigning. You're getting out, aren't you? You can't take it, you'll leave it to the others. Run away. You've got no guts –

'Whoa, there! come aboard my barrel.'

My hand was gripped in mid-stroke and guided to a rope hand hold on... what was it? A barricoe!

'I'm glad to see that,' I said. 'And you. Who are you?'

60

'Stoker Jonathon Darling, in command. Who are you?'

'Dick Fitzallen,' I croaked. 'I used to be in command.'

'Oh... I didn't recognise you, sir. You're all oily.' White teeth gleamed at me across the barrel. 'Me picking up the captain!' he crowed. 'Well, I'll be buggered. Are you hurt, sir? Are you all right?'

'Yes, thanks,' I said guardedly.

'I can give you a drink of water if I can get the bung out of this thing. I think there's water in it.'

'There should be. It should be half-full of fresh water. It's a barricoe, a fresh water cask kept in the whaler for... such purposes as this. But I'm not thirsty.'

'Well, the navy does think of everything. Makes you glad you joined.'

I looked at him sharply. It was facetious, but scarcely insolent and said inoffensively... anyway, I wouldn't want to dress him down in this situation. It would be ridiculous.

'A breaker,' he said, giving it my pronunciation. 'Why do they call it that?'

Oh, well. One had to pass the time.

'It's spelt "barricoe", I said, 'which is an old English word. But you say it quickly over a few centuries and it becomes "breaker". There are lots of things in the navy like that. Take "bos'n", for instance, spelt "boatswain"... '

What piddling rubbish!

Across the barrel we both recognised that we were play-acting. There were issues to face.

'What're our chances?' he asked, in a new, sober tone.

'They're good. They'll be looking for us. *San Juan* and *Hobart* ought to be handy. You keep your eyes open.'

'I'd rather know if... fair dinkum, no bullshit, sir,'

'That's not bullshit. It's absolutely straight.'

We were silent, each with his own thoughts. Then he said:

'What happened?'

'Oh... we got sunk.'

61

'I was in Number Two boiler room. We didn't know what was happening, of course. Just kept the steam pressure up to her, that's all we did. By golly, she was moving! Then the next thing we know the magazine goes up and half the engine room is missing. The PO ordered us out then. We had just shut down, drawn fires, when the airlock went. We were lucky there wasn't a blow-back. Anyhow, we came up, went aft and just stepped off. Easy. I don't know where the others are.'

The story touched me and I responded with a straight narrative of the action, in detail. When I had finished he said:

'Phew! If that's what was going on, I'm bloody glad I was down below. Would've upset me.' Then he bent his head and great gulping half-retches, half-sobs convulsed him.

I did nothing, simply because I didn't know what to do. It was the right thing; he recovered quickly.

'It just got to me,' he spluttered. 'Don't know why. We're the lucky ones, aren't we? Boy, are we lucky!'

Lucky, was he? I hadn't told him about the mishaps and misjudgements, or my talent for being too late with too little. He should still be afloat.

No. It wasn't as bad as that. Take it item by item. The rejection of Martin Field's theory was a massive indictment. In the actual battle, my first torpedo attack failed because of the death of Morley and my second because of an equipment failure – the bad starshell. Just bad luck. I had called off the third in favour of laying the smoke screen for the American cruisers and there were endless moral and practical considerations for and against that. But, say what you like, it failed and that was proof. The system would be unforgiving. I could accept that... indeed I must accept it for my own sake, for to refuse to face it, refuse to take up the burden of so much death could lead to madness. But it did not mean I could not argue my case with honour.

There were other things. I should have tried to use communications more...

My stoker friend was trying to float on his back and rest, but he was being swamped by every wave.

'Lucky to be alive, yes,' I said. 'But there were some problems I couldn't solve and they had consequences. So we're here now. There'll be some music to face. Probably for a long time, I'll be thinking I should have done things differently. Do you understand?'

'Like some bastard's always on your back? Even a captain? Well, the boys say you're a damned good skipper.'

We were tired now and cold. The hard edges of the brass bound barricoe dug into our flesh, which was becoming pulpy and tender. Hems and seams in our clothing chafed the skin. We would slip an arm through the rope handles and hang at rest, then reverse arms when one side became too uncomfortable. Occasionally one of us would struggle on top of the cask but it required too much effort to stay there, for it bobbed and bounced, and hurt.

The time passed better when we talked.

'Well, what are you thinking about?' I asked.

'Getting out of here.' Ask a silly question...

But his teeth were chattering. It was going harder with him. I watched him and saw his eyes close.

'You mustn't go to sleep. I'm putting you on watch. You take that side and I'll take this. We report everything we see to each other, even seagulls. That's an order!'

He nodded but his hold slipped. I brought his hand back to the rope handle and shook him.

'Ah. I was having this dream,' he murmured. He seemed not to realise he'd let go.

'What was it?' As long as he kept talking.

'My sister and I were picking these mushrooms. We went down to the bottom paddock before school, to feed the horses and there were hundreds of 'em. Mushrooms, I mean, not horses. Funny, that's just like it used to be, too. We used to get mushrooms there, about this time of year.'

'Where was that?'

'Coffs Harbour, sir. Do you know it?'

'No, where is it?'

'North coast of New South Wales. Banana country. It's a good place... '

He was drifting off again.

'Look here, I'm thirsty. Let's try and get a drink out of this barricoe.'

'Okay.' He perked up. I really was thirsty, and no doubt so was he.

'Have to be damned careful, though. We don't want to lose it.'

He held the cask while I prised at the bung with my fingers and to my surprise it came out easily. Treading water, with great effort and care I lifted and tilted towards his mouth, grimly clutching the bung in my hand at the same time. It was a mistake; it was too exhausting. He gulped a few mouthfuls and then we changed over. I passed him the bung and sucked some water but the cask butted me in the face and I lost hold. I was weaker than I thought; this time he had to grab me to bring me back to the barrel.

'That was hard work,' I gasped.

He was alert, staring frantically around.

'I've lost the bung,' he cried.

We thrashed round in circles searching, but it was gone. The barrel filled and sank.

Minutes, hours later, I do not know, he called across the few yards of water that separated us:

'I'm giving it away. Good luck.'

'Goodbye, Jonathon Darling,' I said to the empty air, and wept.

Again, minutes, hours later, I cannot tell, I was bundled into an American whaleboat.

CHAPTER FOUR

The paymaster captain was writing busily at his desk. A buzzer rang and he looked up at me.

'CNS will see you now,' he said.

In my borrowed, ill-fitting blues, I went through a green baize door.

'Fitzallen.' The Chief of Naval Staff rose from behind his desk and shook my hand. 'Sit down.'

I sat in an easy chair and instead of returning to his desk, the CNS sat in its twin, opposite me.

Good P.R. Suggests we are just having an informal, cosy chat. Only we aren't.

'I've read your report of the Savo Island night action. It's a good report of a bad business.'

Pause.

'Where do you think you went wrong?'

Well, we weren't going to waste any time.

'In the first place, sir, by disregarding the advice of my first lieutenant.' I had written this in full detail. It was a penance and a promise. 'Obviously, if I had taken it into consideration, I would have been prepared and I might have been able to give warning – '

'No, I don't criticise you on that account. Your first

65

lieutenant happens to have been right, but it was completely intuitive. He didn't have a shred of evidence to support his theory. You had the proper staff assessment and your responsibility stopped there. You should have accepted it.'

I glared at him murderously. What the hell did he know about it? But it would do no good to Field to argue that point, and it was an unexpected bonus for me. I said nothing.

'But what I can't understand,' said the admiral, 'is the total failure of communications. It was general of course, but in your particular situation, you could have pulled the whole thing together. You could have... well, let's take it from the beginning. In the first suprise attack, why did you go off to the north-east?'

'It... it was a pretty instinctive reaction. I think I thought it was a clear area. I felt I needed room to look at what could be seen, form some sort of perspective, check the whereabouts of friendly ships. I thought we had opened fire on friendly ships.'

'Yes. You were not alone there. Look, don't think this is a fault-finding inquiry, it isn't. There will be an offical inquiry of course, but that's a formality. Meanwhile, I want to hear what happened, from you.

'Now, did it occur to you that you were supposed to be escorting *Canberra* and *Chicago*? That you should have been in attendance on them? Under *Chicago's* orders?'

'Yes, it did, sir. But there weren't any orders. That's the point. And by the time it did occur to me, we were in contact with the enemy column.'

'I see. But... ' He shifted impatiently in his chair. 'Damn it man, why didn't you call up *Chicago*? And keep calling?'

I focused on the carpet. 'There just wasn't time.'

'Well, your report has an attenuated quality. When you read it, the time factor doesn't assume the significance it should. I suggest you add a time-scale appendix. That will bring that out.'

'Yes, sir.'

'Now, I think you fought your ship, or tried to fight it,

well, in the first action. You had bad luck. It was a classic torpedo attack. Couldn't know your torpedo officer was... '

'No, sir.'

'But here we have this communications business again. You had a full two minutes before you were in action again and – I am right, aren't I? – You didn't even try to establish communications with *Australia*, with *Chicago*, with the northern patrol?'

'Yes, sir.'

'Why?'

Oh, God.

'I don't want to keep saying I was too busy, sir. But there was damage to assess, there was a very confused situation to sort out on my own bridge, navigation problems, the whereabouts of the northern patrol, trying to find touch with the enemy again – '

'All right! I do know what it's like, you know. And half the trouble was faulty dispositions. The patrols should have been stationed close enough to be mutually supportive, instead of which, they were almost a hazard to each other. But you said it yourself: you were preoccupied with the whereabouts of the northern patrol. You must see, if only you had spoken them, the situation could have been transformed.'

'I was just about to, as a matter of fact, when we nearly ran down that Japanese cruiser. And that was the end of that.'

'Well, yes. I quite see.' A thin smile.

'Now we come to the second action.'

He leant back in his chair, seeming to search for words.

'Fitzallen, whatever possessed you to do what you did? You didn't have a snowball's chance in hell of getting away with it.'

'To me, there was no choice.'

'Oh wasn't there? Then I'll tell you what you should have done. You should have bloody well screamed and shouted and kept screaming on the TBS. If they wouldn't answer you, you should have made them. It is incredible that this whole action went on without any communications. And instead of throwing yourself away like that... I would have carried out a torpedo attack, instantly, at the best target and then stood by for whatever developed, reporting on the enemy. You were a ready-made shadower for those cruisers.'

'But it wasn't like that, sir! They were too confused to use me in any tactical sense. There was no time! They were hit at once and they kept on being hit.' How could I explain? 'It was like a mine cave-in.'

'Well, I wasn't there and I can't argue with you. But if I accept that your action was sound, you tell me this. You didn't get away with it, that is a fact. But if at an early stage you had established communication with the cruisers, you could have advised them of what you were doing. And they could have reversed course. Don't tell me they couldn't have. Then there would have been some chance of them getting under your smoke.'

That had been preying on my mind for days. It was so glaring and elementary, and there was no case to argue.

'Yes, sir. I did think of that. Afterwards.'

'Too bad.'

There was a long silence.

'Fitzallen. I want live captains, not dead V.C. winners and sunk ships. You conducted yourself with spirit, but you lost a ship, to no purpose. That's... you know as well as I do. Well, I need a drink. What will you have?'

We had several and under their influence, talked more easily and generally about the action. The stunning efficiency of Rear Admiral Mikawa's force of seven – not five – cruisers and one destroyer. The mystery of *Blue* – she had turned away on her patrol, presented her stern to the enemy as they were streaming past and nobody looked astern. The sinking of the four Allied cruisers. The destroyer was not mentioned again.

When I took my leave, I was sufficiently emboldened by drink to ask about my next appointment.

'Too early. You've got survivor's leave and you need it. Go and enjoy it.'

'I would enjoy it more if I could have some indication.'

'Well, if you insist. There aren't any immediate commands. And as I have endeavoured to make plain to you, in my view you showed some lack of judgement... blank spots... and over-confidence, in your last. That's putting it more black and white than I feel, but you force my hand. Whether the actualities of the situation will work out like that I don't know; we are still very short of experienced officers. But I will say that I would like a further report on you before you are offered another destroyer. You could go to one of the cruisers. If that is what happens, don't resent it and don't waste it. You are young... how old are you?'

'Twenty-nine, sir.'

'Far too young for a command like that, so you've got plenty of time. And you've other, good qualities.'

Melbourne in winter should have been refreshing after the tropics, but it was chilling to the bone and cheerless. I huddled over the electric fire in the wardroom of the small shore establishment that had taken me in, writing letters to the families of dead sailors. There were 180 of them. Being so new to the ship, I did not know many of them but I was resolved neither to succumb to heartless duplication nor to embroider or invent in the letters and it taxed my powers of expression to avoid the cliches, to say something worthwhile, to vary the formula in each case. An hours labour might produce:

> Dear Mr and Mrs Carmichael,
>
> I write to offer you my sympathy on the loss of your son, Leading Telegraphist Robert Carmichael, when our ship was sunk by enemy action on 9th August, 1942. Words are of little consolation, but I hope my knowledge of the circumstances will enable you to share some of my own pride

in having served with men such as your son.

The communications department in which Robert Carmichael held senior responsibilities performed extremely well in battle, as at all other times. In the action your son was in charge of a watch of telegraphists reading cypher traffic. At an early stage the ship's main roof sling wireless aerials were shot away and under heavy fire, carrying spare wire and tools, he climbed the mainmast to repair them. He was engaged in rigging a jury aerial when a shell burst killed him instantly...

It was important to give as much detail as possible, even in cases where the actual circumstances of death were unknown. But who was Carmichael? Was he that little tubby telegraphist, or the very freckled, red-headed one? I had been told the story but I couldn't place the man.

So went the first days. At night I drank, trying to blot out the nightmares that woke me, shouting and sweating. Unspeakable visions of charred steel swept me along on my back, over black water, holding me captive with their splinter arms. There was little to do after my WRAN typist finished work at 1600 and so I went on a few pub crawls with some younger officers. But the 'six o'clock swill' was uninviting and once I got into an altercation between a U.S. Marine Sergeant from Guadalcanal and a couple of truculent Aussies. Drunken bar-room brawling. Really! It made no difference to the nightmares whether I was drunk or sober, so after that I stayed away from the pubs.

At last the letters were finished. All but one. I officially went on leave, bought some clothes, hired a car and set out for Coffs Harbour.

The green winter landscape rolled away, seeming never to end. More trouble. I had always enjoyed driving. In my younger days I wore out a succession of battered old cars, but now it produced in me a state of acute nervous tension. It was the same in a train, or a rickety Melbourne tram. Any travel at speed, or even walking across a busy street in traffic, or going up in a lift, caused me anxiety.

I knew it would pass with time, and meanwhile I could take the driving slowly. I had some thinking to do.

I might never get those 180 men off my conscience, but that was what war was all about. Unless you were tough enough to live with your split-second mistakes for a lifetime, you had no business in it. Was I tough enough? Or brutalised enough? But Crutchley was no thug and he would live with it. Archie Wavell had the soul of a poet, but he could lead men to their death. Robert E. Lee of the American Civil War was another in the same mould. There had even been a few in my own red-necked clan. One who had distinguished himself in the Sudan had been a minor composer of sacred music. No, the true tradition was mastery of self in the face of necessity.

I had learned from a cousin in the RAF of a phrase they used when they sacked a pilot for evading bombing missions: 'Discharged, LMF', a laconic entry in the record that burned on the musty page forever and summed it all up with precision: 'Lack of Moral Fibre'. Moral fibre was the key, the thin, inconstant stuff that shored men up against their protesting instincts and turned them, introverts and extroverts, poets and peasants, into leaders. It was deceptive to measure, but one of those things you had to store up by mental preparation.

'Lack of judgement.' 'Blank spots.' 'Over confidence.' There was something to it. I stared through the windscreen at the black road winding over the empty hills and remembered.

I remembered Rugby games as a cadet at Dartmouth. I was

71

fast on my feet and so played in the three-quarter line. Once we played our army opposite numbers from Sandhurst. They were older and bigger lads, more developed than us and we were heavily out-gunned. We were losing and somewhat demoralised when, with an inspired leap, I flashed between two of their players as they passed the ball, intercepted it and sped on over the line for a winning try between the goal posts. I was a half-day hero, but even then I knew there was something wrong. In another match I scooped up the ball and ran, deliberately ignoring the outside wing three-quarter's cries to pass to him, which according to all orthodox theory I should have done; and again I dodged successfully over the line.

It was audacious but flashy play. My successes were always risky and relied on inspiration. My failures, just as many and equally spectacular, occurred when the inspired chance did not come off. I was not a consistent player and lacked a football brain.

'Blank spots.' As a newly fledged officer-of-the watch at sea, one night I had taken a bearing of a point of land which read 344 degrees. With this figure in my head and intending to drop the ship's speed half a knot in a simple station-keeping adjustment, I ordered '340 revolutions', when I should have ordered 140. Before I realised the error we had careered right up on our next ahead and were about to mount her quarterdeck. I dropped the speed drastically and pulled out of the line, then watched open-mouthed and shaking as the rest of the column swept past me. Well astern now, I rang on too much speed again and overshot my place in the line for the second time. It took me an hour of heart-stopping experiment and manoeuvre, surging backwards and forwards, before I finally clawed my way back into station. I spent the rest of the watch in a state of near collapse, alternating between hysterical laughter and blue funk.

Most young officers have similar experiences. Most would very properly call their captains in such an emergency, but any that might decide to go it alone would be either over-confident or else too fearful of the captain's wrath. I was neither, then; it simply did not occur to me to call my captain. I had a blank spot.

At Savo, in the first encounter, I had steered instinctively to the north-east and I had been right. Later, I tried to charge down the crippled cruisers and the standard verdict, against which there was no appeal, said I was wrong. I was the boy with the ball again, flying down the wing, unorthodox, spectacular, but sometimes successful. Not always however. I should have taken time to tot up the factors. I would still have been called 'wrong' because it didn't come off, but I could have answered for it on the basis of reason and logic.

And at times my anticipation had been slow. Marks should never have had to ask me what to do when we missed the attack on that Jap cruiser in the rain. I should have been ready. Oh, next time I would be ready, I would be like clockwork, next time I would... next time. Did I really want a next time?

Family or no family, the choice had still been mine. I was a professional in the war business and the answer to that question would have to wait until it was over.

CHAPTER FIVE

There was a pleasant chore to do in Sydney. Some of my men were in hospitals scattered all over the city and I went the rounds eagerly. It was the first thing I had enjoyed since the sinking. I kept the 113th Australian General Hospital, in the sprawling western suburb of Concord, until last, for Lachlan was in there. I found him wandering round a ward in a vivid blue dressing gown absurdly large for him. He fumbled his handshake; his sleeve was too long and he couldn't pull it up with his left hand because that arm was missing.

But how cheering to see him. We talked for a long time and, without shipboard constraints, his personality emerged freely. He seemed to have matured and he showed a wide-ranging intelligence and a blithe nature that it had only been possible to glimpse in our previous formal relationship.

He said he would be invalided from the service in a few days time and would be going back to journalism.

'I started in it before I joined the navy, you know. I'm going to be a war correspondent. And I'm going back there. It fascinates me.'

'Where?'

'Ironbottom Sound.'

'Is that what they call it? What do you want to go back there for? You ought to be chasing sheilas.'

'Oh, don't worry, I'm doing that too. A wounded sailor hath charms. Anyway, so ought you.'

It was a slight liberty to take and he looked abashed as soon as he said it. I let it pass. I didn't know he knew I was unmarried.

'There was another naval battle off Guadalcanal on 24th August,' he continued. 'Between carrier groups. The Japs lost a carrier and a destroyer and the *Enterprise* was bombed up. There was nothing in the papers but there was a wounded Yank in here the other day who was in it and he told me about it. He was an *Enterprise* pilot.'

His round grey eyes stared past me through the window.

'There will be naval battles there the like of which this world has never seen. Battleships blowing each other out of the water at point blank range. Ironbottom Sound, all right.'

'Well, that all depends. You can't really predict that.'

'Perhaps not, sir. But the Japs are already fighting back hard for Guadalcanal. It will be a long little war. They have to resupply and reinforce their troops there from Rabaul, which means armed convoys coming down The Slot at night and plenty of them. They're doing it now; the "Tokyo Express," they call it. At present the Americans control The Slot by day and the Japs control it by night. The Americans must of course intercept and destroy these convoys, which means night actions, pretty well any night they feel like one. And the close, confined waters will do the rest. It will be a real slugging match.'

I had not thought much about the war itself, being preoccupied with my own gloomy introspection, but I could see that, if nothing happened to break the deadlock, what he predicted seemed likely. And I couldn't think of anything that might break it. Damn it, why did my officers have to give me staff lectures?

Lachlan's idea was to observe and record these battles; if not for contemporary publication, for history.

'There could even be academic openings in it later,' he said. 'And there's another reason. I can't get the place off my mind. It's so bloody awful and primitive. I've got a feeling

75

it's brooding, waiting for something. Maybe... '

He broke off and looked at me shyly, to see how I was taking it.

'Yes,' I said. 'Yes, I think I know what you mean.'

As I left, he capped it with a parting shot.

'By the way, sir. The Whitehead Mark II two star torpedo doesn't arm under 500 yards.'

I picked up a bunch of grapes from an absent patient's locker and flung it at him. Grapes went everywhere.

'Tuck into those.' His blue-gowned backside wobbled under a bed, chasing grapes.

I found the Darling farm straddling a series of high ridges behind the town. Rows of dark green, stunted-looking banana trees stretched away in all directions, following the contours of the red earth. As I climbed the steep gravel path to the house, the sun was warm on my back and a triangle of blue sea appeared past one corner of the verandah. It was a cheerful aspect. The farm house was a low weatherboard building in need of paint, but bougainvillea overhung the verandah and there was lush, unfamiliar growth in the garden. Rather like the West Indies.

I was decidedly nervous now I was there and hesitated for some time before I knocked. A fair woman in her fifties in a sun-faded print dress came to the door. I introduced myself and she gazed mystified while I stood, apprehensive and embarrassed.

'Jonathon's captain?'

Perhaps this was not such a good idea after all.

'I'm sorry. I should have written or telephoned.'

'Yes. Well, no. Oh, come in.'

She led me through to what was evidently the front of the house, a wide, half-enclosed verandah with cane furniture

76

scattered about.

'What... what is it?' She looked anxious, fearful.

'Oh... it's nothing official,' I stammered, suddenly seeing that to her I represented Authority. 'It was just that I... we were in the water together. For a long time. I was there when he... I thought you would like to know what happened.'

Her face crumpled, but she regained control.

'And you've come all this way,' she quavered. 'I'll get Jim.' She fled, but was back in an instant and thrust a piece of paper at me.

'That's all we got. All we know.'

It was a telegram from the Department of the Navy, regretting to inform them that Stoker Jonathon Michael Darling was missing, presumed killed in action on 9th August 1942.

It dawned on me while she was gone that I had not the slightest idea how to play this. I might make it worse, barging in and stirring up their grief. I couldn't expect everyone to be on the same wave-length as I was. Another blank spot! I wished I hadn't come.

Jim arrived and all was confusion with the three of us trying to speak at once, while she dashed about making tea.

When we were finally settled, he said, 'Tell us what happened.'

I did exactly that. I started with a brief account of the battle and continued the story in detail from the sinking. However, I left out the few lighter moments, for I thought that might break them up altogether. The lighter side could come out later.

'So,' I concluded, 'your son saved my life, but I couldn't save his and all I can do is tell you about it.'

Mrs. Darling left the room and her husband leant forward on his bare forearms, gazing at the floor in silence. He was the prototype of the son, lean and sinewy, with the same colouring.

She was a type I would learn to recognise. In a gentler place, she might have been elegant, even beautiful, but the

77

years of making do in harsh conditions, battling with the Depression and the capricious seasons, had left their mark on her. In this continent such women pioneered with their men. If the man was a good one, they were happy; if he wasn't, they had no resource but bitterness. Australia had its unsung heroines. But I could see that for these two it was not like that, though it had clearly been hard for them and it seemed to have left her timorously expecting the worst.

Mrs. Darling came back, composed.

'How I wish Pat was here,' she sighed. 'That's his sister...' She choked again. 'There were only the two of them. They were very close. She's in Sydney, nursing.'

Jim stirred.

'If you go back through Sydney, maybe you could look her up? That is, if you could go through it all again.'

I said I would certainly do that.

'What was he like on the ship, as a friend?' his mother asked.

'Mother, he's the C.O., he doesn't have friends on the ship, not like that.'

I explained that in any case I was new on board and had not known Jonathon and many others in the ship's company.

Another half hour passed in questions and answers, then they grew preoccupied again and I judged it time to leave. I declined an invitation to stay for a meal, but promised that I would call and say good-bye before I left town. Perhaps I could fill in the lighter touches then, I thought.

I had not planned my leave beyond this moment. What to do now? Coffs Harbour was a pleasant fishing village and the weather was fine and warm, so while I made up my mind, I decided I would stay there in the little pub.

I spent a couple of days walking the beaches and writing letters home. To my father I had written the barest possible account of losing my ship and his reply surprised me:

'Nobody here has ever heard of Savo Island. Your story has odd gaps in it, even allowing for censorship. You'll be taking it on the chin. We

78

have to make hard decisions and stand by the consequences. That is something your mother doesn't understand. Do you think I am proud of my M.C. at Bullecourt? I lost half my company and but for a stroke of luck I could just as well have been court-martialled. There's a fluky element that dogs us and I sense something of it in your business. So don't feel alone and don't dwell on it too much. Find yourself a woman. It's that celebration of being alive you need now.'

'Incidentally, I knew your colonials at Bullecourt. Too individualistic for massed infantry, but they did well...'

I found a shallow lagoon off the sea and bathed in it for hours, tiring myself out. I was keen to try the boisterous surf across the sand bar, but I knew enough about surfing not to risk it by myself. There were sharks and there would be no means of rescue if I was swept out.

One afternoon I returned to the pub from a jog along the beach and found a note waiting for me from Jim Darling:

'Dear Commander Fitzallen,

'I was in town and saw your car outside the hotel. If you are doing nothing, we would like you to come and have tea tomorrow. If I don't hear from you, we'll expect you. Yours sincerely, Jim Darling.'

I was pleased, for I had found myself thinking about them. It would be a good opportunity to say good-bye, and then I would get away back to Sydney the next morning. Tea, I supposed, meant about 4 o'clock. To be safe, I would get there at 3.30.

But that was the second time I embarrassed Mrs. Darling.

'Oh, didn't he say? I thought Jim would have told you. We don't have an English tea here. Our tea is what you call "dinner". He's still out working. But you mustn't go. No, please, you'd only have to turn round and come back again.'

I had an inspiration.

79

'Will you show me where Mr. Darling is, then? I'll go and give him a hand.'

That was the start of it. Bananas ripen all the year round and there is always picking and packing to be done. For the next few days I revelled in hard physical work; it was what I needed. A silent companionship developed between Jim and me, but his wife was naturally gracious and carried the conversation when we were with her. She had wit and tact and I could see Jonathon in that side of her, though she was softer-shelled, and there was a wistfulness about her, as if she knew she could be shining on a wider canvas. She did not wear her grief on her sleeve, but neither did she bury it, and spoke of both children as a matter of course, often as if Jonathon was still alive. I became engrossed with these people, the first humankind I had known outside family and the navy for longer than I could remember. The old Dick Fitzallen, hard-nosed careerist and conformist, would have kept a calculated distance from an ordinary sailor's kin. I pondered over the change. The disaster must have taken social overlays with it.

If she was trim, Jim was ballast. Outdoors, his was a comfortable presence, like a smooth, sun-warmed rock. Hours might pass between his 'Warm today', and 'knock off for lunch now, eh?'

One day he put down one of the cases and said: 'I'll just say this. Once the boy had seen how the land lay, he'd want to go on his own terms. The way I see it, with no rescue in sight, he wouldn't want to just wait for the end. That's him. He was wrong there, but he was no piker.'

It was painful for him. I told him that was how I'd seen it too.

'Might pay you to lift the boxes this way. Get more of a swing to it.' He moved about the packing shed with long, lithe strides, expertly hefting the cases, a study in economy of motion and effort. I worked clumsily and doggedly. Sweat dripped off my forehead and tiredness entered my bones. On this alien hill-top, I was seeking the simplest of existences.

When I left Coffs Harbour the cure was well begun and I knew the human contact had done it. Left to myself, my sombre musings could have fed on themselves and made me really ill, but now they were dispersing and life was ahead again. The trek up had been a blur, but going back I noticed the countryside. Sometimes the road ran for miles beside wild, clean beaches and I stopped and played on the sand like a child.

Sydney, I saw for the first time, was an attractive exciting place.

CHAPTER SIX

'I'll spell it out again,' I said. 'I am joining *Australia.* The Resident Naval Officer in Brisbane sent me on to Darwin. You will have something about me somewhere. Find it. If you send me back to Brisbane, I'll have your guts!'

A touch of the old Fitzallen there, all right. But this limp book-keeper dressed up as a lieutenant was the last straw. My new appointment and a dislocating journey by train and aircraft had already reduced me to a state of savage misery, and now this mincing clerk said he had never heard of me.

His spectacles flashed defiance. He was not used to being spoken to like that.

'I'll check again, of course.' He was pitching it above my vulgarity. 'But, actually, I'd victual in the mess, if I were you. As far as I know the Aussie is somewhere in the Coral Sea and you'll have a few days' wait. You may have to go on to New Guinea or... back to Brisbane.'

He'd damned well do it!

'We're not playing hotel bookings! I am joining a warship. If you don't get your arse off that chair and produce a piece of paper with my movements on it, I'll have you turned back into a reservations clerk. Jump to it!'

He jumped and disappeared into an inner office. I sat in his chair. The sun beat down like a hammer on the airless corrugated-iron hut.

It was inevitable that I should find the woman my father wrote of. Her name was Beth and I met her through Jonathon Darling's sister. She was lovely, like the golden fruit of her own land, with flecked brown eyes that readily filled with laughter and with tears. The curve of her arm in candlelight set my blood surging and as the days passed the want of her built up until I could no longer tolerate the deprivation. A power beyond me seemed to have decreed that she would be the one to cleanse the drying blood, drive out the still lingering stench of death with her own sweet musk and make the last smashed bodies whole in her embrace.

A week ago we had sat in a café on the Old South Head Road. I reached over meaning to take her hand, but instead I just put mine on the table beside it and we sat there, not touching, looking at our hands, for a long time. Then we looked at each other, with understanding and evident delight.

'Let's walk,' she said.

Outside, she kissed me on the lips and took my arm. There was a thunderstorm coming but we walked slower as it approached, smiling at each peal of thunder, taunting the storm, consciously allowing the sexual tension to mount with the atmospheric. When the first tepid drops of rain spattered down, she stopped and raised her face to them. The rain moulded the white stuff of her dress to her skin and I reached for her there on the dark street, her body wet and seeking, naked to my touch. I kissed her and we clung together with our mouths and limbs. 'Don't be so troubled. Come on,' she breathed, and we ran.

I did not want her just for my own relief, but I couldn't help it. It was a mental and physical upheaval of only seconds. But afterwards, with a growing, marvellous lightness, we talked and made love again and it was all right. Early in the morning I left, still in the rain.

Then, for my last four days, we took a houseboat on the Hawkesbury River. We pottered about the magical inlets, occasionally plopping over the side into the still, green water. At dusk, I would fish and catch our supper of flathead. While we drank our wine, the little toy-like generator would run out of fuel, the lights would go out and I would find her in the dark. The first urgent release would start a cycle of deep sleep, tenderness and passion, a joyous festival that renewed itself like the bright sun each day.

Now, time had passed and I knew this had been no ordinary affair. But I would soon be off again, God alone knew for how long or where in the world I might be... even if I would end up back in Australia.

'In *Australia*,' indeed. I knew I had to expect it, but when I read the words of the appointment, they hurt. What job would I have? Mess deck officer, probably. Seeing that someone else saw that someone else kept the ship's company's lavatories clean. Action station? Damage control officer or in charge of the bridge plotting room, perhaps? A principal control officer at night.

Well, I consoled myself, the *Australia* was a doughty old County Class cruiser and had given and taken much already in the war. At least, I was still at sea. But the flagship!

A flagship's bridge is a place of hierarchical dread. The admiral stares down his nose at the captain and the captain stares down his nose at the navigator who barks at the officer-of-the-watch, half to impress the admiral and the captain. The OOW barks at the midshipman, who, wretched child, cannot bark at anyone unless he has a go at the look-outs. The admiral's staff gets in the way doing their bit, the noise level is appalling and the whole place is awash with tension.

How different from my sweet destroyer! Noise we had and a hierarchy certainly, but we also had an underlying fellowship, doing the job together.

A ship, any ship, is like a kingdom. It is a self-contained, self-propelled environment for many people and the organisation that enables them to live within its citadel is complex. The functional systems of a warship make it even more so. A warship needs a laundry, a bakery and post office, as well as the wherewithal to repair a 500 watt radio transmitter. It carries food, clothing, money and ammunition, as well as propulsion fuel. It has a fire brigade, police force and jail, as well as heavy artillery. Its electrical, electronic and engineering systems must all be maintained from its own from its own resources. It must have a hospital and pharmacy, and a canteen. If all this functions under one man, shall he not proudly be called king?

It takes all sorts, of course. Captain Macintyre, with his quaint, unruffled 'make it so's' and 'if you please's' had no common touch, yet his crew strove only to please him. Others held the kingdom together by driving force, or let it slip away and the arts and sciences of sea-going decline. I had scarcely had time to find out what sort of king I was, but I had tasted the lonely intimacy and power of it; and they had stripped everything from me but my robes.

The lieutenant was back.

'I've checked the signal log and the correspondence register for the past week,' he said. 'We have nothing on you sir. I've sent a signal requesting... '

I cut him short and stalked over to the wardroom.

In the morning, I was in no better humour. I called on the Resident NO, whom I knew slightly and rather liked, but within the limits of propriety – he was of senior rank – I let him know what I thought of his arrangements for transit officers. I was leaving his office when the lieutenant dashed up and flung me an extravagant salute just short of insolence.

'Have you found it?' I snapped.

'Not exactly. But this has just come in.'

He handed me a signal pad.

'Appointment of Lieutenant Commander R.H.U. Fitzallen to *Australia* is cancelled. Officer is to report to Navy Office forthwith for briefing prior to attachment to ComSoPac and duties as observer with U.S. Naval Forces, CACTUS.'

CACTUS was the code name for Guadalcanal. God Almightly!

The paymaster captain was still writing.

'Hello, it is Fitzallen, isn't it? You look a different man. Enjoy your leave?'

I said I had.

'What do you think of your new job?'

'I like it, I mean the idea of it. If I can't have a command, that is... '

The buzzer went and he cocked his head wryly at the green baize door. I knew the drill and went in.

The Admiral looked me up and down keenly.

'Well, your clothes are a better fit, I must say. Fitzallen, don't think you have been dragged back here unnecessarily because you haven't. You can get background briefing here, though you'll have to go back through Brisbane and Townsville for the full works. But I wished to see you myself, as I am responsible for your appointment. I don't often interfere with the Director of Officers' Appointments and I suspect I am none too popular for it, but I wanted to let you know the importance I place on this job.'

Pause. He was sitting at his desk this time and regarded me steadily. The vice admiral's stripes rested in front of him, giving much point to the gaze. The old boy knew all the tricks.

'There is nothing new about an observer with a foreign navy, of course. There have been certain changes in command arrangements and when the probable nature and duration of the Guadalcanal campaign became clear, I asked the Americans for this billet. Admiral Nimitz acquiesced so promptly that we were embarrassed; it should be a commander's job and we can't spare one. It was recommended to me that we defer the appointment, but I pulled you out of the hat. You've had battle experience in the area, you know something about command and, last but not least, you can write an understandable report. There is no question of an acting half-stripe, by the way. No establishment.'

'Now.' He walked over to a wall map. 'The various staffs will brief you in detail – and mind you leave completely up-to-

86

the-minute, especially on intelligence in Townsville. Broadly, as you know, there are two major land campaigns going on; one is the Japanese thrust straight across New Guinea, over the Owen Stanleys to Port Moresby, and the other is Guadalcanal. This is where we hold the line, or you can say goodbye to Australia and New Zealand. It's our last chance and the Allies are committed to desperate fighting. The Australians must force the Japanese back from Port Moresby the way they came and the Americans must roll up the Solomons from Guadalcanal. Then, if the two can join forces and take Rabaul, we can say the Japanese have been held.

'I mentioned new command arrangements. It has been agreed that the Solomons will come under Admiral Halsey, who will soon take over as Commander South Pacific, even though west of a certain point the islands are in General MacArthur's parish, as Commander South-West Pacific. But the New Guinea show comes under General MacArthur anyway, so he has his hands full enough. There will be overlapping, of course, both commands lending each other operational support and so on. The air side of it in particular has to be closely integrated.

'The Australian Fleet properly comes under the south-west command; together with American units, it forms MacArthur's Navy. So there will be no more Australian ships in the Solomons campaign and that is our loss. Our fleet is going to miss valuable fighting experience, which it will need once this phase of the war is over.

'Are you getting the idea?'

'I think so, sir. I can see that it will be a different sort of war for MacArthur's Navy. Convoy work, air attacks, perhaps the odd bombardment, but... you can't have close naval support of the New Guinea land campaign because the water's too shallow to get the ships in there. That north coast of New Guinea is full of reefs and virtually uncharted anyway.'

'Exactly. Unless it is by chance, there will be no set piece, evenly matched naval actions on our side of the fence. But there will be plenty of them in The Slot. You know better than most people about the ability of the Japanese to fight a night encounter at close range. Their eyesight beat American radar and their fleet handling was... well, we talked about that last time.

'So, you are going to get the fighting experience for us. I want you to observe every naval action you can. Don't always ride with the cruiser division commander or the captain D... what do they call them?'

'Commander Destroyer Squadron, sir, ComDesRon. A cruiser division commander is ComCruDiv.'

'Yes. Well, go with them too, but spread yourself, go with the ordinary units as well. In learning how the Japanese fight you will by the same process learn how the Americans fight and I want to know about that, too. Don't hesitate to be critical if it is called for. And above all, keep a continuing flow of recommendations for training coming in.

'How does it sound to you?'

'It sounds fine.'

'Then that's all I want to say, except that you are in no sense a liaison officer, so don't be drawn into any liaison arrangements. These are established and working perfectly well, separately.'

'I'm glad to see you looking fit again. If you get too lonely for the white ensign you can visit the New Zealanders. They should have a couple of ships there soon and some land and air forces too, I believe.'

'Good luck.'

And the interview was over.

And that was that.

Americans need goals. Their preoccupation is with the dynamic and they still believe that the true measure of man is the gauge of his personal exertion, the sum of his striving. Walt Whitman wrote that Americans are always moving on.

These are a poet's carefully chosen words that summon both sharp and diffuse, primary and secondary images. The literal, peripatetic sense is too facile, so he must also be referring to the great spiritual restlessness the founding fathers brought with them.

This took root in the early wars and spread as the frontiers pushed out, eventually transforming itself into material terms in this century, when all the first causes of the continent had been won. In Sinclair Lewis's time, it was called "git". One of Lewis's characters mentions that he didn't care for a certain motion picture as it had no "git" to it. "Git" was the hallmark of the people who ran Main Street; a rapacious, rather frenetic and elastic-principled acquisitiveness.

This energy had a resurgence in another practical form in the Second World War. It was to be the last great cause and it pulled America together in one almighty pulse of purpose and effort, which was also a release for surplus drives. It was not until after this war that the energy turned back into its spiritual form again and produced the anomalies and perplexities that devastated a generation.

After Pearl Harbour, the American at war believed that Righteousness was his sword and God was his shield and that he was invincible in his wrath. He was closer to the German than he knew in his sentimentality, orderliness and approach to discipline and he sometimes fought like him; rigidly and with prodigal waste, but with total conviction.

I did not see all this in 1942, but the first thing I did see when I crawled out of the blister of a Catalina at ComSoPac headquarters, Noumea, was a large sign which said: "KILL JAPS, KILL JAPS, KILL MORE JAPS." Well, undeniably, this was what it was all about, but... it was a bit locker-room. As if "KILL GERMANS" was plastered all over fleet headquarters at Rosyth. Oh we British were too prissy.

Anyway, there was no denying the immediacy of the war. This was the last stop before Guadalcanal a thousand miles away and every day was D day; from here we go forth, to live or die. At first light a group of crew-cut Marine Corps fighter pilots, reinforcements for beleagured Henderson Field, might fly out, followed by an attack transport full of "dog-faces" or a couple of destroyers on sortie.

The first night, enjoying anonymity, I wandered into a smoky dive on the Rue General Gallieni and stood picking up atmosphere and snatches of talk from a phalanx of khaki figures at the bar.

'The Japs can reload a whole set of torpedoes under way, I'll swear.'

'You plug the fuel tank in a Zero and WHOOMF! No self-sealing tanks. No cockpit armour, either; they're a bunch of matchsticks. But they can still out-turn anything we've got. Real split-ass.'

'The point has the highest attrition rate. At Tenaru River, our patrols had 75 per cent casualties with points and the 5th Marines had 100 per cent.'

It was all callous war talk, but that was how it had turned out for them, and they weren't complaining. It was too late for that; they were on the knife-edge of survival.

'Don't give me that low flying crap. That's how Berkowitz got his, horsing around right on the deck. He says "What is this, an oxygen hop," and he's in. Bye-bye, Berkowitz. Boy, that stuff's dumb.'

Strangely, there were no US servicewomen in Noumea. 'Congress thinks they'll get raped,' I was told. That could have been far-sighted, but there was a small contingent of New Zealand girls there and I never heard of any official complaints. There were still some French colonial administrators on the island, stiff aldermen who congregated on the governor's hill and looked down on the crowded quonset huts with apparent distaste. They were said to be divided pro- and anti-Vichy among themselves, though they presented a solid enough front when it came to resisting American needs for real estate and property.

I could see that a good deal of self-projection would be necessary in this job and I spent my first days trying to sell myself and my task. I was unproductive to American plans and efforts, and unless I forced myself to their attention, made an impact, it would be natural for them to overlook me. I kitted myself out in American uniform, following the tradition

90

in such cases that the host force confers this as a privilege and the guest individual accepts it as an honour. Then I made a round of calls.

Like people everywhere, some were courteous and some were rude, quick or slow on the uptake, co-operative or otherwise. There were some who had only the vaguest notion of Australia, let alone its navy. A full commander complimented me on my English and probably does not believe to his day that I *was* English, seconded to the Australians, who spoke English anyway.

But the key to open all doors was Savo Island.

'Say, were you in that? That destroyer that got sunk trying to lay smoke for the *Vincennes* group? In command! Boy, let me shake your hand... ' Casting modesty aside I pushed it shamelessly and within a week, I had an office in the naval operations centre and wads of files on my desk, which included the action reports of all SoPac ships. I read the accounts of Savo Island and relived that ghastly night.

One morning, at the start of my third week at ComSoPac, my telephone rang. It was still a rare enough event to be exciting.

'This is Commander Ben Jones. Still want to get your ass shot off?'

He was in operations and didn't like Limeys. Positively hostile. When I'd called on him and said my piece, he responded that he wasn't sure they could do a whole lot for me and if the British had released their East Indies Fleet to the Pacific as requested, we'd be getting our own battle experience here on our own ships. Washington was, uh, a bit put out about it. But they'd keep it in mind and if something blew up, he'd let me know. I had little hope that he would and determined to bide my time and go round him.

'I'd rather keep it,' I said into the phone. 'What is it?'

'There's a picnic party leaving and you're invited. Come to my office and I'll brief you.'

It was still early but his desk was deep in paper, full ash trays and empty coffee cups. I knew already that he was one of two or three key figures, overworked staff officers with seemingly open-ended responsibilities, round whom ComSoPac revolved.

'Come in, sit down, help yourself to coffee.' He shoved some papers aside and sat back, passing a hand through carroty hair. 'Mister, I don't know what they do in your navy, but this outfit shoots the works *before* the battle. Destroyers' plants are shot, cruisers need boiler cleans, everything's under manned and now we've lost the *Wasp* at Torpedo Junction. You know that, don't you? The word is, we may still maintain air superiority on the island because we own the Goddam airstrip; meaning, I suppose, that we never really needed the*Wasp* anyway. But how do you use the airstrip at night? *Night's* the problem.'

'I see.'

'Oh, you do? Well, I wish to Christ you'd tell me.'

Best ignore that.

'Well, that's, uh, not what we're here for.' He reached for a file of signals. 'Despite what I said, we have managed to scare up another surface task group to run some reinforcements up to Guadal. The 164th Infantry is going up under naval escort the day after tomorrow.

'You can take your pick. You can ride with Admiral Murray's *Hornet* carrier group, away north, or Admiral Lee's battlewagon group in the *Washington*, off Malaita, or with Norman Scott, in the cruisers and destroyers.'

'Well, that's good news.' This was a change of heart.

'Ho, don't be so hasty, you haven't heard it all yet. All groups will be distant support forces for the convoy, but Scott will hang around Rennell Island until the convoy gets in. Then he is going to block off The Slot against the Japs, while it unloads. They're putting fresh troops in themselves every night with the Tokyo Express and, according to intelligence, they'll be coming down again with a major convoy of their own at the same time. I have no details. So, what'll it be?'

'I'll go with Scott. I know the beat.'

'Damned if you don't.' He sat back again. 'You crapped out at Savo, didn't you? I would have thought you Savo

92

Island hot shots had had enough. This'll be a big one.'

'It's not a matter of choice, it's plain bloody orders. What are the ships?'

'Noblesse oblige, then. Task Force 64. *San Francisco, Boise, Helena, Salt Lake City* and five cans. Where did I put the... here they are: *Duncan, Farenholt, Laffey, Buchanan, McCalla. San Francisco* is flag and you're assigned to her; you'll have to get yourself a hitch over to Espiritu Santo and on board. I'll make the necessary signals about you.'

'Okay.' I drained the coffee and stood up, as if he might change his mind before I got away.

'Revenge for Savo Island, maybe,' he muttered. 'But even so it's only a curtain raiser. Things are building up and one side or the other's got to win. The Japs have got organised and the big fleet looks like breaking out from Truk. By Christ, there's going to be some fight up there before we're finished.'

Oh, God! Was I destined to be lectured on how to win the war forever?

'I know. You don't have to be Napoleon to appreciate simple strategy. Thanks for the coffee, Commander; I'll get started.'

'Well, don't get sore about it. You don't have to be Robert E. Lee to appreciate that, "it is well war is so terrible. We should grow too fond of it." I wish you luck, Limey. And call me Ben.'

CHAPTER SEVEN

We had hunted for them for two nights, but we knew they were out there tonight: three cruisers and two destroyers, covering a convoy of six more destroyers and two seaplane carriers that were bringing troops and supplies to Guadalcanal. In the afternoon, they had been reported and tracked by both aircraft and coastwatchers, running at high speed down The Slot, and Task Force 64 was steaming to intercept. It was now 2100 and Rear Admiral Scott estimated that we should make contact between 2300 and midnight. Our long column of nine ships slipped across The Slot at 25 knots, deceptively delicate and feather-like on the surface, but dense with destructive mass and power in their slim hulls. On the *San Francisco's* bridge, the TBS hummed with traffic and life-jacketed figures came and went, conducting their business with encouraging, low-key competence.

We ran north-east, with Cape Esperance and the black bulk of Guadalcanal astern, Savo Island some fourteen miles to the east. The island had been our reference point for days, criss-crossing The Slot, but I was always drawn to it and now searched occasionally out to starboard for the faint outlines, but only as relief to the long, straining stares out to port. Tonight was the night. The second Battle of Savo Island was only hours away.

One thing troubled me... the bridge. It was glass-enclosed, with a roof over it; a pilot house, really. It was weather-proof and comfortable, but I felt claustrophobic, as if I couldn't see out of it properly. Our own bridges were open to the sky and therefore the weather, but you could see and you did. In our ships it was rare for a look-out or even a signalman to spot something before the officer-of-the-watch saw it. With constant practice, normal eyesight developed into abnormal acuity.

But it had taken the Japanese to show all of us what could be done. It was now emerging that for years before the war they had trained in night attack and they selected their key officers and men for sharpness of night vision. In addition, they mounted huge binoculars, three times more powerful than ours, on their bridges. The pre-war naval attaches in Tokyo thought these were to correct defective vision and had smiled condescendingly, while the Japanese went quietly on developing eyesight into a weapon. When Admiral Mikawa advanced down The Slot before the first Battle of Savo Island, he exhorted his ships with a fine Nelsonian flourish to 'attack with certain victory in the traditional night attack of the Imperial Navy.' They preferred these and looked for them.

The train of thought was disturbing. This American combination wheelhouse and bridge, with groups of men and instruments behind glass, put us at a disadvantage against such an enemy. Developments in radar were to change all that sooner than I knew, but on this night of 11th October 1942, I kept moving restlessly out onto the walk-way round the *San Francisco's* bridge, where I could feel the soft breeze and carefully sweep the horizon. I swore my own good eyes were a match for any mis-shapen Oriental's and I would penetrate that fatal blackness first. I came in from one of these prowls to hear Scott order a course change northwards over the TBS.

'Small Boys, this is Blackjack. Execute to follow, Corpen 35, I say again, Corpen 35. Over.'

'Stringray, roger, out.'

'Cornball, roger, out.'

'Haybox, roger, out.'

All eight ships acknowledged smartly and the signal was executed, but it took a lot of time and chatter. This circuit could be dangerously overloaded if the long column had to be manoeuvred in a battle mêlée.

TBS, or Talk Between Ships, was fairly new and a marvellous advance on the old method of communication by Morse code and blinker light. One simply picked up a telephone-like instrument, pressed a button and spoke. However, the tendency to use it for both fire control and manoeuvring purposes caused clutter at critical times and the strictest circuit discipline was necessary. At the first battle it had failed, partly due to atmospheric conditions. There was much static and background noise that night and I learned afterwards of vital messages put out on TBS that I did not receive. The Japanese did not have TBS but their manoeuvring did not suffer.

Even so, Admiral Scott seemed to have its vagaries well in mind and was taking no chances with it. He required acknowledgements of his orders, believing that the time spent and the bottleneck in transmissions was a better price to pay than a missed signal. If the pace became too hot, he could adapt accordingly.

I looked at him now on the darkened bridge and felt a sudden wave of compassion and sympathy. On his shoulders lay the burden of reversing Savo Island; the dented reputation and bruised morale of the United States Navy were his to smash or restore. In a few savage minutes it would all be over and Norman Scott would either be a disgraced, broken man or a "hero." No matter if luck ran against him, if it was not his "fault"; there would be no excuses. At least I had had options in my own ordeal, but he had none.

He turned towards me and I started guiltily.

'We'll get them this time, Fitz.' His bleak good looks broke into a grin.

'Yes, *sir*,' I said, like the Americans. I took "this time" to be a reference to our joint baptism of fire at First Savo, one of his touches that made me feel at home in the flagship.

Scott had been an agonised spectator there. Stationed to the eastward with *San Juan* and *Hobart,* he came on the scene to pick up the pieces. The lessons of that night were burned into his mind: faulty dispositions, divided command, failure of communications, lack of preparedness. For three weeks he had trained this force in close range night encounters. His communications procedures left nothing to chance and he was determined to keep the tightest possible control over the column.

The ships swept on like charging locomotives on level tracks, yet silent and elusive in the gloom. How could such Titans lose a battle?

Then Scott gave the start signal: 'Reduce speed to 20 knots and launch planes.' Each cruiser carried a Kingfisher float plane and drawing a leaf from the Japanese book, Scott planned to use them to track and illuminate the enemy, with flares.

'... like greyhounds on the slips, straining upon the start. The game's afoot... '

Three Kingfishers shot from the catapults and climbed away, engines labouring and exhausts sputtering. Three only? One was missing.

'Coughdrop, this is Blackjack,' said the TBS plaintively, 'Has your fieldmouse left the barn, over?'

'This is Coughdrop. Negative, I had no executive signal on that... '

Oh, good God, *Helena* had missed it. Despite, perhaps even because of, the careful communication procedures, it had still happened. One of those extraordinary things... But what was this? One fieldmouse was throwing off bursting fireworks from the rear. It did not seem to be an explosion, it was a mass of white fire and it would not subside. It grew endlessly into a huge pear-shape that lit the whole heavens. This thing stuck to the molten rump of the tiny plane and with insane purpose drove it, twisting and writhing in useless evasions, down hard into the sea. The plane plunged straight on, scarcely seeming to pause on impact, but still the white scourge would not die. It fought the sea itself, spewing out harsh light and white-hot fragments, for interminable seconds. It was only then I realised what it was: magnesium illumination flares.

'God, what was that? Whose plane was that?' demanded a horrified Scott.

'That's the *Salt Lake's*, Admiral. The Japs will have seen it. We've lost surprise!'

'Give me that thing!' Scott snatched the TBS handset.

'Cornball, this is Blackjack *himself*. That rotten foul-up could have cost us a battle, let alone a plane and two men. I want to know why that happened and I want to know *now*. Report on air forthwith!'

'This is Cornball. Sir, we can't say with any certainty. All I can say is, the illumination flares in the observer's cockpit appeared to ignite on take-off. That's what we saw here. In the circumstances, I doubt we'll get much further, I'm sorry...'

Scott slammed the phone down. 'Nothing we can do about it,' he blurted.

Shaken by the frightful accident and its even worse implications, we stared out in the supposed general direction of the Japanese, trying to fathom the darkness.

I turned my eyes away too soon and I missed it, a single flash of light against the clouds, far away, they said. A couple of ships reported it and Lieutenant Brubaker, the staff communicator, saw it.

'What was it? Lightning?' asked Scott.

'There's none about, Admiral. I'd say it was a searchlight,' said the lieutenant.

'A searchlight? That's crazy. Why would the Japanese be flashing searchlights at us... unless... the flares. They saw the flares. What colour are Japanese flares? White, the same as ours. Soc – are you thinking what I'm thinking?' This was to Captain 'Soc' McMorris, in command of *San Francisco*.

'Could be, Admiral. It could be. What's the distance? Sixty... seventy miles? That's no sweat. Yes, sir, it makes sense.'

We were all thinking it now. It would be inconceivable to the Japanese that we had fired those flares. They should not even suspect we were there at all. They could have taken the conflagration for a signal from their own forces on shore.

Flashing a searchlight on low cloud was a recognised method of signalling over the horizon. It was an attractive idea. But it was still pretty vague, only a theory.

'Too nebulous to alter our assumption of the worse case,' said Scott finally. 'We still presume we've lost surprise. But it's something to keep in mind.'

Time had marched on. At 2230, Scott altered course for Savo, intending to skirt its north-west shore, from where he considered we could be in the best position to thwart a landing. All was quiet again and I watched the flat cone shape of Savo rise out of the darkness, mesmerised with dread. Sacrificial offering to the gods: two incinerated airmen. But they would have more than one sacrifice this night. Extinct volcano? There were miasmas still alive and they pulsed with the wolfish appetite of war.

Farenholt, Duncan and *Laffey* were in the van with *San Francisco* and the cruisers following, then *Buchanan* and *McCalla* in the rear. There were six hundred yards between ships; not enough room for much freedom of movement, but perhaps too much to reverse the line quickly, which we might need to do.

The next twenty minutes were deathly quiet. Taut nerves grew tauter and every man fought that worst of all battles, with himself. I could not stop waves of rising panic that swept over me like nausea. It was the waiting. In the silence, the ticking of the gyro compass repeaters on the bridge was very loud. We heard the helmsman shift his feet and when someone cleared his throat, everybody looked at him. I longed for something to do. I edged over towards the walkway with my binoculars. I must search; couldn't expect any look-out, however conscientious, to recognise that first hallucinatory smudge in the general blackness that meant a ship.

But they were talking and moving inside again. Something was happening. I hurried back.

Our own float plane had reported sighting 'one large, two small vessels off the northern beach, Guadalcanal.'

What were they? They could be friendly. If they were enemy, where were the rest of them that had been reported that afternoon? We would wait for clarification and further reports from the aircraft. Meanwhile, we were getting close to Savo and Scott ordered a turn to port in column, to the north-east, to parallel its coast. The quietness settled once more and I returned to the walk way.

Now both shoulders of Savo showed up as faint lines against the sky. I had read somewhere that the proportions of things are most attractive to the human eye when the length is one and half times the height; the Golden Mean, they called it. What I could see of the island had this now, but it didn't obey the law and seemed as ominous in aspect as in atmosphere. Spanish sailors had named it centuries ago, but no one knew for what, or for whom.

Out here, the throb of engines was less distinct and the rush of air and water created the illusion of coolness. The sea was like black silk, merging into the sky within a few yards; there was barely a horizon. A bad night to see ships. I thought of the countless ships round the world I had seen in hundreds of nights and all at once doubted if I could do it now. Had I missed any? I had forgotten what they *looked* like! The binoculars under my hands were slippery with sweat.

I turned my back and watched a white bird swoop up and hover at the masthead. They were always there, planing above the funnel gases and diving for scraps in the wake. Here, close to land, where it could give nothing away to the enemy, ships could throw their trash overboard and the only thing that drove the birds away was gunfire. The masthead traced an errant path among the stars, which were brighter now, for the milky overcast was lifting. A white point of fire scored itself against the sky – a shooting star. Lucky I'd seen it clearly for I could have taken it for Japanese fireworks.

They must be there. I took up the glasses again and, letting reflexes take over, covered a long arc. Now I was confident I'd see them; but how close? These night operations were the devil; so deluding.

Another twenty minutes had passed and I went in to the bridge in time to hear the float plane report that the three vessels had now moved sixteen miles east, along the Guadalcanal shore. Pretty fast; destroyers. But those sixteen miles gave us some leeway; we were now poised to intercept either the approaching force, assuming it was still approaching, or the one off the coast, when it retired back up The Slot. But to do either, we needed to reverse course, now. And that raised grave dilemmas.

To reverse the course of a column of nine ships requires both time and room. There were several methods. The simplest and quickest way was for each ship to turn 180° individually, but that would displace the flagship to the rear of the formation and was unacceptable for fighting. Another method was for ships to wheel astern of the leading destroyer, *Farenholt*, in follow-the-leader fashion, but that would be too slow. Crucial time would be lost while the line doubled on itself and the big cruisers charged round behind each other in a kind of seaborne version of musical chairs.

The third way would be to wheel the ships, by squadrons. This would require the column to split. *San Francisco* would lead the five ships astern of her round, while *Farenholt* would lead *Duncan* and *Laffey* round in a separate turn. However, these three must then race up the long line of ships now ahead and regain their former position in the lead of the column. It was messy, but on balance it was best and Scott chose it.

But that was the easy part. The question now was, which way to turn?

A heavy cruiser wheeling 180° at 20 knots displaces itself sideways for over a mile. If we turned to starboard, away from the enemy, the cruisers would fetch up so close to that cursed island as to be cramped for room, if not in hazard of running aground. But to turn towards the enemy meant *Farenholt*, *Duncan* and *Laffey* would pass up the engaged side of the other ships, in the line of fire, if they did fire.

All this was canvassed in urgent mutterings in flag plot. Finally Scott straightened up from the chart and said, 'No use wishing we were some place else when we aren't. Wheel ships to port. And hope to hell,' and the fateful order went out. There was none other he could give.

The *San Francisco* wheeled and our five ships negotiated the cumbersome hairpin turn in slow succession in her wake, while far behind us now, the three destroyers made their own turn and wound up to 30 knots, to overtake us. They had a hair-raising haul, in pitch dark, at close quarters and with the prospect of being shot at, or through by their own side. Nine minutes would pass before they were clear of our guns.

The vast blackness out to starboard was empty. Five minutes elapsed and there was still nothing. Over the half-way mark, our anxiety abated. Any second now, a ghostly *Farenholt* would loom up astern and steal past with hushed, measured tread and splashing wake.

The TBS burst raucously into life. It was *Helena* again, who carried the new SG type radar.

'Blackjack, this is Coughdrop. I have a skunk, bearing 285, six miles. Course south-east, speed 20 knots. Three echoes.' I froze. A 'skunk' was radar talk for an unidentified surface contact.

This was it. This was the covering force coming down The Slot. The light *had* come from them. And the van destroyers were still in the line of fire.

Things happened quickly. *Boise* started chattering about 'Bogies', unidentified aircraft, in the same position. It was a confusing and harrassing slip of the tongue, for he had meant to refer to the same skunk. While that was being sorted out, Scott spoke to Captain Tobin of *Farenholt* and in a voice sharp with anxiety, demanded:

'Are you taking station ahead?'

'Affirmative. Coming up on your starboard side,' said Tobin calmly.

And overall rang out the triumphant cry of Scott's chief-of-staff:

'Admiral, we're crossing the T!'

And by God, we were. With geometrical precision, an enemy force in line ahead was steering straight at us on the beam. The full armanent of all our ships could bear on the enemy, while in theory, only the forward gun mountings of his leading ship could fire at us. The classic naval manoeuvre of Beatty at Jutland, the tactician's dream, was ours by accident.

But Admiral Scott was not so cock-a-hoop.

'How the hell do we know? *Three* echoes. That contact could be our own destroyers, Goddamnit.'

It was far-fetched. Yet the accuracy of *Helena's* new radar was still unkown. We did not know how wide Tobin had turned, or even remotely where he was. The possibility had to be admitted.

'Well, let's order the destroyers straight into line where they are, Admiral!'

'No, wait! This radar picture will clarify any minute. Don't want unnecessary manoeuvring if we can avoid it.'

And immediately he spoke, *San Francisco* herself made radar contact with echoes at 5,000 yards. Now, with radar under our own eye, we could see. Were they the same group as *Helena's* and were they the enemy or Tobin's destroyers?

I dashed into flag plot once more and tried to follow the feverish calculations of the staff, craning over their shoulders at the table while the contacts were marked down and appraised. It was frustratingly early to say. We needed more reports, but they had dried up. Nothing came through.

Scott stood still, a block of controlled tension. His khakis were soaked with sweat.

'Have they lost it? Cy, get up to that radar shack and see what's going on,' he said softly. Brubaker left and we waited, in silence, dragging on cigarettes.

The star of the show blared on TBS again:

'Blackjack, this is Coughdrop. Interrogatory Roger, I say again, interrogatory Roger, over.'

'Roger,' said Scott distractedly and the word went out.

'Blackjack, this is Coughdrop. Confirm "Roger" to my last transmission, over?'

'Judas priest! Tell him "Roger", for God's sake!' cried Scott, beside himself with vexation and the word was passed again. The damned fools were cluttering up the airwaves getting acknowledgements of acknowledgements. *Helena* had already been passed a 'Roger' for the radar report.

Scott swept impatiently out onto the bridge. The plot team was still in balk, there was nothing happening and I followed him.

I was in time to see *Helena* fire her 6-inch broadside. The unmistakable flash, smoke and noise burst from her position as fourth ship in the line. I stood transfixed. Then the whole of the line, including *San Francisco* herself, split the night with a loose, ragged crescendo of blast and flame. *Helena's* breach of discipline ran like wild fire to operators lined up on targets, from trigger finger to nervous trigger finger.

I fell over flat, unprepared for the staggering blast of 8-inch guns. I picked myself up to a bedlam, shouting, angry voices and figures scurrying to and fro.

'CEASE FIRE! CEASE FIRE!' yelled Scott.

'But Admiral – '

'CEASE FIRE, I tell you.'

But *San Francisco* fired her second shocking broadside and I nearly fell again. For a few seconds, utter chaos took charge. Crew members trying to proceed with the firing were impeded by staff officers bleating protests. People milled about in confusion.

'Captain McMorris!' thundered Scott. 'What is going on on your bridge? I ordered you to cease fire!'

Oh, God, this was unbelievabale. All eyes turned on McMorris.

He muttered something to his gunnery officer and somebody hit the check fire button. Then the captain faced his enraged admiral, tight-lipped and dignified.

'You gave permission to open fire,' said McMorris evenly. 'You passed the word to *Helena*.'

'I did not! What are you talking about?'

Scott strode towards him and the two men glared at each other, uncomprehending. But other ships were still firing and at that moment they happened to synchronise in a reverberating volley.

'Jesus CHRIST!' Scott was off again. 'Get that order out to those ships and have them STOP! We're firing at our own ships! They're not firing *through* them, they're firing *at* them. I'll court-martial every son-of-a-bitch officer in this rabble. Am I the commander of this task force or the Goddam side boy?'

Cy Brubaker was squatting over the TBS repeating 'This is Blackjack, CEASE FIRE, I say again, CEASE FIRE; this is Blackjack, CEASE FIRE.' But with his other hand he balanced the signal book open on his knee and ceased transmitting to shout above the din:

'Admiral, there's a hell of a fuck-up in the signal book. "Roger" also means "open fire", as a separate signal. Coughdrop wasn't asking for an acknowledgement of her previous message; she was asking permission to open fire!'

There was a stricken silence.

'Oh, the bastards! The forlorn, useless bastards,' groaned the suffering man and clutched his head in his hands. Then he grated between his teeth, 'You have to lose a battle to find that out.'

Through my own paralysed astonishment, I registered something. The admiral had made a mental shift. From merely suspecting we had fired on our own ships, he was now convinced of it.

But he had not lost the battle, he had won it. The Japanese, taken completely by surprise, now had exactly the same problem of reversing their column, while trying to struggle away under an avalanche of accurate radar-controlled shells. The range was now down to 4,000 yards and we could see a dim shape running the gauntlet as it came to the turning point. The second in line was afire and looked like sinking. Crossing the T was paying off. This was First Savo reversed with a vengeance; every blue jacket knew it and threw himself into it. And orders or no orders, they weren't going to stop.

But poor Scott didn't know. Still deceived by who knows what phantoms of the night, he was convinced we were firing on our own destroyers and while our own skimpy radar plot remained inconclusive, he would not be shaken in this faith. All that could truly be said with certainty was that somewhere out there, these ships were in the line of fire. Unless they had had the common sense to get out of it. Quieter now, but with grim insistence, Scott kept repeating his order and not even Soc McMorris, perceiving prime targets slipping past his guns, dared remonstrate with him. At last, the firing died away, four minutes after it started. Act One of the miscarried tragedy was over.

Now Scott seized the TBS phone and called Captain Tobin.

'How are you?' he asked fearfully.

'I'm okay.' He sounded slightly surprised at the admiral enquiring after his well-being at such a time. He added: 'Coming up on your starboard, still.'

'But haven't we been firing at your ships?'

'Admiral, I don't know what you were firing at,' said the imperturbable Tobin. Come to think of it, how would he?

Scott was still not satisfied.

'Pancake,' the destroyer squadron's collective call sign, 'this is Blackjack. Switch on your recognition lights. Over.'

'Haybox, lights on.' This was *Laffey*. We searched for her out to starboard but could see nothing. Then somebody called:

'There she is!' And pointed astern.

Slightly out of line, somewhere in behind *Helena*, bobbed the green and white lights at the masthead. When the firing started, *Laffey* with cruiser shells screaming past her, had taken off her 10 knots of extra speed by going full speed astern and dived into the nearest space. Good for her.

'Crossbow, lights on.' There was *Farenholt*, half a mile to starboard and ahead, never deviating from taking her appointed station. But she was not as 'okay' as Tobin said; it transpired that she had in fact taken damaging fire on her port side and that could only have come from American ships. Scott wasn't right, but he was not entirely wrong, either!

But nothing had been heard from *Duncan*.

'What's happened to *Duncan*?' demanded Scott. 'Stingray, Stingray, this is Blackjack, over,' he transmitted. No answer.

'When did you last sight her? Over.' To Tobin.

'During our turn, twenty minutes ago. She was astern of

me then.'

'This is Haybox. She was next ahead of me on the turn. Half way through, on a westerly heading, she just left formation. She just proceeded westwards. I don't know what she was doing. I last saw her at about 2335. She was headed straight at the left front of the enemy and firing.'

We looked back to the north where there was a ship stopped and on fire, hull down on the horizon now and barely visible except for a steady blaze. We had thought it was a Japanese destroyer. What ever had possessed her? She would have charged straight into a storm of American and point-blank Japanese cross-fire.

'Sheer suicide. What the hell got into him?' asked Captain McMorris.

'Cowboy stuff,' muttered Scott. But it was an overwrought judgement. How did we know what the dead men of *Duncan* had seen? This black night was blacker for the shadow of death. No two super-charged imaginations interpreted the same thing in the same way and the caprice of human response ran riot. Demons plagued the shifting scene and one split-second stimulus over-rode another. Distortion and disorientation ruled. In officers' clubs afterwards, there were endless argumentative post-mortems because we could not reconcile post-battle accounts. This was the kind of thing historians would cover with 'certain details of the action remain obscure.'

At last, Scott swept the whole field carefully once more with his binoculars and stepped down. Then he looked deliberately round the *San Francisco's* bridge. There was silence in his own line and the flagship's people faced him, expectant. He had got control again.

'Open fire,' he said for the first time and turned again to seaward. Time, 2351.

There was a bad patch, then. Numb with noise and fright, no longer caring how the battle went, I clung to the bridge bulwark as the pyrotechnic storm broke with searchlights flickering and groping, starshell bursting and the orange flames stabbing out at me across the water as the Japanese fought back. Each second that passed brought the one with my name on it nearer and I thought only of the dwindling odds on my own survival. At least, it would bring release, into nothingness. Who said it was better to travel than to arrive? They were never in a battle; and watching one with nothing to do was a hundred times worse than fighting it. Moral fibre be damned; I was having trouble controlling my bowels...

Far away, a voice called: 'Fitz!'

It was Captain McMorris. That stemmed the flabby panic.

'Yes sir?'

'Is that can over there ours or theirs?'

They were watching a destroyer steaming parallel to us on the beam a bare 1500 yards away to the west. She appeared to be narrow-gutted with the typical high trawler bows. There was desperation in the way the little ship careered about, first butting across the swell in scuds of spray, then wallowing uncertainly in a new direction. It was lost. As we watched, it showed strange red and white lights and began flashing incomprehensible Morse.

'She's theirs, I'm certain.' With even this to do I felt better.

'But what's it doing there, headed this way?'

'It's become detached and disoriented, sir. It happens to them too. It could have been the Jap's port escort, or a picket. It probably thinks we're friendly.'

The captain studied the ship intently.

'We can't have any more foul-ups. I'll take a snap searchlight look at her.'

I was thoroughly alarmed and said so. I practically ordered him to do no such thing or the Japanese would pinpoint it, fire on him and probably knock him out.

'Sir, you don't know what they're like. They react like

bullets,' I said feelingly.

His blue eyes crinkled at me from a round, ruddy face. 'If you were one of my officers, I'd put you in hack for talking to me like that. As it is, I'll bet you five bucks nothing terrible happens,' he said and ordered the searchlight on.

It switched on, and off, but the smoky blue-white beam caught the ship squarely for three seconds, still plunging on as if in company. Sure enough, it had a lattice mast and a white band on the funnel. Awful realisation struck it and it darted off like a frightened mouse. The whole of the line was arrayed against it and the cats pounced.

It was prostrated under shell fire. The superstructure disintegrated like cardboard. The wrecked hull broke apart and sank as we passed by, leaving not a rack behind, save one last wisp of steam blowing away in the wind. The little kingdom was demolished almost casually, in passing. But that strange king must have died on his own pulverised ramparts; he would not be brought to account, nor wrestle alone with his fatal indiscretions. In some odd way, I was pleased for him.

But that classic piece of T-crossing was the last, for we had run past the enemy now and had to swing north-west after them, in a rattling stern chase. Cape Esperance was four miles due south, on the turn. Now the Japanese were broad on the starboard bow at 6,000 yards and they were fighting back strongly. As usual their fire was tightly grouped and accurate. And very close astern of the flagship, a forest of the familiar discoloured fountains rose out of the sea on either side. I glanced at McMorris but he was busy. My five bucks would keep for a broadside or two.

We were going to get the worst of it now. One Japanese cruiser was labouring and still sinking but one seemed to be scarcely scratched and the third, though riddled with shot, was never out of action.

'Cease fire!' called Scott.

Jesus wept, not again!

But it was not so drastic this time. In the fury of the chase the column had become scattered and he merely wanted to reform the line. He was going to keep a tight rein, no matter what. Ships burned recognition lights and adjusted their positions quickly but again, some ignored the 'cease fire'. I scarcely dared look at the admiral but beyond some ripe language, he let it pass. There was no time to lose bawling out the miscreants now.

But we lost sight of the targets in the interval and the flagship drove on, not firing, searching for their gun flashes.

'Captain, *Boise's* turning towards,' the officer-of-the-deck reported. I looked aft and made out her black shadow lengthening between white water of bow and stern waves, as she peeled away from the line, in a flurry of wash and spray.

'What's she doing? Ask her.'

But we didn't have to.

'Blackjack, this is Gadfly. I am combing torpedo tracks... what? Put the light on it, then.' This last part was less distinct, as if the speaker was addressing someone on board his own ship and had not meant to transmit. Then, sharply:

'Blackjack, I have a target. Out.'

And so did the Japanese. *Boise* had shone her light and at once she was smothered in a fusillade of shell splashes.

'She's hit! That's the forward turret.'

'There goes the magazine! God!'

An enormous ball of fire billowed up from her forecastle higher than the masthead, lighting up half the sky. There could be only one sequel: she would blow up. She stopped and drifted helplessly, dwarfed by the raw consuming blaze. We waited for the explosion, sick in our stomachs. It was too much for a young look-out in *San Francisco*, who turned inboard and covered his eyes.

'Just go on with your job, son,' somebody said quietly. The boy swivelled his stool back to his look-out sector, glasses to eyes again, the bravest man there in that moment.

But the explosion didn't come. Slowly the fire ball died down.

Scott was on TBS.

'What's your situation? Are your magazines at risk? How disabled are you? Over.'

'Blackjack... it's a miracle. The shell holes in the hull have let the sea water in and flooded the magazine. We are getting the fires under control. But I have many casualties... '

'Roger, thank God. Now get out of it. Retire south-west at best speed.'

'I will.' The voice shook slightly. 'I believe I can make 10 knots.' A sitting target still, engulfed in smoke, she began to turn painfully, screws thrashing, and finally inched away.

'And here comes the cavalry!' It was young Brubaker and he let out an all-American whoop of delight.

From further astern, another shadow, *Salt Lake City*, was snaking out to starboard and overhauling *Boise*. She knifed over towards the Japanese and struck. She was firing continuous rapid groups from 8-inch guns. She got between *Boise* and the Japanese, steadied, forged ahead, then swung hard, straight at the enemy line. Then she danced back, in a tight, erratic fishtail. Shell splashes began to climb around her; first one, then three, then the full orchestrated concentration, but her own sledgehammer assault never faltered. I had never seen a big ship move so nimbly and it was grand to watch. The Japanese must suspect it had a steering failure; surely it would fill them with terror, if anything could. To them, it would be a clanking robot, run amok. But the *Salt Lake* was very much under control. She drew the fire from *Boise* and *Boise* got away. There were cheers and back-slappings on our bridge and the young look-out was weeping unashamedly. Only Scott watched, saying nothing. It could equally well have been disastrous for both ships. 'Cowboy stuff' was all right, if it worked. Anything was all right, if that fluky element went your way. God help you if it didn't.

Scott called it off, then. Though *San Francisco, McCalla* and *Buchanan* had resumed firing and were scoring hits on a cruiser, with *Boise* out and *Salt Lake City* off on her own errand, the line was scattered once more and ships were still turning this way and that, dodging torpedoes. We'd had half an hour of it.

'They'll become disoriented and turn against each other,' he said. 'We haven't time to reform the line again. Sorry to spoil your party, Captain.'

A slight stiffness had settled between the two men since their confrontation on the bridge. Scott now treated his flag captain formally and no longer called him 'Soc'.

'I think I've had my money's worth,' said McMorris and visibly relaxed. He took a few steps round the bridge, flexing his shoulders. As he passed by me, he put his finger to his lips and slipped me a five dollar note with comical contriteness.

As we turned away to the south-west, *San Francisco's* Kingfisher, now circling overhead, reported that the Japanese cruiser was going down at last.

In the long, straggling aftermath, assembling the flock and shepherding the cripples home, even the tired ships' companies could not relax, for it might not be over yet. There were still the Japanese convoy destroyers to reckon with, last heard of off the Guadalcanal coast, and our ships would stay closed up for action until nearly dawn, when they could count on air protection from Henderson Field. *Boise* rejoined, fires under control and making 20 knots, while *Farenholt*, with new waterline holes, was detached to Tulagi under escort.

I stayed on the bridge with the staff and the muddled, disjointed battle turned over and over in my mind. Anticipatory phrases for my report kept forming; and suddenly I felt contempt for the bloodless, academic words. It was the same, grim old story, of fallible, desperate people put into some Godforsaken arena to kill or be killed. But I would reduce it to: 'Inflexibility of column formation; restriction of destroyers' high manoeuvrability and fire power; no organised torpedo attacks; a critical imbalance between requirement for control and capacity for independent action'. A what imbalance? A critical what? A capacity for what? Cant, catch-phrases, supercilious perversions!

But in the meantime, we did win, didn't we? There was no sign of the convoy destroyers and *Duncan* was our only confirmed loss. 'Morale restored; ship for ship and man for man as good as; cool, determined leadership... '

Rear Admiral Scott was slumped in his chair. I wanted to say something. It was a good moment.

I walked over and saluted.

'Congratulations, sir. We did get them this time.'

'Uh-huh. Thanks.' That was all. Flat and dispirited. He was utterly drained. I went away.

'Fitz.' He called me back. 'They will claim it was a great victory. But we know it wasn't. At Savo, they didn't get in amongst the convoys. Here, we didn't prevent a landing. In attrition, loss of ships, they're still way ahead. We're still losing.'

On the following morning, with the task force still a day out from Noumea, we got the news. The Japanese had contemptuously struck back. In the small hours, the battleships *Kongo* and *Haruna* had swept leisurely around Savo Island and unopposed except for a few torpedo boats from Tulagi, poured a ninety-minute storm of 14-inch bombardment shells onto the American positions. More than half the aircraft at Henderson Field were put out of action and the fuel supply went up in flames. They followed up with two heavy air raids in daylight. Again that night, Admiral Mikawa retraced his steps around the island with two cruisers and pumped another 750-odd 8-inch shells into the shaken defenders. At dawn, a Japanese convoy landed another 4,500 troops at Tassafaronga and when night came once more, two more heavy cruisers ripped the airfield with yet another 1,500 shells.

What had Task Force 64 fought the battle for? What hope did we have?

CHAPTER EIGHT

Noumea, with its grubby nickel mines and cobbled, dilapidated streets, remained aloof from ComSoPac celebrations of the Battle of Cape Esperance, so called to distinguish it from the 'first' Battle of Savo Island. But there was an irresistible public thirst for good news and reassurance abroad in the US, at ComSoPac and in the navy in particular. As Scott had foreseen, anything short of disaster was bound to be hailed as a great victory. We relied so much on collective morale building. On balance, it was probably beneficial to encourage this at the time, but in the process some folk lore became enshrined and dubious tactical notions passed into doctrine. One of these, to the navy's later cost, was Scott's single line formation. Even so, the rejoicing at ComSoPac had an air of sophistry about it; everyone really knew we were still far from winning but it was not the moment to spoil a party.

I wrote my report to Navy Office and was at a loose end. There were still files to read in the office, but after the battle I could not settle down to printed words; they seemed to be meaningless moonshine. The base was as colourfully transient and busy as ever and I wandered round looking for things to see and people to talk to. Ben Jones, as I got to know him, was good for pithy comment on the affairs of ComSoPac, though it was hardly a case of popping in for a chat, but rather of keeping a foot in the door until I was thrown out. After the last encounter, I gave Ben as good as I got and this took the prickliness out of him. He was still combative, but he respected a light insult.

The best place for me was still at sea, on operations; and to make matters worse, it looked as if I was going to miss a battle. 360 miles east of Guadalcanal, off the Santa Cruz Islands, Japanese and American carrier task forces were shadow boxing. It had the makings of an all-out Japanese effort to retake the island. The indications were that they would try to recapture Henderson Field on land, while at sea the carrier task force, having beaten off its American counterpart, would fly aircraft in and turn the field to Japanese advantage. It could be the decisive phase, but as Ben put it, we didn't have to win decisively. All we had to do was hold on and hold out. The Japs couldn't keep the pressure up.

'You're like everyone else. You don't understand that this is the defensive phase and that's the right posture. They won't shift us.'

'So there's an optimist in the camp.' I said. Henderson Field was still rubble after the battleship bombardment and the Japanese now dominated Guadalcanal by day and by night. After Cape Esperance, Admiral Nimitz, the Commander-in-Chief Pacific, had acknowledged that we were unable to control the sea in the Guadalcanal area. 'Thus, our supply of the positions will only be done at great expense to us...' he wrote.

'All great strategists are optimists,' said Ben deprecatingly. 'Nimitz is a messy thinker.'

'Is he? So am I, then. If you lose this, you are going to have to pull out.'

'Not at all. But you should worry, it's not your war. It's mine and I'm trying to run it. Beat it, will you?'

Ben's trouble was overwork, but he brought it on himself. He had to have a finger in everything and he accepted the price of attracting tasks like a magnet. He was a middle level staff officer, under a captain, but he created a broad canvas for himself which included both conceptual thinking and detailed problem solving. He had the rare combination of practical flair and a cool analytical brain... and surprisingly, in a traditionally rigid system, his colleagues and superiors let him run. He became a minor legend in the South Pacific. Nothing could happen without Jones and it was not in his nature to let it; but at the same time, he knew he was trapping himself in ComSoPac. He was a line officer and above all he wanted to get back to sea.

He reacted to these warring sides in his make-up with aggression and an excruciating enlisted man's vocabulary. At least, no one was going to call Ben Jones a sucker or an egghead.

But I suspected that his real mainspring was on another level and he did not recognise it himself; he was driven by a personal sense of responsibility for people at deadly risk. If he could produce the best answers, might he not save lives on a grand scale? He had the brand of leadership born of concern for people.

The carrier battle started on 26th October. All day the two sides launched air strikes at each other. The American carrier *Hornet* was an early casualty, to be abandoned and sunk the next day, along with a destroyer. No Japanese ships were sunk in this action but two of their carriers were so damaged that their fleet was forced to retire to Truk. But *Enterprise* also suffered bomb damage again and the American commander Kinkaid had to withdraw, his task force no longer operable. Aircraft losses were even, about seventy each.

But in the meantime, on Guadalcanal, the Americans fought the Japanese land thrust to a standstill in the mud. It was another stalemate, but it took pressure off the Guadalcanal supply line at a critical time. This battle was never inflated into a victory, but it marked a perceptible change in our attitude; before it, we said 'How long can we hold on?' but afterwards we said, 'They are not going to give up yet,' albeit just as grimly. It was a start.

For the two days and nights of the battle I haunted the operations room, absorbed in the blue Perspex plotting boards and charts as the drama unfolded. When it was over, I went back to Ben again.

'Ben, what are the chances of another run up The Slot?'

'Another task force? God's teeth, I don't know. I don't

run the show, you know; I just do all the work. But if I was Halsey I would sure grab the opportunity to reinforce and resupply. And if I was Tojo, I'd do exactly the same thing.'

'Well, can you work out a time scale?'

'I can guess one. I'd say a major convoy could be on its way in a couple of weeks. Why?'

'I'd like to go up to Guadal. If I flew up, say in the first week of November, I could be back in time to go with the next convoy escort.'

'What a very terrible idea. But it's no skin off my ass.'

'Then here's a signal already written out, saying I'm on my way. I'll just fill in the dates and you can send it.'

'Hold on, fireball! Suppose I say no? You can't just go.'

'I'll take a no from up there but not from down here. If you don't like it, I'll get Captain Browning to do it. No skin off my arse.'

He signed it, grumbling about lousy Limey fireballs, but he didn't mention the one thing I was afraid of, that they would be too busy on Guadalcanal to cope with visitors. I would have to watch the timing, which I might have to adjust, depending on convoy schedules.

The earthy Admiral Bill Halsey had taken over as ComSoPac and was making an impact. He was a 'sailor's admiral', popular with the men, who, after all, win battles. One might recoil from his public crudities and Jap-hating – and I was not alone in this – but he knew what he was doing; the superman image of the enemy began to crumble under his constant denigration. Halsey fostered images of evil, subhuman creatures, ape-like 'little yellow bastards', who were to be exterminated, not feared. 'KILL JAPS.' Like insects.

Halsey was a grey man. Grey, straggly hair, thick grey eyebrows and sometimes a grey complexion, for he lived hard and it showed. Some called him the 'Ancient Mariner'; he would have had that 'long grey beard' and he certainly had the glittering eye and skinny hand.

But his personality was far from grey. The sharp jaw was

always set and on a good day, his crackling exuberance was electric. He was a tough Indian fighter throwback. He had one ambition, to fight battles, and made no pretence otherwise. And fight them he would, later, wheeling great aircraft carrier task forces across the enormous Central Pacific with craftiness and dash.

In Noumea, oblivious and uncaring, he divided his associates down the middle into supporters and detractors, lovers and haters. But it mattered not a jot. He had a natural fire and when Bill Halsey spoke, you not only jumped, you jumped with him, like him or not. Even his detractors said he was the man to pull SoPac out of its despondency and set it rolling towards the enemy.

I came closest to him during the Santa Cruz battle. For hour after hour, he roamed about the operations room chain-smoking, spilling coffee with a trembling hand and delivering a rapid-fire commentary as the tracks of the opposing task forces inched towards each other and away again. It was not the responsibility that set him on edge, or the awesome stakes in the balance and their irreversible consequences. These he could take in his stride. But he could not abide not doing the shooting.

He spoke mostly to Captain Browning, his likeminded but long-suffering Chief-of-Staff.

'If the sons-of-bitches hold that course and speed all night, they might be trying to dodge round to the south, Miles, and do an end run for home. But they'll use up a mighty lot of fuel. Jesus Christ and General Jackson, don't they want a fight? What did they come out for?'

Then he would turn his back on the information display boards, lean his bony frame against them, thrust out his paunch that sat awkwardly on a man so spare, and ruminate on the enemy's intentions. 'Getting into his skull', as he called it.

'No-o-o, the yellow bastard, that ain't his drift. It could still be a trap. The hyenas will double back in the night, say about 0230... Christ, you've got to think triple for these monkeys. But on what we know, I say we ought to come south-west and be here at first light, in reconnaisance range whichever

118

way, right? Get 'em with their kimonos up. Okay. Now put this into your gobbledegook: One. You should now be guided by principle of keeping between enemy and his base, to ensure he brings you to battle while fuel reserves allow. Two. We estimate he has... how much? A hundred thirty? One hundred twenty hours total, repeat total fuel remaining...'

At last, Kinkaid sent him a signal outlining propitious options and the long ordeal was over. He sent back:

'Attack, repeat attack,' and sat down. Soon I heard his old man's cackle and saw him thumbing through an enlisted man's dog-eared 'Snappy Stories'. Hardly irredeemable, but it gave a clue to lack of depth, to seat-of-the-pants propensities that would lead him into extravagance and folly in days to come. Because of this, he will likely be remembered as just the man on the spot and not the last great naval hero in the world.

Halsey and his staff might complain that they were running the campaign 'on a shoestring', but to me in my naïvety the scale of the American build-up was breathtaking. Ships, planes and men arrived in Noumea in a never-ending stream. In the last days of October, there seemed to be a new population in the crowded officers' club each night.

They were a motley collection, like no other officers I had ever seen. They were broad-band middle America, from the ethnic and polyglot ends of the earth and some, hastily trained, seemed not to have made the transition from civilian life entirely. The exec of a destroyer, later to lose his life and his ship, always remained for me a New York restaurateur. A naval fighter pilot was still a priest. Serene and lethal, this man fought his war in inner peace, and after it was over, returned to the Solomons as a saintly missionary. Others were like slightly overweight businessmen, B-grade movie stereotypes.

But these were cheerful evenings. There was always a group round the piano bawling out some inventive wartime parody:

'Oh Maryland my Maryland,
The harlot of the battle line,

The bloated bitch of Market Street,
The bastard daughter of the fleet,
She'll bugger up each battle plan,
Will Maryland, my Maryland...'

One night a destroyer commander, a cigar-chomping, moustachioed extrovert accosted me with:

'I'm Jackson. I got the *Moncrief.*'

I shook his powerful hand, uncomfortably aware that on his heels strutted a lieutenant in gross impersonation of the speaker's manner.

'I'm Pogonoski. I got the clap,' announced the newcomer, to my disbelieving ears. What happened now? A fist fight? A court martial?

'Bastard's my exec,' beamed Commander Jackson fondly. 'Probably has, too. Why, there was this waitress in Townsville and he – '

'Aw, Captain, you're just jealous. Just because a good-looking guy gets to talk to a dame once in a while.'

'Yeah, well, she did something to him. Ever since Townsville our gunnery's gone to hell. Couldn't hit a bull's ass with a bass fiddle right now.'

'If you keep throwing the ship around to beat Jesus we never will,' said Pogonoski genially. He added in an exaggerated aside to me: 'The captain thinks he's a real cowboy on that bridge. We have to ride herd on him.' The two strolled off, still amiably scoring points off each other. The *Moncrief* would be an interesting ship.

There were also those who weren't going to make it. They had a look in their eye. Their behaviour was not natural. They did not drink socially but were by turns abstemious or got soddenly drunk, gulping their liquor down for its effect. They were either over-animated, or preoccupied and silent. You could be talking to one of these and see the eyes drift off to some real or imagined horror, being burnt or blown to bits or mauled by sharks, but they would never talk about it. If they broke under fire, they would become whimpering war neurosis cases... shell-shocked, as the British called it.

120

It had nothing to do with courage, but no-one has ever satisfactorily explained exactly what it *has* to do with. I knew a carrier pilot, a sick, exhausted bundle of twitching nerves who vomited before every take-off, but he lasted the distance, while an athletic, healthy-looking type from one of the submarines had to be shipped home after three months. There was no way to tell.

'That's the Galloping Horse down there and over to the left is the Sea Horse. See 'em?' shouted the pilot.

The C-47 banked steeply and I bent over the pilot's shoulder. At 4,000 feet Guadalcanal was a picture post card sight; clean, deep blue water shading to light blue-green in the shallows, bordered by a ribbon of sand. Then the matt green of the trees stretched away over the hills, broken up by grassy clearings. One of these was in the shape of a galloping horse, another looked like a sea horse and a third was called the Snake. I had seen them many times in aerial photographs and I picked them out easily. Savo Island was ringed with little breaking white caps, looking as innocent as a cow pat in a paddock.

It would be good to get down. The C-47 or Dakota was slow, uncomfortable and at an unpressurised 12,000 feet, cold. These aircraft ran a daily shuttle service from Espiritu Santo, bringing in food and taking out stretcher casualties.

'Strap in. We're getting down while we can. It's nearly Tojo Time.' The crew were searching about nervously for Japanese aircraft, which habitually bombed Henderson Field at noon, Tojo Time. I fastened myself on to the cold aluminium bench among cartons of K rations and waited for the landing.

It was a wild one. The touch down was perfect but we went straight into a hole and slewed violently to port. The pilot gunned the motors and we lifted over the rim, swinging hard the other way, I felt sure on one wheel with a wing tip scraping the ground. There was a clatter from outside as the wheels hit something metallic and another bad bump; then we got on to smoother ground and braked hard to a stop.

'Fuck.' Said the pilot, slumped over the control column. I climbed out shakily.

So this was it. A wound in the jungle. A crude scar on the earth's surface, bordered by shattered palm trees. A bit of dirt, all coral dust or mud, covered in potholes. Or, rather, bomb craters. Pieces of Marston matting poking out of the holes like bones in a bad fracture. That's what we must have hit, some loose Marston matting. Puddles, swamps really, with water inches deep in places. Impossible for planes to operate from this, surely.

The control tower was a rough pagoda of coconut logs and as we picked our way towards it through the mud, somebody ran up a Japanese flag on it. What was this, a joke?

'Scramble,' said my pilot. 'The Japs are coming. Get off the strip!'

When they ring a shark alarm at an Australian beach, the spectacle of thousands of swimmers streaking to the shore for dear life has an irresistibly comic aspect. It was the same here; a hundred or so engineers and Seabees working on the strip ran to the edge and the bulldozers churned after them at full throttle, like maddened pachyderms. The strip was suddenly deserted.

But out of dispersal in bomb shelters and trees came the aircraft, the Grumman F-4F fighters and Dauntless dive bombers, the slow ones that had to get up and out of the way before the Japs came. First come, first served, they swung on to the strip and roared off in pairs. They hopped and bumped along, gathering speed, swerving wildly and throwing up clouds of spray. They all got airborne.

Then up went a large black flag at the pagoda.

'That's air raid red,' said the pilot and made for shelter. I tumbled after him into a stinking, stifling hole in the ground.

One of my worst fantasies was being bombed in a fox hole. You would be unable to go anywhere or do anything, but, a prisoner of your own making, you would hear the bombs creep closer; it would seem always that the next one would bury you, choke you to death in the mud. The nearest I had been to this was sitting out an air raid at St. Pancras Station in London and that was unpleasant enough. In a ship, you could dodge the bombs and fight back. You had a chance.

It was exactly as I had imagined. We heard the pattern approaching; crump... crump... BANG... W H A A M ! The earth jumped and the logs of the dug-out shifted. The next one must kill us... but no, thank God, it was further away. They were going. I risked a squint up through a chink in the roof and caught a glimpse of about twenty silver aircraft, flying high, in perfect V formation. Going away. I climbed out, raw-nerved and brittle-tempered. The pilot pointed out General Vandegrift's headquarters and went about his business. Already the Seabees were dashing about the strip in jeeps, inspecting fresh damage.

I walked towards the headquarters, aware of my nuisance value, but still rattled and edgy. I was also aware of the unflattering view of the navy held by the defenders; they said we had let them down at Savo Island. Neither had the navy prevented 'The Bombardment' by Japanese capital ships after Cape Esperance, nor stopped the flow of enemy reinforcements. The navy had not yet won its spurs with them. Admittedly, their lives were dominated by this wretched strip and the even more primitive fighter strip under construction nearby. There would be no getting away from it; every plan and tactic, perhaps nearly every waking thought of every man would come back to its defence. Some 20,000 soldiers and marines ringed it in a rough semi-circle, so close that they did not need formal staff work to communicate between units, facing outwards at an equal number of Japanese to the east, west and south, while less than a hundred fighters and dive bombers, a rag bag collection from the navy, army and marines, called it home and fought over it in the air. Henderson Field did bear the brunt and its defenders considered the navy not only ineffective, but also comfortably insulated from its rigours.

But I was in a mood to challenge that. Given half a chance, I would tell General Vandegrift and his staff a few home truths. And why was there no one to meet me, a senior foreign officer? No wonder the Japanese beat them, they were slack.

Even as these thoughts flitted through my mind, there was a greeting.

'Are you Commander Fitzallen? You came off that C-47 didn't you?'

He was a youthful captain, in fresh green fatigues.

'Bates' my name, sir. I've been looking for you. I'll see you're okay whilst you're here. I've billeted you with the coastwatchers; they're Australian Navy, kind of. Meanwhile, I'll show you round.'

'Well, that's good to know. Thank you; it sounds fine.'

I learned later that they were used to visitors on Guadalcanal and had a well-oiled system for handling them. It was part of the P.R. for visiting congressmen and lobbyists.

Soothed, I climbed into Captain Bates' jeep and we set off round the perimeter. It only took half an hour, for there was little distance to cover. But there was a great deal to see, if you were looking for it.

They were tired. You could tell an original from the First Marine Division; anaemia, weight loss, fungoid infections, tropical ulcers. Malaria had cut a swathe through them. They were hollow-eyed and had a certain droop to the shoulders where the vee of sweat ran down the back of the neck. They stood on virtually the same ground that they had occupied on 7th August, but since then they had fought at Tenaru River, Matanikau, Ilu River, Tasimboko, Bloody Ridge and held off the October counter-offensive. There were no rest areas in the perimeter; whether you got a night's sleep or not, it was all front line. They needed to get out.

The army Americal Division troops were fresh but rivalry between the two divisions seemed to have an edge to it. There was some graffiti in the army lines – 'Piss on all the broad ass marines', 'B Coy, Ist Bn., 164th Inf. Welcomes All from North Dakota except Feathernecks – ' but my guide said they were merely jealous of the marines' achievements and that was healthy. This division had a name instead of a number, made up from the words 'America' and 'New Caledonia', where it was raised. This was unique in the U.S. Army and the men felt it conferred a reputation on them.

It all reminded me of something... Rorkes Drift! That was the British feat of arms at the back of my mind. It was not really the same; this was not an outnumbered garrison in defence but a strongly fortified position which carried the attack to the enemy now. In fact the more you thought about it, the less similar they were, tactically. But it was the same old fashioned frontier stuff of earthworks and logs. And the subtle, human essences, the fortitude in a man's body as he laid telephone wire, a sergeant's quiet monosyllable to some riflemen and an evocative, motionless figure searching through field glasses, made me think that these men could have stood at Rorkes Drift. They had already; Tenaru River, Matanikau... And San Juan Hill, Chancellorsville, Shiloh... Why not? They were the same people.

The coastwatchers' headquarters was an important place, by the look of it. It was a valuable hole in the ground, convenient to General Vandegrift's HQ, though unfortunately also near the infernal strip. But it was theoretically shrapnel proof, being lined with old Japanese boiler plates to protect the teleradios. Few other sites on the island could boast such amenities. Even the latrines were sumptuous; neat holes in the soft earth made by Japanese bombs which had exploded some way under- ground, leaving commodious chambers. Their possessors were proud men.

They were gathered in a tattered mess tent near the dug-out. Australian Navy 'kind of' was right. They had been put into naval uniform in the hope that the Japanese would not shoot them as spies on capture, but the uniform sat awkwardly on them and there was not much of it. One wore a complete marine 'goon skin', another was Australian Navy to the waist and U.S. Army below, while a third, in baggy navy shorts and stockings, was a marine from the belt up, except for a disreputable naval cap. They were rakishly insouciant but quite unaware of it.

The officer in charge, a lieutenant commander, had in fact been in the regular navy but had left it in the twenties to roam in New Guinea. The four other Australians had been plantation managers in the Solomons before the war and there was one Englishman, a former Colonial Service official in the islands who stayed on. He thought he knew my brother.

It was a comfortable environment after the American one, which could still disconcert me. At one point I said something to this effect and there was a general murmur of assent. The Yanks were 'funny buggers' sometimes; you never knew which way they were going to jump. They got on well with them but... one told a story of having just returned from a perilous trip up The Slot in a Higgins boat, under fire at times, to rescue a downed pilot who was being cared for by natives and the man never said a word to his rescuers.

'Just stood in the bows the whole time and when we touched the beach, he walked off. And do you think the marine section we had in the boat with us would help us unload? Not on your life. They walked off too.'

Yes, there were some strange ones. But, there were good blokes among them too. Oh, real princes, some of them. They didn't want to give me the impression they were 'whingeing,' far from it. The Yanks were doing a tremendous job and they would get all the help they needed from the coastwatchers.

They got a lot. There was at least one coastwatcher stationed on most of the islands in The Slot, living off the land with the help of natives and reporting Japanese movements by radio. They claimed that, given clear weather and some luck, they could give Henderson Field hours warning of an air attack. On Guadalcanal itself, they patrolled and scouted with small parties of native irregulars, bringing in intelligence.

But it was mid-afternoon and they were drifting away to whatever it was they did, so I went off to look round on my own. I was walking towards Lunga Point when Captain Bates caught up with me.

Before I left Noumea I had arranged for Ben to signal me advising a date to return. It was also understood that I would keep in touch with the reinforcement situation and convoy sailing dates from here, if I could, though I had done nothing about this yet. Bates had a signal from ComSoPac:

'Presume you are watching convoy situation expecting your return 7th November.'

That was tomorrow! I had planned to visit the Tulagi side. Oh, well, I'd miss it; better book a seat, if that was the expression, on the C-47.

I went with Bates to the headquarters and we arranged this with no difficulty. There were eight malaria cases but no wounded to be evacuated, so the plane would be half empty. That taken care of, through Bates' good offices, I got a briefing on reinforcement plans.

Admiral Turner was to sail from Noumea with the 182nd Infantry of the Americal Division at 1500 on 8th November. A task force of five cruisers and some destroyers at Espiritu Santo, under Rear Admiral Callaghan, would join him; half Callaghan's ships would escort the troop transports and the other half would form a distant support force. Norman Scott, in the cruiser *Atlanta,* with another four destroyers, would also depart from Espiritu, on 9th. All ships were due off Guadalcanal on 12th November.

I wrote a signal to Ben saying that I was returning to Espiritu on 7th November and asking for a berth in a non-flagship this time, preferably a cruiser. I would work down to the destroyers next time.

Then I took the road to Lunga Point again. I poked about the rudimentary small craft facility on the point for a time, then trudged along the foreshore towards Beach Red. Obviously nobody ever went here. Outcrops of rock and coral barred the way and foetid secondary jungle came down to the water's edge in places. I had to make detours through the bush. The thorns and 'wait-a-while' creepers, the soldiers' name for them, snagged clothing and held me back. I jumped a small stream but landed short and half a dozen leeches fastened on my leg in an instant. I pulled at the slimy little bodies to no avail, then remembered you had to burn them off with a cigarette. I did that, trembling and sweating, then sat on a log and took some letters from Beth out of my pocket; at least it was a quiet place to think in. Before long, however, hordes of mosquitoes drove me with flapping arms back to the beach again. Mad dogs and Englishmen. It was a pointless excursion. But I wanted to see it.

When I did get to Beach Red, it was a deserted, dreary strip of grubby sand, bordered by poisonous-looking coral nigger-heads and outcrops. Even the water was turbid here and the wash on the shore made a sullen, mournful sound. The palm trees were still shattered from our shelling and an abandoned landing barge lay rusting in the shallows. The rubbish of war was unutterably boring. I thought of that marine who had vomited from his landing barge on D-day and suddenly I was sure he was dead. Surveying the chill, tossing sea, where on that first placid August morning I had looked back with such interest and expectancy, I could find no trace, neither sight nor sound of the intruders. Beach Red had shrugged them off and the Sound had buried its dead. I picked my way up to the road, flagged down an air corps jeep and asked the driver to drop me back in coastwatchers' country. This road had been fought over and the jeep leapt from crater to crater.

When I got back, Snowy Rhoades, an Australian approaching middle age who had one war behind him already, was the only person in the tent, sitting over a mug of their eternal tea. He proffered me a mug without asking, squinting up askance at my damp, dishevelled state, through bushy eyebrows and cigarette smoke. Snow rolled his own and he was never without a limp 'racehorse' fag stuck between his lips. It turned out that he had recently been on Savo Island.

'We have a look at it every now and then to make sure there are no Japs on it,' he said. 'Just the sort of thing they'd do, sneak a raiding party or a field gun in there in the middle of the night and stir up trouble. Some of the bodies from the sea battles washed up there too and we had to go and recover them. The captain of the *Quincy* ended up there; they identified him by his Annapolis ring.'

'Is the island inhabited?'

'Not now. The natives reckon it's spooked. Evil spirits.'

'Oh? What sort of spirits?'

'Hell, I dunno. Hey, Sergeant Vouza!' Snowy called to

128

one of a group of native scouts, squatting near the tent. 'This bloke'll tell you.'

But 'this bloke', a muscular, dark-chocolate Solomon Islander in a wrap-around 'lap lap' skirt, spoke only Pidgin English. Snow did the talking and the conversation went something like this:

Snow: Vouza, you savvy dewil 'e stop along Savo, along haap?

Vouza: Me savvy. 'Im 'e number ten. Itambu.

Snow: Orright, what name belong 'im?

Vouza: All 'e got one kind bigfeller balus. Kerosene belong Jesus Christ 'e bugger-up-finish, orright, byamby 'e come up. Bigfeller master, na lik-lik master, na boy, 'e fight 'im altogether strong too much. Kill 'im 'e die. Number ten.

'He reckons they're like big birds,' said Snow. 'They come out after sundown and sort of fly around. They don't like humans, white men or black and they hunt them. He says they kill 'em. It's typical.'

'Has he ever seen them?' I asked, suspecting it was a foolish question.

'You look 'im?'

'No got. Mepeller no look 'im.' None of his people had seen them.

'What about the battles? Does he connect the spirits with the naval battles? It's a bit of a theory of mine,' I said, smiling for Snow's benefit.

Snow rattled off some more Pidgin and Vouza said:

'Itambu.' Forbidden. It was no use pressing for he was clearly uncomfortable and didn't want to say more.

'Orright. 'im 'e tassall,' said Snow. Vouza padded out and, as he lifted the tent flap, he muttered softly, not looking at us:

'Me got sorry along master.'

'Sorry along what? What's he mean? Does he mean you or me, Snow?'

'I'm blessed if I know; you, more likely. He's not sorry for me, the old bugger; knows me too well. But he'd know you're a seagoing type and all that about the Savo Island battles... it fits that way, maybe.

'Look, if you're all that interested, I'll get you a ride out there. They'll run you out in a Higgins boat from the Point.'

'Oh no, I was just curious. Thanks.'

But I put my private construction on Vouza's words and I shivered at their cold message. Of my own free will, I was never going near that island.

In the morning there was a signal from Ben saying: 'Assigned *Juneau* keep your feet dry.' She was in Callaghan's distant support force. Fine. I said good-bye to my hosts and the punctilious Bates, who I discovered suffered being called 'Master' by his friends, and went to the strip.

But it was not fine. It went badly off the rails. When the C-47 landed it burst a tyre in a crater, caught a wing tip and slewed round in a hard belly slide with a collapsed undercarriage. There would be no flight out that day.

But I could still get out on the 8th, in time to join Scott's ships before they sailed. I hurried to the headquarters to arrange my passage – and found there was no C-47 flight scheduled for that day. Something about rotation arrangements for the crews; they were sending up two aircraft on the 9th. There were other flights in on the 8th, but none out. I stopped short of asking them to lay on a special flight; they knew and I knew I wasn't worth it. I was stuck.

There was nothing for it but to stay and hope that I would be able to join one of the ships after they arrived. But it would be chancy; if they were not in action they would certainly be busy and underway, patrolling and bombarding, with no time to stop for a useless passenger. Yet, however I looked at it, it was all I could do.

It was of monumental unimportance to anyone, but I still had to signal back and explain the situation. I tried to put the best face on it and keep it in low key, but every word was a humiliation. 'Intend to embark here in any available ship,' I concluded and boiled impotently at Jones' smirk. Would he read between the lines? I was sick of this stuttering apology for a job, sick of myself, sick of the Pacific Ocean and most of all, sick of Yanks. And I had not advised Navy Office of my little jaunt. If I missed a naval action I would have some explaining to do. It could look bad. 'Did remain absent over leave so many hours so many minutes and thereby missed his ship on sailing.' How often had I glared across the defaulter's table at some hapless sailor who had done the same thing?

But it was nearly Tojo Time again and I had better find a slit trench or something. God, how I hated this place!

CHAPTER NINE

But it was never dull. You never knew what was out in the Sound at night, for at sunset, it became Japanese territory. In the first part of November, the Japanese put most of their 38th Division into the western end of the island in destroyer loads; we heard nothing and saw nothing because we had nothing to oppose them with, but the morning would confirm they had been there. A few days before I arrived the Tokyo Express landed 1,500 troops at Koli Point, east of the perimeter and the marines were out in force, clearing them out. In the evenings, when all other sounds except the whine of mosquitoes had died away, the faint crackle of rifle fire still came to us in the coastwatchers' tent.

One day, a dawn flight from Henderson Field caught two destroyers retiring up The Slot and attacked them; and the destroyer *Lansdowne*, bringing up ammunition for marine artillery, bombarded a Japanese strongpoint, then dashed about the Sound hunting a submarine. She made a brave sight, but... one lone destroyer! The navy was trying to stem the horde with single ships. It was hopeless.

The sailing of the convoy from Noumea duly coincided with stepped up air-raids on Henderson Field and intelligence reports of naval movements at enemy bases. The build-up had begun. Air searches from Guadalcanal north and west, towards Truk, intensified. Simmering with frustration, I offered my services as an observer; with the 'seaplane tenders' débacle of First Savo in mind, I tactfully suggested that my particular expertise was ship recognition and this could be put to good use. I simmered another day while the planes flew off without me, then I was offered a job with a stray Catalina, or PBY, that had put down at Tulagi on some errand and been pressed into service.

It was good to be occupied. I sat in the blister of the great Cat as it droned over hundreds of miles of ocean, searching, searching, but nothing did we see. Air searching is tiring work, however, and I slipped into a satisfying routine of work and rest straight away. The crew was good company.

On the second day the PBY captain suggested that I might be better employed with a Royal New Zealand Air Force Hudson, the forerunner of a squadron that was soon to arrive, or the Marine Corps SBDs. Catalina crews were, after all, navy men and 'knew a ship from a hole in the ground' when they saw one. The image of Martin Field trying so desperately to impress his sleep-sodden captain with the same words came vividly to mind and I fervently agreed. Could he get me on to the Hudson?

He couldn't, as it turned out, but the marines were short-handed and wanted a tail gunner for one of the SBDs. I said farewell to my Catalina friends, flew across the Sound in an amphibian and headed for the coastwatchers' tent again for the night. Tomorrow would be my last flying day, for the naval task forces were due the day after.

I had been warned to report to the SBD squadron at 0500 in the morning, for briefing and issue of flying gear. I found the squadron dug-out after several false starts, floundering in the dark among coconut trees, fuel dumps and general litter. There was a fat corporal inside it who knew nothing about me. I explained.

He seemed fascinated.

'You British?' he asked.

'Yes.'

'Navy? English navy?'

'Yes.' I was used to it. 'Look, hadn't we better sort this out? Can't you check with somebody? I am rostered to fly with you this morning.'

He kept staring at me. 'Hot damn. I got cousins over there. Winthrop? Topping Ugly, Prickets Hatch, Nutfield, Hants. Via Nutfield. Runs a milk delivery?'

'Really? Well... '

'My name ain't Winthrop; it's O'Reilly. They're on my mother's side.'

I gazed back patiently.

The spell broke at last and he was galvanised into rummaging among some papers. 'Hot damn. Never figured I'd... ' Another thought struck him.

'And you want to join the Marine Corps?'

'No! I'm just flying with you as an observer. Will you just try and find a list or something?'

He returned to the papers and shuffled.

'Ah. This here,' he announced, holding up a clip board, 'Is the flight sked. Schumaker, Hollidge, Brinker, Lemprière... Fitzallen?'

'That's me!' I cried. 'I am on it.'

'Well shoot. First time this sked's ever checked out. It says here you're flyin' with Lootenant Forrester!' This was something else to marvel at. 'Now, what about some equipment? Helmet and so on?' I asked.

'Well, hold on, now. I never issued stuff to no-one like this before. Just sashay in and ask for it... don't seem regular. I gotta think her out.'

He was not the first soldier to be caught between the dictates of bureaucracy and the demand for military action and there comes a time when each of us must face this alone. I sensed that if I said anything, I would lose.

'Aw, heck! Step right into the store, Commander.' His mind made up, he bustled about with a proprietary air and fitted me with parachute, life jacket and helmet and goggles, in no time.

'Y'oughta have a forty-five and a watch, too, but I ain't got the key for them and I'll have to get another guy up. You want them?'

'There probably isn't time. Don't bother,' I said. 'Now where can I find my pilot?'

'Best thing'd be to wait over by his plane, I guess. It's in back there, in dispersal. Called Fancy Pants. Got a picture of a lady on it with a yaller rose on her butt and sweet nothing else.' He made motions with his hands indicating robust female curves. 'Nicest piece of ass that ever shat behind a pair of high-heeled shoes. Barney Forrester's from Texas.'

'Well, thank you,' I said and made towards the open air.

'Why, I'll tell the world it's a great day for this U.S. Marine, to have assisted one of our gallant British Allies fighting with us on Guadal. Thank you, sir! You ever get to Nutfield... '

Outside, there were already dim figures of aircrew moving about the line of aircraft. I found Fancy Pants and leant against her, smiling.

'Y'all done much flyin'?'

He had come up on me unawares, a hunched outline like an ape in the half-light.

I told him.

'Huh. Well, first thing is, don't lean on the fuselage, it ain't no bar. Now, if I have to aerobat, don't start tryin' to get outa Goddam thing. Just go with the airplane. Check the gun out and fire a couple test rounds when we're over the sea but warn me first. Then search, sea and air. You gotta fight off attackin' planes.'

'That suits me.'

'Well, let's go.' He swung a foot up on to the wing root, paused, came down again and shook hands.

'Australian, ain't you?' he asked.

'No, English.' Don't let it start again, I prayed. He peered at me to see what manner of man this was, then abruptly hopped up into the plane. He was really a small man, and square, but agile. Swarthy, blunt features.

'C'mon. I need wakin' up.'

I got in and then he had to get out again to show me where to plug into the inter-com. He barked some monosyllables about the cockpit layout, all of which went over my head, and stood by while I strapped in.

'Tight?'

'Very tight.'

'Take 'em down again some.'

'As much as that?'

'Yep.'

I pulled the straps down till they cut into my shoulders and fastened them. The pilot hopped back to his seat again and started her up.

In the Dauntless dive bomber, or SBD, the tail gunner sat facing astern and I hung pop-eyed in the straps, looking past the puny tail-plane at the ground. We bumped out between the trees onto the strip and were off before I was ready; the world reeled by backwards, there was a jerk and then we were hammering up into the sky. The scenery diminished in front of me at a dizzying rate; yet these were supposed to be slow crates. Top speed 220 knots.

Disoriented and queasy, I did not begin to get the hang of flying backwards until we had formed up and were flying straight and level. I risked a look out at the other aircraft in the flight fanned out in the search pattern. There was a constant nervous staccato chatter on the R/T, which I could not read, but the dour Forrester did not join in. But that was good radio discipline; pilots habitually jammed the ether with inconsequential chatter and prejudiced the passing of important traffic.

Twisting round in my straps, I could see the trailing edges of the wings directly underneath but no further forward. This meant I could only search that part of the sea we had already flown over, but it was still a useful thing to do. I cocked the Browning and told the pilot I was ready to fire the test rounds.

'Check,' he said and it was the last I heard from him until we were back in the landing circuit.

That done, I settled down to searching, beginning to enjoy flight now in the pure element. The wrinkled sea stretched itself like a skin and the sky was cloudless. I scanned once round the whole field of vision, then searched it in quarters, to and fro, up and down. It was mechanical but required concentration and effort.

Nothing happened. We flew out to our 400 mile limit, turned 90° to starboard on a short leg, then cut back to base in a thin 'pie slice'. The islands came up out of the sea like a green and brown necklace. In contrast to the take-off, landing backwards was gentle and easy. When I got out, the ground crew had already started to refuel, for it had to be done by hand pump from drums and was painfully slow.

Forrester was kicking one of the tyres and muttering something about the port oleo leg being 'down'. It looked all right to me, but I wouldn't know. I waited patiently in the hot sun.

'Go get some lunch,' he said. 'Back after Tojo Time. 1230.'

Lunch? Where? I turned on my heel and stalked off to the coastwatchers.

'Hullo, here's Lindbergh,' they said. 'Find any Japs?'

'No, only one of your funny buggers,' I growled, dumping my gear on the ground, 'but this one takes the cake.'

Tojo Time passed in relative security in the teleradio dug-out and I made a mental note to be handy to it in future, if need be. As soon as it was over I went back to Fancy Pants. She sat well in among the trees, safe from Japanese bombs, looking gorged and comatose and smelling vilely of high octane avgas. She made digestive, ticking noises as her parts expanded in the mid-day heat.

I was deliberately early and climbed in before Forrester arrived. I saw him coming with his swinging gait and determined to give exactly what I got. He sprang up with a simian bound.

'Okay.'

'Right-oh.' With these civilities, we taxied out and took off again.

Equilibrium restored after take-off, I cooled down gratefully in the higher air. The R/T circuit still buzzed with pilot gabble. I settled down to the task once more but there was nothing on my side. We turned at the end of the outward leg and I searched as far as I could to the north-west on the short cross-leg, giving the whole field a final hard scrutiny. There were no Japs today. It was my last chance to see them. Allowing two hours for the return leg, we ought to be back on the ground at about 1700; a welcome prospect. The PBY boys described flying as 'hours of boredom interspersed with moments of terror'.

We flew on for another few minutes and the moment of terror came. The pilot called sharply:

'Can you see smoke?'

Smoke! I looked wildly round the horizon – and found it right under my nose. A tiny wisp of grey smoke was trailing astern. Fire! We would roast alive, like that Kingfisher crew.

'Yes, underneath!' I shouted. 'What's the matter?'

'Oil pressure's out. I'm climbin'!'

Oh, my God! He jerked the stick back and the nose rose but immediately fell again. The engine was clattering and sounded choked. The smoke was much thicker.

'I'm gonna put her down, boy!'

It all happened very quickly. Nose down, we dropped like a stone.

'High Yaller, High Yaller, I'm ditchin'. I am ditchin'. I have a power failure. Can you see me?' He yelled on R/T. 'Mayday, Mayday, Mayday.'

'Okay, Barney, I gotcha!'

' – luck. Coming left. I see you at nine o'clock – '

'– easy, Barney. I'll mark you and send that PBY out –'

The nervous voices babbled and cut in on each other. I braced back hard and grabbed the release pin of my straps. Then I lifted a foot and began snatching at my shoe lace; you couldn't swim far in shoes. I came to my senses just in time to brace again before we hit; the tail flipped down and there was a solid crunch, it was flung hard up again and then there was just violent deceleration with white water rushing past overhead.

I was out on top of the canopy in a second but a white-faced Barney Forrester was there before me.

'Shit,' he said and threw a yellow package into the sea. The thing blossomed instantly into a substantial-looking life raft. He tumbled in and I jumped, landing across it. We sat up, rocking gently and regarded Fancy Pants.

She lay snuffling mournfully into the swell, nose down and tail high. The wing tips were under. Sometimes these sorts of aircraft floated and sometimes they sank. It didn't look as if she was long for this world.

'What happened?'

'Lost oil pressure and run the bearin's. Overheated. Engine was breakin' up. Oil line fracture, I figure.'

A couple of our SBDs swooped overhead and dropped a green dye marker. They circled once and were gone.

It was a wretched moment, but I felt a rush of gratitude for this tough little Texan boor. I knew enough about flying to know he got us down damned well.

'Well, we should have both been killed. You did a bloody good job. That PBY'll find us, I know that crew. We'll be home tonight.'

'The hell we will. The Goddam PBY won't get here till mornin'. Be dark in under three hours.'

Of course, he was right. Even if the PBY happened to be standing by ready for take-off, it couldn't make it there and back in daylight. We had reason to celebrate being alive, but being safe was another matter.

'How far out are we?'

'Why, we'd be 400 miles off base. North-west.'

'That's what I thought.' It couldn't be worse. 'Well, at least the weather will push us in the right direction.'

'What? Oh, yeah.' He hung his head, shivering and miserable. He was probably in shock; he had certainly had a shock and you need not necessarily be injured to suffer the effects. I had nothing to put on him except my own wet shirt and no 'strong cup of tea', as the first aid books recommended. I told him to lie back in the sun and relax and he complied meekly.

I hadn't meant the remark about the weather seriously. The wet season had just started, when the rain-bearing north-west monsoon blows for six months. In some of the rain squalls, the wind could reach hurricane force, though these squalls were usually brief. The rule of thumb was that if the wind came before the rain it was only a squall but if the rain came first, you were in for a soaking. But if a gale blew all night, it could not shift this aeroplane two hundred yards nearer home; and we would be wise to stick close to it and the dye marker. There was only a gentle breeze now but we had drifted a little down wind already and I started paddling back to Fancy Pants.

'What're you doin'?' asked Forrester.

I explained and he let it go. It marked a change in our relationship; in the aircraft he had been in charge but now he seemed content to let me take the initiative.

Fancy Pants was much lower in the water and while we were up close to her, she sank. She rolled over with a snore of bubbles and slid quietly down on one wing. The lady cocked her yellow rose at us in a final obscene gesture.

Barney had no pangs of sentiment. 'Sidewindin' coffin bastard,' he said. 'These single fan dingbats is shit. This is my second power failure in six months. I oughta be on bombers. At aviation school I come through cross-country navigation without losin' a mark.'

It was a long and deeply felt speech, but I could not think of a reply.

Night came. Barney settled down for the night and dozed fitfully, taking up more than his share of room. But I had the habit of wakefulness on water and I felt that our troubles might not be over by the morning. I kept a watch and paddled up wind occasionally towards the dye marker. The patch of green dye was dispersing and it was increasingly hard to find in the dark. To keep awake, I concentrated on hating Barney and his mother and father and girl friend, the school he went to and the town he grew up in in Texas; then I would switch to loving him for saving my life with his skills and training and good reflexes.

There was much life and movement in the sea. Fish jumped and splashed in swirls of phosphorescent bubbles. Flying fish skimmed the water and flew into the side of the raft. Once a great sail fish surfaced near us and crashed down with a noise like a cannon shot, in a cloud of spray. There were sharks and in the small hours, one brute nudged the raft. It woke Barney and he produced his .45 pistol, trying to get a shot at it.

'Hey, I shouldn't do that,' I said kindly. I was loving him at the time.

'Why not? I ain't aimin' to get tipped out and et.'

'The muzzle flash would show up. You can see a match flare at sixty miles, you know, if you're high enough.'

'Aw, for Chrissake! Who's to see it? Fish!'

'Maybe. But you don't show lights at sea in an operational area. And we are.'

'Yeah? Anchors away! Man the torpedoes, full speed ahead! Aw, you navy guys give me a pain. Pantywaists.' But he put the gun away.

At last, eyes prickling with fatigue, I watched a dazzling sun float up behind some streaky clouds on the horizon and dumbly prayed my thanks. I was aching and shivering and very light in the head, but we had got through the night and it was a sober probability that the PBY would come. We cocked our ears for it.

'Won't be long now,' said Barney.

No, it would not. I gaped past his shoulder at a catastrophic vision. But I knew I wasn't delirious; it was no fantasy and it wouldn't go away. It was real. A ship was approaching from the north. A Japanese ship.

141

CHAPTER TEN

They threw us a jumping ladder and Barney climbed it with his astonishing agility. I was stiff and made hard work of it. When I got to the upper deck, he was nowhere to be seen and I never saw him again.

Destroyer. Huge torpedo tubes. Familiar ship smells with a musty odour of food and latrines. Turbines whining beneath my feet; increasing speed. A blast of dry, hot air from a boiler exhaust fan.

As if in a dream, I stumble along the oily deck between two diminutive escorts. Mental processes are shocked into suspension, but I am acutely aware of surroundings and see small details.

Except for the tubes, everything is diminutive; this ladder, now: ridiculously narrow and the rungs too close together for my feet. But, good, solid construction, nevertheless; 3/16 inch plate on this bulkhead here, riveted. Sturdy little ships. Tiny doorways into compartments... oh, that stink of food! Sickening. Another ladder; two chaps prodding me from behind. No need for that. I balk, they prod, I prop, they jostle roughly. It's ridiculous, they have to win so I let them. On we go. A bloke in a khaki shirt meets us and starts jabbering. Petty officer? But we are going back down the ladder again. Why? Captain too busy, not ready for me? Understandable; regaining station in the formation. Back to the break in the forecastle; roar of exhaust fans and galley fans. They open a sort of mesh cage just abaft the funnel and motion me inside.

What? I can't get in there! I spread my hands in appeal and shake my head; it's not physically possible. Pointing again, threatening.

'I can't,' I say helplessly, still gesticulating.

They close on me, menacing, saying words full of hate. It's deliberate; they are looking for an excuse to beat me up. It's my choice.

Down on my stomach and scrape through on to piles of seaweed, in bags. Food locker; open to the air, at least. Pull one foot in; can't get the other one in... keeps just missing the... a fellow shoves it home briskly as if he is loading a shell into a gun. Knees in stomach; door shut and stapled.

One left on guard. He circles, inspecting, pleased with his catch. Mustn't lost my temper; grimace at him painfully. Unexpected response; he opens his mouth wide, holds one hand close to it and makes rapid two-finger motions towards his mouth with his other hand. Rice bowl and chopsticks — food! I nod vigorously. He goes into the galley and comes back with a tin bowl of soup; hands it in. Chin on chest, manage to sip it down. Not bad at all, fishy. Bang the tin on the cage for more; he grins and gets another one, with some rice. Hungry. I think he's actually pleased.

Still can't *think* of anything. Just as well; Beth and the war and the navy are all finished. I can think that much. I'm out. Years of it. Unless they kill me... oh, can't be bothered. All I want is sleep. But I haven't a hope in this cage; wriggle round on to my side, more comfortable. Foetal position; most appropriate. Fitzallen's carcass shall end as it began.

Nature provides a sort of don't care insulator effect when the worst happens and there are no alternatives left. A sort of reverse calm, a block anaesthetic for the mind. Interesting, that. Fitzallen's Insulator Effect...

I awoke agonised with cramp and banged on the cage, calling out. I had to move my legs. I jerked about like a landed fish, trying compulsively to stretch, hitting my head on the mesh. The guard looked at me and went away. He returned with another fellow, they opened the locker and my feet shot out. They pulled me out on my back and I struggled up, gasping with relief. They'd never get me back in there.

They let me recover, staggering and stretching and stamping. Then we went up the ladders again by the same route and this time emerged on the bridge. The insulator effect had gone and utter wretchedness engulfed me.

Three officers paused in what they were doing and stared at me. This one with the wispy goatee beard would be the captain; he was the oldest and he was sitting down. The young chap by the pelorus with binoculars round his neck would be on watch. The third approached me.

'Did you sreep werr-uh?' He asked in a nasal American accent. Sarcastic sod. Name, rank, number; name, rank, number.

'Yes, thank you.'

'Name-uh, rank-uh, number.' He said.

'Fitzallen, Lieutenant Commander, Royal Navy – '

It was out before I could stop it.

'Royarr-uh Navy?'

'Er, yes. On attachment to the... '

I stopped, flushed and embarrassed like a midshipman who had committed some stupid gaffe.

He came closer and peered at my collar pins, then at my shirt front.

'You are not air-uh clew. Why were you in that prane?'

That reminded me.

'Where is the pilot?' I said.

'Ah so, you are not pirot-uh. Why is Royarr-uh Navy officer in back seat of American prane?'

Oh Lord. Every time I opened my mouth... keep it shut, you fool.

The Japanese chattered to the captain who was looking at me

keenly. The captain said something to my interrogator and he said:

'If you do not answer questions-uh you wirr-uh doubrr-r round the island.'

What was he saying? Double round the island? I knew only one island you doubled round: Whale Island, the naval gunnery school at Portsmouth. Paddy D'Arcy, in my term, boasted that he had the record: twelve minutes flat. Remorseless petty officer instructors had sent me round twice. *'Keep silence during gun drill* ! Mr. Fitzallen, you seem to have a lot of breath to waste this morning; I will relieve you of it. *Round the Island, Double... March!'* Oh, school days, happy days. Now this...

I goggled in amazement at this Japanese. He couldn't mean Whale Island, could he? Then the captain said in good English:

'Carrying a six inch dummy charge.'

That settled it. They made you carry one if you were in more than usual need of correction.

The captain roared. He rolled in his chair, clutching the arm rests for support. Tears started in his eyes. I stared at him until the joke wore itself out.

'I was at Whale Island in 1932,' he said pleasantly and turned back to give an order to somebody.

The first officer, whom I mentally nick-named 'Froggy' because of an unfortunate lack of proportion between mouth and chin, seemed uncertain whether to go on and we stood in silence. I was to notice this again; once the captain stepped into a situation, they seemed to require his express direction for the activity to resume.

Well, they hadn't touched me yet. I had time to take stock. I couldn't read any instruments on the bridge except the clock, which said 0930 and possibly the log, indicating the figure 18. Yes, 18 knots would be about right. The little ship sliced along quite comfortably through the swell. I couldn't see a compass repeater but we were obviously steering near enough to south-east. Of course we were! This was the Truk crowd, heading for Guadalcanal. If we were 300 or so miles away now, we would be in The Slot at about midnight at this speed. Oh, I'd see another night action in The Slot all right, and it would be the greatest show of all. I needn't have worried.

But my watch said 1130. They must be on a two hour time difference.

What other ships were there? I had a cautious look round; there was a next ahead, another destroyer, but nothing on either beam. They must be in line ahead, which meant they had virtually no anti-submarine defences. Extraordinary for an ocean passage.

I was turning my feet so that I could look aft, when Froggy started again.

'When did you reave Guadarcanarr-uh?' he asked. I didn't answer. He stepped up and hit me hard on the chin. I staggered, recovered and went for him. I was about to seize him and throttle the life out of him when the captain shouted something like *'Yammeh!'* very sharply. It stopped us. Now I had done it. Attacking a Japanese officer; nothing less than death.

But the captain turned on Froggy and delivered a stream of savage abuse. Froggy stood stiffly, jerking his head down in perfunctory bows and hissing respectfully. Then the captain turned to me.

'I do not permit my officers to strike my men and I will not permit them to hit anyone else on my ship, prisoner-of-war or not,' he said, in his dry, even tone.

'It is not the policy of the Imperial Japanese Navy to rescue enemy personnel. They are a nuisance and a hazard and we leave them in the water. That is what I should have done with you but I was ordered to rescue you. We require intelligence on Guadalcanal and I speak English. If you do not answer my questions, I will execute you. Myself. I will behead you ceremonially. This will be an honourable end to your shame as a prisoner. Any Japanese officer in your situation would choose it. I extend this privilege to you as a British officer.'

Comprehension cut out again and the dire words made no impact. Instead, I warmed to a London accent. Not Cockney, or BBC, but somewhere in between; stressed back

146

to front and fleeting but unmistakable and redolent of the swarming humanity I knew so well. London Polytechnic!

'You will go to my cabin for half an hour and consider what I have said. Then I will send for you. In your deliberations, do not overlook the factor that you are merely a nuisance to me and it is up to you to save your life, not up to me to spare it.'

Down one ladder, through a louvred door and they left me alone.

Then I went out of control. I crouched on the bunk a primitive, with no defences. The illusion of fellow-feeling vanished; a male aggressor of my own species was going to kill me and I could only gibber. God help me, I killed, but remotely, for concepts, because someone told me to, not for life and food, not with bone and sinew. This one-for-one resurrection had me helpless. My instinct for it had been bred out, I had no resources, no chemistry for counter-strokes, no atavistic ducts. I was a cornered animal bereft of its birthright.

Beyond that, reason faltered. Images tumbled over in my mind: Beth, the sword raised over my kneeling form, my mother, a bare winter field somewhere in Victoria and a random but rational manifestation, a butcher's sign in Knightsbridge that said 'Joe D'Eath Supreme Meats'... Admiral Crutchley, the sword... watery, random flickerings having no connection, leading to no conclusion. The life of a rudimentary creature 'flashing before its eyes'.

Gradually something stable distilled out of it and settled on my consciousness. The flickering images stopped. I sat on the bunk and began to think again.

What did he want to know?

There was only one thing to do. Stick to the truth except in one particular: that I knew nothing about the convoy or its escorts due at Guadalcanal that day. If I had been alone I might have carried off some subterfuge but they would be comparing my answers with Barney's. I hoped that Barney knew little or nothing of the convoy; he had never mentioned it – but he never mentioned anything. Apart from that, I hoped he would have the sense to stick to the truth too, for it

147

could give little of any value away.

Well, then, I'm ready. Up to me to save my life, is it? Then I will. 'Privilege' for a British officer. Offering me an 'honourable' death. Who says we have to play your rules? I'll take you on and I'll beat you. You pompous, insufferable sod, playing God ... If I could get my hands on you I'd kill you. There's some killer in me yet, thank Christ. I'll break your nasty little neck, I'll kick your head off –

But I'd have to appear to go his way a bit. Mustn't be combative. No good raving about the Geneva Convention and all that useless rot. If I played it carefully, I'd have a chance to spin it out until we got to Guadalcanal, that's all.

His cabin was only six feet by nine, bare and bleak. Desk, chair, bunk and cupboard. I tried the desk drawer, for something to do. His papers were neatly laid out and face down on them was a framed photograph. It showed him in high-necked tunic and white gloves, standing behind his family; a smiling wife in her kimono and two sweet-looking, chubby infants; girls, probably. The monster was also human; in spite of myself, I had a sense of prying and was annoyed. I wondered what I looked like after all this but there was no mirror in the compartment.

Something scraped in the cupboard as the ship rolled. I opened the door and there, hanging on a hook at the back, was the sword. I slammed the door shut and faced away. I paced about, hesitating between revulsion and morbid fascination and finally took it out. It looked very old, genuine samurai. They said the test was in the hilt; it should come off and inside there should be a scroll giving the sword's history. I tried it and found it had a spring-loaded bayonet catch; sure enough, there was a parchment in it. I could not bring myself to look at the blade.

The half hour went past and longer. He must be busy again. It was a little like waiting outside the headmaster's study for a caning; extra time was a reprieve, but you also wanted to get it over.

When they came for me, it was nearly 1100, their time. I dragged myself up the ladder, heart thumping. The scene was as before, except that Froggy was not there. Before the captain could speak, I launched into a pre-emptive and, I hoped, disarming address on the whole matter.

I said I was conscious of the honour he had done me, but he must be aware that I did not think like that. There was no shame to me in being captured because the circumstances were beyond my control. My religious and philosophical beliefs inclined me away from the view that death was preferable to life in any situation. Indeed, in our society, suicide was a misdemeanour. I therefore rejected that alternative and would answer his questions. I would be truthful, but I knew very little of strategic value to him.

I blew it. He was obviously a sucker for the pompous, rolling phrase and it was an attempt to get on his wave-length as much as anything, but the timing and delivery were off. It lacked conviction and his own sonorous gravity. I gabbled it, pausing for breath, not emphasis, and tended to go embarrassingly falsetto. It was just a rigmarole.

He regarded me with sour contempt, beard thrust forward. Then he consulted a pad of notes. Barney's answers? A list of questions sent to him by the flagship?

'What carrier do you come from?'

Ho! They would certainly be worried if they thought there was an American carrier within range. This could be a breathing space.

'None. I flew from Guadalcanal.'

'Your pilot does not say that.'

'You must know what squadron he comes from. Your intelligence people will confirm that it is based on Guadalcanal.'

'That will take too long. What are you doing there? What were your duties?'

I clutched at a straw. The best form of defence is attack.

'Take too long? You mean your headquarters is not able to signal you that information in time?' I tried to feign incredulous interest.

He coloured angrily. 'We are not playing games. I ask the questions.' It was your mistake, old boy, not mine. But mustn't make you repeat your question; that would be my mistake.

It was a question that suited my scattered wits. My attachments and wanderings made a strange tale, even if true. I let the story track back and forth of its own accord, however, glossing over essentials and tediously inflating details. It grew vastly complicated and convoluted; I began to take a pride in it. He scribbled notes for a while, then gave up and gazed at me with glassy incomprehension. It was my first break; it seemed he had no head for interrogation.

But that was to be expected, I should have seen it. He was pretty bright, but he was just a destroyer captain and this task had been thrust upon him. Interrogators are specialists and like any others, they require particular skills, training and experience. There was hope yet.

At the end of an hour, we were back where we started. He took a few turns round the bridge and lit a cigarette – a Lucky Strike! How I longed for one.

'So,' he said with a faint sigh. 'You are English. I know your navy. When were you at Whale Island?'

'I was last there in thirty-three.' Was this the alternating hard-soft technique? I was on my guard.

'We missed each other by a year, then. You would have been very young, on your sub lieutenant's course, I guess. You realise that we might have sat at that table on the same guest night and passed the port in the silver gun-carriage ... an ingenious piece. Miniaturisation is more usually our talent. Did you pour beer down the piano?' If he was trying to be jocular, it fell very flat.

'And drunk the health of King George the Fifth?' I'd rather have him back in the old mood.

He was genuinely affronted. I'd overdone it, thrown a reasonable overture in his face.

'How you dare,' he said with passion. 'You British. You could not be anything else but British. I had forgotten your ill manners. Barbarous! You trample on civility with your big feet. But the most ugly thing about you is not your arrogance, but your ignorance. You do not know that you have nothing

150

to be arrogant about!' It was as if he had been waiting twenty years to say it.

'You are finished, my friend.' He spoke more matter-of-factly. 'You think you have tradition; your silver gun-carriage stands for four centuries of sodomy and the lash. You think you have statesmen but you have self-deceiving word-spinners. You claim you have soldiers, but you have a lower class obeying an upper class of hedonists. You have affectation and no culture; ego but no pride. Britain is a dead fish, rotting on the shores of Europe.'

'And the shopkeepers,' I said faintly. 'Don't forget a nation of shopkeepers.'

'I should be reluctant to quote that,' he said. 'You turn the other cheek, but like your bull in the china shop. More quotes for you.' He was amused now; the black lozenge-eyes had a positive twinkle.

'You brought this' – waving his hand towards the fleet – 'on yourselves. You will gain nothing out of it, even if you win. But it is a temporary situation and I admit ... sometimes this war can be a joke, in hellish taste. I will drink your king's health again, Englishman – if you still have one.

'But now, you will remain on my bridge until this mission has been carried out. You will continue to be questioned and at the first evidence that you have lied, I will kill you.'

He gave orders to the watch and went below. Now what? I stood for some time and nothing happened. No one took any notice of me and the tremor in my limbs subsided. It was scarcely as if I had been accorded the freedom of the bridge, but if I could move about a little, I should get some idea of what was going on. I took two steps towards the chart table but one of the watch motioned me back again immediately. The two fellows came up the ladder with a small stool and some rope. They were going to tie me up.

'Benjo.' I called. I had an idea it was Japanese for latrine.

'Benjo, no,' said the little officer. They sat me down alongside the bridge bulwark where I could see nothing and tied my ankles to the stool, but they left my hands free.

But in my case, the thought was father to the wish and the

151

wish grew rapidly into a primary need. All right, my son, we'll have to have it your way. I tilted back the stool, unzipped my fly and peed. And sheep as a lamb, etc... Aim, correct for optimum trajectory and maximum range... there was an ominous drumming on the steel deck a good four feet away.

A sailor cackled and the young officer flew at me with fists swinging, shouting imprecations.

'You dare lay a finger on me, sonny,' I yelped, 'and I'll report you to the captain.'

Ridiculous, but it worked. He stamped back to the front of the bridge and sent a sailor below, who returned with a bucket and cloth.

This was what I had hoped for. They untied me and I cleaned it up, pottering about almost at leisure, bending and stretching. I had aimed so I could sneak a look at the chart table. As I thought; the course was laid east-south-east, entering The Slot between Santa Isabel and Florida Islands, then passing close west of Savo Island. I straightened up and as casually as I could, turned aft.

Christ Almighty! One, two, three ships back in the line, was a battleship. And astern of it was another. Twin turrets; *Hiei* and *Kirishima*. Couldn't be anything else.

I allowed myself to be tied up again, deep in thought.

There was no point in taking battleships into The Slot unless you were going to bombard. They were too unwieldy to fight effectively in those restricted waters, at close range and especially at night. They would tend to become muscle bound and a hindrance. So, it seemed the Japanese were not expecting surface opposition and this was a bombardment run. A couple of thousand rounds of 14 inch shells on to Henderson Field in the night ... it would be ravaging. It could well tip the balance.

But, there would be surface opposition. And these battleships would be loaded with their special bombardment shells, which were impact-fused and thin-skinned. The shells carried dozens of incendiary bombs, not high explosive. They would be spectacular but not very damaging to ships;

152

they would tend to bounce off. For ships, you needed semi-armour-piercing stuff that would penetrate halfway through steel plate and explode, blowing a maximum hole. If the Japanese got sufficient warning they could change the projectiles but it would be no easy job to replace all those one ton monsters from deep in the shell rooms, through the hoists and to the turrets. It would take time. No wonder they wanted intelligence.

I closed my eyes and tried to recall the composition of the American task forces. Norman Scott was in *Atlanta,* with four destroyers. Callaghan had five cruisers; what were they? I thought *San Francisco* was still the flag and also that Callaghan was the senior officer of the two and so would be in tactical command. Yes, that was right, I remembered thinking at the time it was a bit odd that they hadn't changed the flagship; if anything had been learned from Cape Esperance, it was that the admiral needed a new radar under his eye and *San Francisco* didn't have it. There was *Juneau* of course and *Portland* and *Helena.* There was another cruiser but I seemed to recall that she was to be detached on arrival for some other duty. *Pensacola*! And she was. What were the destroyers? *Sterrett, Cushing, Laffey, Monssen, Fletcher* ... I could not remember any more. But there were thirteen ships in all. I must count the Japanese ships as soon as I could.

The watch changed. They brought me a bowl of rice for lunch and we passed through a rain squall. I was unprotected and gratefully let it cool and clean me.

At 1330 the captain reappeared, but he took no notice of me. Both he and the new officer-of-the-watch were obviously concentrating on something else; conferring, looking about them, examining papers or charts. They seemed expectant.

Then a sailor bent to a voice pipe and relayed a message to the captain, who nodded to the officer and he in turn spoke in another voice pipe. It was all very familiar. The helmsman spun the wheel and the telegraphman wound her up. We were changing station. Belatedly, to my way of thinking, the admiral had decided to get into some kind of screening formation.

We headed out to starboard and from the look of it, or rather the feel, we would end up on the starboard wing of the screen. We ran for ten minutes and I became absorbed in the officer, who was taking his bearings, watching the range and the speed. He seemed a smart young chap, the counterpart of Toby Marks perhaps, or Lachlan. Then he put his foot in it – turned too early or too late – and the captain duly bawled him out. In spite of myself, I smiled at them, feeling almost sympathetic. Same old navy, whatever flag it flew.

The captain was about to go below again when he saw me and appeared to change his mind. He walked over slowly.

'Have you remembered anything that may be to your advantage?'

'No. I have told you everything I know.'

'Do you know the work of Sun Tze, Englishman? The ancient Chinese classicist on warfare? Two and a half thousand years ago, he said that if you know the enemy and know yourself, you need not fear the outcome of a hundred battles. You see the advantage I have over you. The great Japanese swordsman Miyamoto observed the swallow's flight and said: "When the enemy thinks high, swoop low. When he thinks low, hit high." He accompanied this with a show of vigorous, two-handed sword strokes.

Where was this leading? What did he do all day down in that cabin, read philosophy?

'I have a problem, English. I regret that I do not have time to discuss its interesting abstractions with you and must leave further questioning to my officers for the present. But I will state the problem to you: I have two prisoners. Each gives different answers to my questions; therefore one tells the truth and one is lying. Which is which?'

He studied me with mocking gravity.

'If I ask that other prisoner whether there are American ships waiting for us at Guadalcanal, what would he say, English?'

'He'd say there are no ships at – Oh, what rubbish, that's just a – it's a – it's a – stupid joke, it doesn't mean anything!'

He tipped back his head and laughed softly. He was still chuckling as he marched out of sight down the ladder.

But by God, it was neat! This fellow could catch me off balance, he was clever. Unnerving. I'd have to watch him so carefully; he'd got on top again.

Now I should try to get a look at this new formation. I was puzzling about how to do it when the officer produced a large perspex covered manoeuvring board, a thing of concentric rings for marking distance and lines, like the spokes of a wheel, for bearing. We used them, too. He was going to plot the new formation on it, in plan. If I could see that, it would give me the exact picture, better than hours of gazing around.

It was raining again and getting heavier. There was now a thick black sky. Where was the wind? I couldn't see from my position.

Froggy came up. I guessed he was the first lieutenant. He had a few words with the officer-of-the-watch and then approached me. Oh, hell! But he wasn't going to come out into the wet and he ordered two sailors to shift me under the flimsy shelter of the bridge canopy. Now I could read that manoeuvring board, if only he'd shove off.

'What ships are at Guadarcanarr-uh?'

Over and over came the same thing, with variations, threats, doubling back, would-be traps and trick questions.

But Froggy had no idea. I recalled from some course or other that the art of interrogating is in making the subject feel guilty. A good practitioner can play on this subtly until the burden of guilt becomes insupportable. Then the subject not only confesses but he also tells the truth, for only the truth can absolve him. It is a highly psychological game. We were told that torture techniques were useless, for though a man will 'talk' for relief, he is likely to say anything but the truth.

Poor Froggy had neither technique and it was only a matter of lasting him out. It was trying, but very simple. I thought it wise not to let it appear so, however, lest he lose more face and deal me a quick, covert kick in the shins, so I tried to appear acutely uncomfortable under his merciless will. He must be burning with resentment against me for his humiliation by the captain.

Then the captain called out from the front of the bridge and Froggy went below, apparently to attend to something else. I was glad he wasn't my first lieutenant. I hadn't noticed the captain come back though, and heard that voice with a stab of alarm. But he stayed in his chair. Warily, I began to study the manoeuvring board.

Good heavens, they had put a double screen out. Five destroyers fanned out ahead, then there was a gap to seven more, spread the same way. Astern of these came the two battleships. Unless that centre ship of the second arc was a cruiser; it had a different symbol. Anyway, the whole thing was like a double arrowhead and it looked very tight indeed; there would not be much distance between ships. Our ship – I realised I didn't know its name yet – would be on the starboard side of the leading arc, with one other ship outside her.

Fourteen ships. Hm.

The rain still poured, heavier than ever. This was an extraordinarily long squall. The canopy leaked and now everyone on the bridge was soaked. And the captain was worried. He and the OOW searched constantly through their binoculars, first over one side and then the other. I don't blame you, old boy. I wouldn't care to be doing 18 knots in this formation and in this visibility. I doubted whether they could see their nearest consorts.

Bouts of misery assailed me again. So tired of being scared to death. Scared *of* death. The nobody-lives-forever game, the same old variations on the theme chased around in my mind. We do not live forever. Then, face it squarely. It's been pretty good, hasn't it? No complaints. And I'm glad I met this girl ... Oh God! She always did that, put me back to square one. I needed something to happen to get my mind off it, even interrogation by the captain would be a relief.

The afternoon wore on. This rain! It had been going on for over two hours. I searched my memory to recall anything like it in this part of the world. Looking up, I could see it was slanting before a wind, so it was just a rain squall after all, but it must be huge.

Then it hit me. This rain was slanting dead ahead. We were not running through a rain squall, we were running *in* it! The thing was travelling to the south-east on the same course and at the same speed as we were. Oh, it was perfect! Neither American radar, nor aircraft, nor submarines could find the formation in this.

'Benjo!' I called. I must look at the sea and confirm the wind direction. Then I lost my temper.

'Captain!' I burst out. 'There is no need to keep me sitting here trussed up like a dangerous criminal. I cannot escape. I am an officer of equal rank to you. Will you please release me!'

He was at the binnacle and tension was in every line of his crouched figure. I knew precisely what he was going through; he would have no thought of me. But he jerked his dripping face round, muttered something to the officer and resumed staring out to port. They untied me and I stepped forward.

'You are not of equal rank,' he snapped. 'I am a commander. Stay out of the way, at the back of the bridge.'

I would do that, happily. And if I was any judge, there was exactly 18 knots of wind propelling us into the third Battle of Savo Island, from dead astern.

CHAPTER ELEVEN

I rode the rest of that wild advance with the Japanese almost as if I was one of them, sharing their apprehensions of disaster. The rain may have shielded them from prying eyes but they paid a price for it. The ships were running blind in close formation; inevitably they would get badly out of position and there was a constant risk of collision. I doubted whether any Allied fleet commander would have risked it, wartime or not. The Japanese captains stayed on their bridges keyed up for instant response to emergencies and they entered the battle already tired.

Our faithful squall rained on us for over seven hours. It was a cloudburst, a suffocating wall of water that fell into the sea like molten shot, raising vapour. Lumps of it pummelled on the ship. It sapped the energy and clogged the mind. We had the illusion that we could not breathe in it, for I noticed the Japanese opening their mouths to gasp like fish and then realised I was doing the same thing.

We turned into The Slot between Florida and Santa Isabel Islands with a drastic alteration to starboard that would have made my flesh creep in normal circumstances. In this weather, the Japanese could not possibly have fixed their position since the noon sun sight, so the navigational problem of where we were in the wide Pacific Ocean was just as critical as the dangerous blind march. But nobody ran aground and we settled on a southerly course, which would leave Savo Island fine on the port hand.

Quietly, without fuss or alarm bells, they went to action stations. The turrets whined round and gun muzzles sniffed the wind. The bridge became crowded with extra officers and men. They bent to voice pipes, spoke into telephones and read dials. Three little chaps swung up into the director control tower: trainer, control officer and range-taker. I looked at them with interest, for they would have the best eyes in the ship. The officers reported to the captain and I knew what they were saying:

'Gunnery department closed up, ready for action, sir.'

'Engine room and damage control parties closed up; condition Z set.'

'Torpedo tubes closed up, ready for action.'

Shrinking back into the shadows in case I should get in the way and be removed somewhere down below, I watched Froggy's comings and goings and worked out that he must also be the gunnery officer. Good. That was a bonus for the Americans.

But it was all very well; how were they going to fight in these conditions? We still couldn't see a ship's length away and they had no idea where their own ships were, relative to each other. They could not bombard like that. It was now 2130 and high time they got out of the rain squall, in my view.

The captain clearly thought so, too. He paced restlessly, spinning on his heel, jabbing binoculars to eyes. He was wet through but I was sure he was also sweating. He concentrated his search over the port side; Savo would be about abeam there now, I thought, but there was not a hope of seeing it through this.

A fascinating new prospect unfolded: if they kept on like this, within half an hour we would be aground on Guadalcanal, and for the first time, I thought of escape. Running aground might suit me very well... but it was Japanese country there; I would step out of the frying pan into the fire.

But they did keep on. The captain now divided his time

between searching ahead and rushing frantically to the chart table. We all began to stare ahead in mounting tension, but I also kept a close eye on the voice pipe from which their fleet communications seemed to issue. But nobody went near it; we got no orders to turn. By God, we*were* going to run aground.

By my watch and what I could remember of the chart, we had five minutes to go when the captain stopped in his tracks, banged his fist down on top of the chart shelter and spat out an order. Instantly the little ship swung hard to port, away from the land.

Well, now, this was interesting. If he had had to turn, the other four destroyers in the van arc would have had to turn too. Yet so far as I could tell, there had been no comm-unication with any of them and more to the point, there had been no communication with the flagship. It was crazy; with the van arc doubling back on its tracks – and heading for the on-coming main body – whatever semblance of formation remained to the Japanese would become a hopeless, dangerous tangle. I was beginning to enjoy this.

So we ran north, looking for the others, but we might as well have been in mid-South Atlantic, for all we saw.

Ten minutes later, the communications voice pipe came to life and from the disgusted groans and exclamations of the officers, I surmised that the flagship had at last decided to slip out of the rain squall and order a reversal of course.

'*Now* he tells us, for God's sake. Fat lot of bloody use...' I hid my face and almost chuckled. But I, too, was disgusted, though not for that reason: now they would pull the formation together.

Our ship slowed to about 12 knots and fishtailed, still trying to pick up its consorts. No luck. Half an hour passed. Presumably, somewhere up ahead, the main body was sorting itself out.

We passed into clear weather at last and the first thing we saw was a blue light dead ahead – a shaded stern light! It belonged to another van destroyer, close at hand. Had they known? It was impossible to say but from their reactions, I thought not. The two ships exchanged messages by dim blinker light and the newcomer fell in astern of us. Then the voice pipe issued new orders, evidently for a return to the original course, for this time we complied and swung south. We increased speed.

I believe I saw it first and with the naked eye. I probably had a presentiment it was there, for I was looking out to starboard, straight at it. We were turning through east and broad on the bow at about a mile, I thought I saw the merest tracery of white, just a hair-line on the water... then it was gone. I flicked my eyes away and back, away and back... and caught it again, at the outer edge of vision. Now there was that suggestion of box-like shadow above it – destroyer. Bows on, American. Heading across our track. It was my death warrant.

They saw it and I ceased to exist for them. They stampeded round the bridge shouting a plethora or orders and commands. An officer spoke down the communications voice pipe and I knew exactly what he said that time.

'Enemy in sight, bearing – '

Bearing what? He couldn't give a bearing, or a range relative to the main force because our ship did not know where the force was. It was the sort of vagary a battle could turn on; as an enemy sighting report, it was practically useless. Out of long habit, I noted the time: 2341 Japanese time, 0141 American.

It was a very brief encounter, however, for our captain turned and fled. Quite right: don't 'do a *Duncan*' on us. Only a moron would tackle the whole American force with two ships.

Our ship shot forward like an eager horse, lifting out of the water at an almost instant 35 knots. She must be on 'immediate overboost'; I had heard of it. They had some emergency full power arrangement whereby they could hit the turbines with maximum steam pressure for short bursts, no matter what head of steam was in the boilers. It had to be done carefully though, for there was a risk of fracturing the turbine blades.

What now? Why was there no gunfire? The one advantage the Americans did have was radar; they must see the main

161

force clearly on their screens and they should have opened up at once. Long ago, in fact.

And what of the Japanese? I pictured an exquisite scene on the flagship's bridge at this moment. Somebody would report to the admiral:

'Signal from— , sir. Enemy in sight.'

'Where, for Christ's sake?'

'We don't know, sir. We don't know where— is.'

Well, you brought it on yourself, old boy. And what are you going to do about the bombardment shells? You don't want them littering the place when those American shells hit you. I'd reverse course for another half hour if I were you, give yourself time to strike at least some of them down and get up some SAP. But you'll have to hurry.

The ship was running hard to the north-east now and we appeared to have lost our consort. I supposed we were still trying to find the main body. Visibility was now quite good, with a dark, moonless night and a clear atmosphere, but we still saw nothing. And I grew increasingly disturbed that I heard nothing. What on earth were the Americans doing? Surely they were not going to throw their radar advantage away? I looked at my watch; good God, four minutes had gone by!

It was utterly quiet, with the same taut, expectant stillness as before Cape Esperance. We continued on, searching about, with no friends, no enemies. It was a perilous time for me; if they took it into their heads, they could shoot me where I stood during one of these lulls.

But only Froggy remembered me; he would. He sidled over to me in his burst sandshoes and hissed:

'Of course, you ried. *Yatsu!'* He brought his hand down in a chopping motion and whistled horribly. 'Whh... t!' He'd got a silver lining out of it, at any rate.

I licked dry lips. The only certainty seemed to be that the captain had far too much on his plate to attend to the matter at present.

Froggy liked to press home an advantage.

'We wirr-uh win this batt-rr. Americans-uh do not open fire. So kind, haw haw!'

He turned on his heel and did a sweep with binoculars. He should have his mind on the job, not on gloating over a prisoner.

'You won't win it firing bombardment shells, you bloody little ghoul,' I muttered after his departing back. He wasn't meant to hear, for in the church-like atmosphere neither of us raised our voices above a whisper. But Froggy had sharp ears.

'What you say? What you know about-uh shells?' he demanded, coming back.

Oh, Lord, my big mouth...

'Two battleships.' I jerked a thumb across the water. 'Boom! Boom! I used my fingers to indicate turrets firing. 'Bombardment, okay?' I said ingratiatingly. Even he ought to be able to see how I knew.

'*So desu ka*. But we have-uh, changed! All-uh, shells changed.'

Barney had talked! I couldn't believe it.

'Changed shells, eh? Just now? Fast pigeon, eh? Chop chop, lickety split. Japanese sailors pretty damn quick!'

'Sure. Japanese-uh smart. Work hard. You, not talk.' He went off again.

'Very smart,' I said reverently and shook my head in admiration.

Utter balls. He was lying. Expecting me to believe they had changed shells in eight minutes... eight minutes! What in God's name were the Americans doing? Froggy was right about that; they were losing the battle.

Then, at last, we heard it; the crack of gunfire astern. Our captain spun us round and headed for the fray.

Something of the enormity of what had happened was plain at once. From our right a searchlight shone full on an American cruiser at a bare 1,500 yards' distance and held it. The ship's pale-grey elegance was caught brilliantly in the blue-tinted light and she glided straight down the beam of it,

163

like a moth trapped in a flame. At a steady 20 knots, she dipped in the swell as she crossed our bows and the light went off. But it was this ship that had fired, for coils of dirty smoke still curled and rolled in her wake.

It was almost beyond belief. The American ship must be charging straight into what was evidently the Japanese centre. The Japanese on our bridge also seemed to doubt their senses for they twittered and pointed in amazement. How could it have happened?

However, there could be no doubt about what would happen next. First, the sight; a multi-headed mushroom of flame and smoke burst from where the searchlight had been, as a battleship fired its eight 14-inch guns. Then the sound; an assault on the ears that seemed too deep-toned for earthly chemistry. Then the blast; a distinctive little puff of wind that even at that distance lifted hair and ruffled papers.

It was almost point blank range for the battleship and all eight shells hit. They burst with deep red rosettes all along the cruiser's hull and especially on the bridge. In the light of their fierce burning I recognised *Atlanta* and choked with rage and swore at the senseless death of Norman Scott. No one could have lived on that bridge. Old Joe Death's butcher's shop. Briskets, forequarters, rumps, brains, livers. Already cooked.

A furious incandescent storm started. Now we could see that there were ships in line *ahead* of *Atlanta* and the battleship's searchlight had made a beautiful point of aim for them. They tore at her like a school of piranha fish. The leading ship, a destroyer, was a scant hundred yards away, pouring 5-inch, 20mm and machine gun fire into the Goliath. Red tracer bounced into the sky through the blue-green glimmer of starshell and searchlight beams and the flashes of the 5-inch lit the water. The battleship swung to port and thundered back. The fitful play of lights and shadows dazzled and danced.

The whole American force, in its beloved single column of van destroyers, cruisers and rear destroyers, must have struck straight into the centre of the Japanese. The formations would have clashed head on at a combined closing speed of over 40 knots. It was a staggering calamity. And there was something else: that battleship wasn't firing bombardment shells, but high explosive. They *had* changed shells! The entire crews of the two ships, perhaps three thousand of them, must have left their battle stations and worked like madmen. It would have been absolute pandemonium, but they had done it somehow. It was an impossible, Olympian performance.

I was still grappling with this realisation when we were in the thick of it ourselves. Our sharp little 4.7-inch mountings opened up at the rear half of the American line and we rushed straight at it. The captain stood woodenly in his conning position, looking right ahead and calling small course corrections to the helmsman as we bore down. He had no time to turn away now... the maniac was going through! Calmly, he drew a bead on the stern of a light cruiser materialising out of the murk and conned the ship at it. It was demented; surely he had more common sense. Could he have been committed before he realised? Even some crewmen watched slack-jawed and aghast with me.

But he got away with it. He sliced between the light cruiser and the four rear destroyers. He was already swinging hard right as we went through the gap and our ship's stern skidded down towards the oncoming American destroyers. The leading ship jammed on hard right rudder and clawed itself clear of that spinning stern by a hundred feet; she was just a grey streak hurtling past but I saw a patch of red lead on her side and glimpsed stunned, gaping faces on her bridge. And loud and clear across the water came a strident shout on her broadcast:

'Now stand by for collision port side... '

To hear that tongue and accent was unutterable anguish. 'Ahoy! Hey, wait for me!' My lips moved, but no sound came. A hill of confused water built up between the two ships, a great pressure wave that surged in all directions. Then the American was gone, trailing a curving wake into darkness.

I looked ahead. The captain had steadied up and we now bounded after the cruiser, rapidly overhauling it. He would probably diverge from it at any second and fire torpedoes from the quarter. Then the press and noise and sheer monstrosity of events swamped my senses.

There was a paralysing roar behind us. The second Amercian destroyer had pulled up short to avoid entanglement in the extraordinary scene ahead and now sat immobile under two descending cataracts of water and gobbets of flaming oil. As the water and steam cleared, a bright and fiery break showed in her hull amidships, its jagged edges glowing with molten metal. She seemed to have been cut in half, above the waterline. Then the last section of plate must have sheered, for the gap grew wider; she was cut in half. The bow and stern sections impelled themselves away from each other, each part settling at the break, singeing the sea and shrouding the jagged ends in steam.

A deep rumbling sound, as if her boilers had broken loose, came to us. Then the forepart rolled and plunged down amid white jets of spray from escaping air and at the same instant, the after part duck-dived. Its round stern reared skywards, heaving up the naked red belly and spilling black dots of men into the sea. Everything went straight down. There was nothing left. It took twenty seconds from first to last. The screws were still turning as they went under.

Only torpedoes could do such a thing and she had been hit by two. Sick and shaking, I searched the field of view for some clue as to where they had come from, but it was impossible to say in this kaleidoscope. But I did catch sight of something else: a shell splash on our starboard bow. Then two more climbed over the forecastle, on the other side. They were ranging shots from the cruiser.

The captain darted at them; six more appeared, short, on the engaged side and he held his course. He was working up to his torpedo attack, exchanging guttural shouts with the control position and taking target bearings. He must hold a steady course to fire and he was having difficulty timing the torpedoes' release, between broadsides. Over the side, I saw the lips of eight tubes swing out, shifting slightly in adjustment. The light cruiser, now broad on the bow, fired again but before the shells had fallen the captain had started a turn away; and inexplicably at that moment, there was a call from the control position and the eight torpedoes launched.

From their tracks, I could see at once that they would miss ahead. It was a wild shot. There seemed to be some misunderstanding between the control position and the captain – who would now bang some heads together. This was going well.

It was going rather too well for my own comfort. Having botched the attack, our ship was now the unequal partner in the duel and at her most vulnerable, under powerful guns. We bolted south, stern tucked down like a dog's tail, with shells leap-frogging up the wake. Heart in mouth, I started forward-observer spotting to myself. But some avid young American in the cruiser would be doing all the spotting required. He would be glued pop-eyed to rangefinder eyepieces in the fire control tower, yelling: 'Up ladder, SHOOT! A falling – , B falling – , A – short. C falling – , B – short. C – over! Down 200, zig-zag, SHOOT! A – short. B – over. C – *straddle!* Rapid groups, SHOOT! Short. *Left...., left...* RIGHT TWO. Straddle. Short. *Straddle. Straddle.* WAHOO, fire for effect!'

Well done lads! But if only I could warn you, I'm at the wrong end of this...

And suddenly the shells stopped. I saw the bright flash and the sickening glow, the smoke and the descending waterfall boiling away in steam. Seconds later, I heard the bang. Torpedo. She stopped and lay over like a beached whale, down by the stern. She spread smoke. Would she sink? Oh Christ, was there nothing they could do to stop this? A light cruiser gone... either *Helena* or *Juneau*. That was a grim touch; I'd have been no better off on board her.

We were now south of the action, reprieved and unharmed, but there was no celebration or respite. The captain took us round to starboard and still at top speed, we closed the main tumult, a whirling, tempestuous fire fight three miles to the north-west. We ran towards it with silent guns, but regrouped and ready to hurl the ship at targets of opportunity.

Midnight, Friday 13th. We approached a dog fight, a savage, shocking free-for-all. There were American ships where Japanese should have been and Japanese ships where American should have been. They twisted and turned round

167

each other, manoeuvring violently to avoid collisions and trying to distinguish friend from foe. It was not a naval engagement but a sea-borne street brawl. In the centre of it, the battleship that had disabled *Atlanta* was under attack herself from the American van destroyers. She was a battered monument, enveloped in flames and evidently trying to retire, for she was floundering slowly round to the south and west. As the Japanese exclaimed and pointed at her, I caught the name *Hiei* several times. So this was *Hiei;* and she was flagship too, for she was ahead of her consort. She struggled on like a giant prehistoric lizard with mortal wounds, and some numb reptilian instinct kept her lunging out, gutted, brainless but still dangerous. The long black cannons, slim as showgirls' legs, still swung round and punched.

But now there was a fiery shape ahead, pointing at the sky like a forbidding finger. We swerved sharply and passed it – an American destroyer, evidently a victim of *Hiei's* fire. She had been abandoned but trapped buoyancy caused her to hang half-sunk, burning and vertical, a stark and stunning spectacle. I was staring at her when there was a burst of automatic fire in my ear; a Japanese crewman was firing the bridge starboard machine-gun, and he had it jammed down at maximum depression. Survivors!

I had a powerful impulse to spring at the man, wrest the weapon from him, turn it on the bridge and kill them all. I even did jump and shout, but before I could attempt anything so rash, the captain silenced the gun with an irascible wave of his hand. He was merely distracted by the noise.

I could not see over the side from my position but I heard high, wild cries from close aboard, ending in a shout of 'Eat shit!' Then their voices rose again in hoarse, broken screams of terror as they were dragged into the screws. The machine-gunner, a squat, bandy little dwarf, craned his bull neck aft and Froggy glanced round and smiled briefly.

Could this be real? Stop, stop, retire, cease fire, all of you, get away from this stinking ditch!

In answer to that plea, a destroyer, entirely lit under its own barrage of fire, came up on our starboard quarter and made her run at *Hiei*. Spearheaded in the van of the American

168

attack, it had no option but to charge and it spent itself in a tigerish onslaught. It seemed intent on ramming, but at the last moment, drew away from the battleship, then flew down her length within a stone's throw, spouting machine-gun and 20mm tracer at the bridge and pounding the cliff-like hide with main battery shells. The point-blank outpouring reached a blind, wholesale spate as she came abreast and two perfectly timed torpedoes joined the barrage with a flash of silver; but they had scarcely hit the water before they were out again. They were too close to arm and glanced off the target's underwater bulge, breaking surface like playful fish. There was a brave and heart-choking logic to it: as in nature, every weapon and system came together in climactic function before extinction. The roar of the assault subsided and I lost her in the smoke; she must be clear of *Hiei* now... there she was again, plunging through the maze of lights towards the dark perimeter. She'd live yet. She might have merely prodded the battleship, but she had run her gauntlet.

A torpedo hit her in the stern. She stumbled to a stop and two searchlights fastened on her, one from *Hiei*. Now she sagged and wallowed in the swell, a prisoner caught red-handed outside the wire. The useless stern sank down. The 5-inch guns stammered out one last blustering round apiece, then she sat there. Nothing moved, nothing showed, nothing sounded. The *Hiei's* first broadside was already in the air.

At spitting distance, it blew a whole gun mounting off, ripped through side and upper deck and left red gaps in the hull and superstructure. It blew bodies and bits in the air. It felled the foremast, which lay abaft the bridge, across a blazing motor whale boat at the davits. If the first broadside punished, the second razed her. When the smoke cleared she was a husk, with no funnel, a gap in the side that spread out tent-like below the water and a reeking, mangled bridge. A pillar of flame surged up from her amidships and the crew were jumping for their lives. It would be a relief to see her go, to pitch down abruptly into the peaceful depths.

But her depth charges exploded. One charge would have been enough to kill them all but the whole set of eight on the stern rails went up, like a gargantuan bomb. There was scarcely anything left; the hull filled and disappeared at once and bite-size pieces showered down from the sky after it. They were just splinters, scattering on the water. The crack of doom was not only seen and heard, but also felt, as if a giant sledgehammer had hit our own ship underwater, for the hull throbbed with metallic reverberations. The blast jarred rivets loose and probably fractured a steam line or a stern gland, for someone started jabbering down the engine-room phone.

But otherwise, every man froze with shock. There was a petrified quiet over the whole field, a moment of recognition when some individual impulse or initiative... say the dipping of a battle ensign, or a green rocket fired, or some ship turning on its peacetime lights... could have taken hold of their imaginations. The notion that they need not go on with this might have caught and spread, on both sides and they could have called it off. But the uproar started again, even as this fatuous fancy entered my mind. It was as out of place as a dirty joke.

But I could not look at it any more. I shut my eyes, faint with horror. In the name of God, what next? Three destroyers were lost, two cruisers blasted... but the sound without sight was worse, it was an amplified, terrifying welter of destruction and our own ship opened fire, after several minutes' silence. When I looked again, the few unsighted seconds had cost me such orientation as I possessed. I no longer knew whether we steered east or west, nor could I identify our target or guess our errand. Originally we had taken up some sort of support or screening position for *Hiei*, but now we had left her, a blazing log on the port quarter. There was no mistaking *Hiei*, at least.

And here was battered *Atlanta,* dead in the water and by the look of the shell splashes round her, under fire from her own side, for they were 8-inch, undyed. It would be one of the ships astern of her in column; probably *San Francisco.*

But ship was firing on ship firing on ship and when I traced these shells to their source, it was under heavy fire itself. Enormous splashes cascaded round it; 14-inch! They were unlikely to come from *Hiei* at this stage so it must be *Kirishima*, though I couldn't pick her out. She must have turned out of it, in the opposite direction to *Hiei*. She too was trying to retire.

We shot past both *Atlanta* and *San Francisco*, perilously close and came on a Japanese destroyer, burning under heavy cross-fire. Vengefully I watched; she would have little chance in it. I saw them get rid of their torpedoes; four, followed by four, fired at nothing. That was telling; they couldn't aim, it was just a safety measure. Then our ship turned suddenly and superstructure blocked my view.

Now I saw our own target, one of the cruisers, *Helena* or *Portland*, about three thousand yards away. We had dashed half-way round the battle to find it; cool thinking, Captain. He had positioned himself well for a torpedo attack, and from outside the lights. But that was their trump card, of course; at the outset, their destroyers had been spread more or less in screening formation, on the outskirts of the maelstrom, from where they could nip at it with their torpedoes like dogs after sheep. On the other hand, the American destroyers had been pitchforked into the centre, where they had no chance.

Our gunfire ceased and we swerved in for the attack. There was not even the distraction of enemy fire; the target's guns were blazing – but not at us! She was fully engaged with something she could see, probably *Hiei*. I noticed we ran in on a curve, with small alterations of course, at intervals. Strange. Oh, but he couldn't miss. There was silence, except for the staccato shouts to the control position, while we lined up. I could be doing this myself: 'Twenty seconds to go... ten seconds... *fire* one, *fire* two, *fire* three...' Off the torpedoes streaked, we swung away and waited for their run. One thousand miserable yards! It was just a training exercise.

Up went the cruiser's stern in another orange geyser of fire and water. With no rudder, and damaged plates dragging below the waterline, she sheered lop-sidedly round to starboard, out of control. It was *Portland,* a heavy cruiser. *Helena's* light cruiser class was distinctively different. *Portland* was still firing, at *Hiei*.

There was a roar of approbation on the bridge and the captain permitted himself a little skip. His droll Foreign Legion cap fell off and in a sudden glow of light, I saw the staid Mongol features unguarded, abandoned in delight. It was undignified, degrading. But wouldn't my face have looked like that?

171

Their rejoicing was short-lived. High over the din came a cry from a look-out perched on top of the bridge and we turned and froze. We were about to ram a very big ship.

Two Japanese expressions have stayed in my mind from this time and very clearly in the sudden silence, the captain croaked one of them then. It was *'Ridari magaru'* – turn left. I had heard it before, when we nearly ran aground on Guadalcanal.

The black bulk of the ship moved across from right to left – the fool should have turned the other way! Too late now. Our bows were beginning to move, picking up momentum. We keeled over. We'd scrape at least. The stem was clear of the silhouette. We might do it...

We had! Inches to spare. Square steel plates towered overhead like building blocks as we swept clear.

What was it? It was an American heavy cruiser hull if ever I'd seen one, but it had no turrets.

It must be Japanese; was it the famous 'seaplane tender' at last? But how did it get here?

The Japanese goggled at it, equally mystified. It was dead. Nothing showed or moved save the ship itself, travelling purposefully straight ahead at 15 knots. There were no signs of alarm, no noises, no one fired so much as a pistol shot at us. If there *was* anyone. At this stage of the whole mad misbegotten frenzy I could have believed it was a spectre, the Flying Dutchman. Just as long as it didn't fight!

But I had seen some large, dark shadows on its side, undoubtedly shell holes. It was no ghost. The poor devils were probably so busy trying to save it and coping with carnage that they were hardly concerned by a mere near collision.

Suddenly the captain gave an order to Froggy and our group of watchers broke up. Froggy passed the order to a man on the searchlight platform and to my consternation, he switched on the light. Of all the dangerous, stupid things to do...

The spectre was *San Francisco*. Every one of her turrets had been bashed out of shape or half shot away. The bridge was a flattened shambles. Gaping holes rent the scorched and blistered hull. The whole outline was saw-toothed with gaps and missing pieces. Battleship fire had done that. In the piercing searchlight it looked more blank and lifeless than ever.

Callaghan must be dead. And Soc McMorris – but he had been transferred and she had a new captain now. Dead. They were all dead. But *somebody* must be steering, they must be manning fire-rooms and machinery.

The Japanese leapt into action. The guns poured rapid-fire point-blank projectiles into the hulk, the close range weapons draped ribbons of tracer across it and our last four torpedoes went on their way, thumping harmlessly off the target's side – too close to arm. But every shell was hitting home; we felt the heat and blast of them on our own bridge. Scores of salvoes pummelled into her but there was no return fire. The apparition wobbled slightly and passed on. Our fire followed her still.

But they had left the searchlight on. I saw it and Froggy saw it. I watched him fascinated as he wrestled with a dilemma. The captain had ordered that light on and the captain must order it off, no matter if he had forgotten it and it beckoned destruction. The sweat coursed down Froggy's worried face but he would not act. Thirty seconds, forty, passed.

A tight bracket of 6-inch splashes rose around us almost as a relief. For a moment, they thought *San Francisco* had fired back; then there was a hit aft and more splashes on either side. The captain screamed something and the light went off. An officer spun the wheel; but she wouldn't answer. The hydraulics had failed and they couldn't shift the turrets.

The chance I had prayed for and dreaded, despaired of yet clung to fiercely for hours, could be close.

They ran this way and that, shouting orders, taking action, I could not tell what. But somebody calmly put the telegraphs to the 'stop' position.

What the blazes! They weren't trying to change to manual steering, were they? They would have to ship a great clumsy wooden tiller aft; it would take minutes. Why couldn't he steer on the main engines?

173

But it was what they were doing and it was suicidal. Two shells laid her open along the flush deck and penetrated the machinery spaces. Rosy jets of steam spurted in the air in several places, roared briefly and died away. Her life's blood had gone. The main steam arteries and God knows what else were shot away, too bad to isolate. The bridge instrument lighting failed. The funnels coughed up yellow smoke, like gobs of phlegm, from water in the fuel.

This was the chance. This ship would never move again. It was done for and must sooner or later be cut to pieces. Death, by one hand or the other – Christ, I was not going to stand here and wait for it. It was time to go.

I braced for the next shell bursts. The cruiser had got the range now; a spatter of shrapnel from a near miss hit the forecastle and set something burning. Dense, acrid smoke poured over the bridge. Then I was down, fighting for breath, with blinding red, white and green flashes zigzagging across the sky or behind my eyes, and pain eating like acid into my face. Was I blind? No. I wriggled; everything worked. The pain abated, but blood poured from my face; something was badly wrong there, but it seemed local. It could have been worse. I fought back upright quickly, testing limbs, recovering senses.

The scene was predictable, even familiar. The bridge had taken a direct hit. It was blown out at one side and the bodies had pitched towards the hole like scraps of rubbish washing down a scupper. At least four of them were on their feet though, staggering to bodies, to voice pipes, to telephones, trying hopelessly to revive the dying ship. They could only patch minor nerve-ends. But my eyes were drawn to a grisly figure who tottered and swayed in a corner.

It was the young officer who had caught my attention... was it only yesterday?... when he had conned the ship to her new station on the screen. Now he kept himself upright by gripping a stanchion with his left hand; his right arm was just pink, splintered bone below the shoulder, his whole right side was a bloody pulp and his right eye a red, shredded mess. He was shuddering with shock. But his other eye was bright, and darted bird-like round the ship and round the battlefield, and he ground out ceaseless orders through bared teeth. God, those grinding teeth, shining even through eddies of smoke that hid the smashed trunk – he should be dead. But for these last few minutes he was in command. I had patronizingly compared him to my own junior watchkeepers, but he was unearthly. This was the Spirit of Bushido paying mythological fealty to ancient, unforgiving gods who made a swordsman fight without an arm. How could we defeat such people?

But where was the captain? I found him over to one side, on his back, gazing with wide-eyed wonder at the canopy. His back was obviously injured. And he was to one side in another way, the old bull ousted by the young. He seemed a diminished figure already. But he had loyal subjects still; a wounded man dragged himself on his arms towards him. As the man finished his painful pilgrimage and raised himself on his hands beside the master, the captain lifted his head and uttered the second phrase I still remember.

'Chikusho. Baka,' he breathed. He fell back and died, I think, of his broken back and a broken heart. His last words meant two different forms of 'stupid bastard'.

Another barrage hit and I ran for it. I don't know what those shells did, except for a volcanic upheaval forward. I dodged to the disengaged side of the bridge and leaped down the ladder, knocking someone flying in my path. If anyone else saw me go, they didn't care. I could have walked off the ship. Now there were fires both forward and aft, but the upper deck was dark and deserted here. I paused, filled my lungs and glanced at my watch. I thought it must have stopped; it said 0013. That was just thirty-two minutes since I had sighted the first American ship.

Now! I swung over the guardrail and jumped. Before I hit the water, I realised I had forgotten two things; one was something to keep me afloat and the other was Barney Forrester.

There was no cause for concern about staying afloat, however, for the Sound was littered with debris. An empty oil drum came my way at once and I kicked clear with it, then studied the popping, burning ship almost absently. Ecstatic surges of reaction and relief buoyed me up along with the drum, yet the escape had been unremarkable, a simple consequence of what had occurred. Things will go well now, I thought. And they did; soon a small empty flat-bottomed Japanese punt came along and I transferred to it, drifting easy in my mind, being carried gently on a light wind out of the battle towards Lunga Point and safety. In this mood, I had little doubt of being rescued at daylight and later, when the firing died away, I even curled up on the dry bottom boards and slept.

I was somewhere south of Savo Island this time, close to where it had all begun a few months ago. On any terms, I was a real survivor now. Drifting in the punt, I reviewed the crowded span of life in those three months, and reflected almost peacefully on it. The symbolic bearing away from the bloody horror turned my mind to cosmic riddles, and I came as near to profundity as I have ever been. I suppose I was praying. At any rate, my spirit was calm and there was hope.

But from time to time some vivid flash or loud concussion brought me back to the battle. Using the fiery carcass of the Japanese destroyer as a mark, I tried to follow its progress. It ebbed slowly in the centre as the Japanese retired, but half a dozen wrecks littered their path and the gutted *Hiei* still crabbed along west of Savo. Immobility put its own macabre stamp on the conclusion, for the hulks still struck at each other like boxers battered insensible on their feet. The gunfire flickered on for hours.

Then at last the night drew a decent covering over it, the violated stars shone out and the tide began to wash it clean. I slept.

But at first light, deep in the after shell-room of *Hiei*, a gunner stirred.

'With full charge and SAP, load the cages. Load, load, load.'

The man shook himself awake, matched a telltale and pushed a lever. Motors started, the hoist pawls collected a shell each under the driving band and rose up the shaft. The shell ring stepped round two spaces. In the magazine, two flashless cordite charges followed. Steel carriages came up through the turret floor and tipped forward on to the loading trays, shell married to charge. The trays slid to the open breeches and the rammers swung over and thrust the package home. The giant breech blocks thudded shut, smooth as silk. Breech closed, gun out, tray back. High in the fighting top the gun-ready lamps came on, as another gunner centred crosswires in his sight and pressed a trigger.

The obscene rites began again. As the shells rumbled over thirteen miles of water, the cruiser *Portland*, still circling helplessly like an injured bird, gathered her strength for a last few salvoes at the Japanese destroyer I had left. It blew up, obliterated. I still did not know its name and was obscurely gratified by that; we were all guilty but let any who could, pass nameless.

The *Hiei's* shells fell about a shattered American destroyer but did not touch it. I counted eight ships adrift on the brassy sea. But here was movement: a tug, come to tow a cripple home. She must have made an early start from Tulagi, but the rest would not be far behind. The tug bore over towards *Atlanta*.

And here they came from Henderson Field, SBDs and Avengers, not bothering to gain height in their haste to get at *Hiei*. Another 31,000 tons for the pile on the sea bed of Ironbottom Sound. They bombed and strafed behind the island and that was good. I did not want to see.

Now the Sound was dotted with small craft, dark against the sun, searching for survivors. I waved to a Higgins boat, but another boat had already approached me unseen and came alongside. A huge bluejacket jumped into the punt, jabbing the air peremptorily with a Browning automatic rifle.

Oh no! Speechless, I gazed at the legend 'D.R. FOLLANSBEE' in thick black letters on his shirt.

'Hey, Ed, this guy's no Jap!' He called.

I slumped down and started to laugh. It was the name – *Follansbee*. That was rich. *Follansbee!* It was the funniest name I'd ever heard. It was hilarious, I had never... it was such a weird name! I was weak with laughter.

The sailor slung his B.A.R., grinned in a puzzled way and took hold of me.

'Hup there, Dandy. This joker's got a head wound and gone nuts. Coming up, Ed!' he called and deposited me gently, still hiccuping, on the gunwhale.

They took us in in Higgins boats and 'Yippies' and administered their rough comforts. Hundreds squatted all along the strip awaiting passage home. I stayed with them, half naked and anonymous. For the time, I rejected the burden of identity, any place in an organism, incumbencies and encumbrances. I sat and hugged the ground. Cigarette smoke and the hum of conversation rose up from the blue-clad lines in the trees. Medics moved among them with field dressings and litters. It was a battlefield at one remove, though they still seemed tense, as if it was not over yet. A fellow went past at a dead run, looking for someone. Somebody bent over me and pronounced my nose broken. 'You're okay, Bud.' Now they were taking nominal rolls; I prayed they wouldn't come near me.

All day, out on the strip, the fighters and bombers skidded down nose to tail, refuelled and took off again. They said more Japanese were on the move; another convoy was heading down The Slot in broad daylight. Some of the boys cheered the planes. The first flight of C-47 air ambulances landed and word was passed that *Atlanta* had gone down off Lunga Point.

By late afternoon the litter cases were thinning out and some C-47s were taking both walking wounded and fit men. Most of the burn cases, always the worst, had gone. I saw that the blue ranks near me had dwindled and I joined a group of twenty, waiting in single file on the edge of the strip. C-47s criss-crossed the ground like taxis in an after-theatre crowd. One lurched up and stopped abreast of us. A navy medic ran up and down the line, calling out something. What was it?

'Is there an officer on this plane?'

Must pull myself together. Must rejoin the human race.

'Yes. I am.'

'Well, why the hell didn't you say so? I've been yelling out for five minutes. You got two guys on this plane might need morphia; that big steward's mate there and the other one's had his thigh half-bit through by a shark. The steward's mate's got shrapnel in the back and a fractured clavicle. Here.'

He thrust a packet into my hand and hurried off.

'Wait! What'll I do?' I called.

'Read the dope on the package,' he yelled and was gone.

A sergeant waved us forward. Forward, check. Forward, check. Then a long wait. They kept the engines running. The line shuffled forward again. We struggled up into it and they shut us in the aluminium cave.

'Okay, let's haul ass.'

Thank God, thank God. If there had been a Tojo Time today...

We took off. The steward's mate, a black, slept, muttering to himself. The other fellow was quiet at first and I was near sleep myself when someone called:

'Hey, Doc, he's screamin'!'

A couple of us swayed beside him as he twisted on the metal bench, calling: 'Oh, Jesus. Oh, Jesus,' in a high-pitched wail. He had been sick. Was it pain or nerves? We could get nothing out of him but 'Oh, Jesus' and the bloody dressing on his leg was getting bumped. A chief torpedoman pinned him down while I got a syringe into him and we held him, talking to him until he was still.

'Easy, son. He's from my ship,' said the chief.

'Which one?'

'*Laffey*. That battleship sank us and our own ash cans blew up on the fantail. Somebody didn't set 'em to safe.'

It was *Laffey*, was it? 'Lucky *Laffey*' we had called her at Esperance. It was still a miracle; people had survived even that! But I did not want to know any more. I sat down and willed my mind into a blank.

Night sky over the New Hebrides. We got down and bumped to the apron where a crowd of welcomers and ambulances waited. They got the wounded out and I stumbled down, past the line of faces. It was raining.

'Welcome home, boys.'

'Cushing survivors over here... *Cushing* survivors.'

'Anyone from *Barton? Monssen?*'

'Limey! Limey! I thought you were gone! What the hell, boy – are you all right? How was it?'

It was Ben Jones, grinning hugely and thumping me.

'A milk run,' I said and brushed past him.

CHAPTER TWELVE

I had a very long shower. Then I wrote a laborious, halting letter to Barney's parents, who lived in a place called Lubbock, Texas. I scrapped it and started scribbling at random. The writing began to flow, and in a sudden burst of energy I tried to write down every thought I could capture. It was a self-indulgent testimony of only a few pages, but the strenuous concentration cleared my head of horrors.

Then I wrote to Beth:

'I have just had an experience that has changed my life. I can't tell you about it, but the important thing is for you to know what I'm like, because I love you and you hardly know me at all. I tried not to love you for reasons I see now were wrong, but during the experience I've just been through, I knew it was true and it was this that brought me through it.

I think of us now on the Hawkesbury River. How I think of it! But I'm not the man you started to know there, I seem to have acquired new bits. If you think that's daft, wait till you read *this*, (enclosed). I just wrote it. It probably won't make much sense, but it's true, Beth, and I want to share with you all my thoughts and feelings.

Beth, I love you. Please try to puzzle together

what you remember with what you read and say
you could love this being who wants nothing
else...'

I dropped it in the mail box there and then, and slept.

In the cold light of day, I knew I had made a fool of myself.
It was farcical; she'd think I was hypochondriac, crazy. But
she wrote back telling me to 'come home and we'd take it
from there'. She was non-committal, though tender, and said
she cherished what I'd written if only because I'd written it to
her. I wasn't crazy and I still had every chance to win her.
And come 'home', she had said. There would be that
decision too. Of course, that Japanese captain had mistaken
strengths for weaknesses in his excoriation of England.
Neverthless, he had underscored the sense of England coming
full circle, of a race run, and won, but finished. Then some
people in the old world were already saying that beyond the
provincial crudity, and rough edges of the new, lay another El
Dorado, a sort of last frontier of modern times. A race yet to
be run.

I rationalised that, as millions of peaceful and useful lives
attested, the world did not have to be a threatening place and
that if I turned my back on the king's enemy, he might well
turn his back on me. It was half guilt, half subterfuge, but
after the reality of this killing ground I could be no other way.
But it would be heresy in Sussex. And as for my golden Beth
trudging the windy Sussex Downs wrapped in a knitted scarf
like my mother... *with* my mother! Oh God, no, the future
did not lie there.

After I posted the letter, I slept for fifteen hours. I awoke
refreshed, starting out of bed with a schoolboy appetite and a
light, summer holiday feeling. Then memory came seeping
back; the aircraft crash, captivity, the murderous battle and
escape... recollections settled on me like dark clouds.
Appetite gone, I sat back on the bunk brooding and distressed
and reached for cigarettes with shaking hands. This was the
real reaction; I was not far from cracking up and I knew it.

'Ah no!' I groaned. I threw on some clothes and went to
the mess building, where I got some left-over lunch from the
startled mess boys and ate it mechanically, staring at the wall.

I had to find survivors. I flung office doors open, asking for ships' officers: *Fletcher, Helena, Cushing*, anybody. All the stupid clerks and yeomen would say was that they didn't know where they were and my agitation mounted. I hurried up the passage-way and a door opened behind me.

'Well, long time no see. What are you doing?' It was Ben.

'Come in.' He tugged me by the sleeve into his office. 'Got someone on the phone. Take the weight off.'

I sat down, struggling to control myself. He eyed me warily as he took up the phone.

'Bert? What I want to know is the repair estimate and whether I'll have to send her Stateside or if they can patch her up in Pearl. It's also a question of seaworthiness. Call me back, will you? Well, get aboard and see for yourself, can't you? That's what I'm asking you. Yeah. No, the ship has already signalled its assessment, but without an inspection and ServPac advice, we can't... that's right. Okay. Bye.'

'Still picking up the pieces,' he said cheerfully, 'and you're one of them. Been waiting for you to surface. What happened to you? The face looks cute. What were you rampaging round out there for?'

'My nose got broken. Who was responsible for that shambles?' I said with forced, icy detachment.

'Take it easy! You mean the battle? Callaghan and all the staff were killed. Nobody knows why it happened that way but – '

'It's stinking, it's intolerable! Butchery! Charging into a formation like that is cold, bloody murder! What happened to the radar?'

'Hold it! it's not your party, remember? You're out of line. You go round talking like that and they'll hang your butt so high – '

'My butt! This was my whole skin, I was there! And that gives me a voice. I'm not taking any more of these bloody defeats. A midshipman could have done better! I've worked it out, that thirteen-ship column was over three and a half miles long, waddling around like a conga line in a brothel – and those destroyers just sacrificed, thrown at a battleship like throwing stones. Why?'

I was on my feet. He edged past me and shut the door, letting me run on while he got out a bottle of Scotch.

'Shut your damn fool mouth! You can't talk like that, they'll have you out of here so fast – they'll bust you, your own people will. You know that. For Christ's sake straighten out!'

'I'll tell you what I know. But you can't hang dead men. And you've got some explaining to do yourself; last I heard you were in an airplane crash. There's a rumour going round that you were picked up by the Japanese, is that right?'

'Yes I was. I – '

'Well, you might have told somebody before you crawled away and holed up like a hog in your sack for two days. Obviously, you were in that battle. You were reported missing to the Admiralty and the Australians, but I've fixed that. Here.'

Here!

I gulped down the whisky he gave me and held out the glass for more. Ben splashed us both one.

'The Japanese ship I was in was sunk. I was a prisoner-of-war in a battle, not a British observer with his arse in a sling at a cocktail party, so that gets me off *that* hook. I saw hundreds of men die unnecessarily. You think I care a fish's tit what they do to me if I can take just one incompetent bastard with me?'

I recognised bitterly that it was intemperate nonsense, but I couldn't stop it coming out.

'Suffering Jesus... ' He passed his hand through his hair. 'They're all dead! The same circumstances won't occur again and win or lose, the next battle will be different. Nobody disagrees with some of what you're saying... you're not the only one belly-aching, believe me... but where does it get us? You're dead wrong about the battle anyway; it was not a defeat. The Japanese were prevented from bombarding and turned away. And a battleship and two destroyers against two cruisers and four destroyers? That's about even in my book.'

184

'Ben, it's the cost I'm talking about,' I spluttered. 'That's what I see, the cost – two cruisers? *San Francisco* didn't make it, then?'

'Yes, she did. She's in Espiritu now. But, uh, *Juneau* got the hammer on the way home. Submarine.'

'Oh... shit.' Slaughter piled on never-ending ruin and despair.

'You're lucky you weren't on it or you wouldn't be here now. Listen, Limey, you're way behind. Get hold of yourself and shut up and listen. You missed another fight; two fights. It was while you were doping off in your sack. And, boy, we won these ones. We've won, Limey! We've won the Goddam war!'

That had a calming, not to say stunning effect. I quietened down and gradually, in snatches interrupted by Ben's telephone calls, the stories came out.

In my battle, it was the old communications-radar bogey again. The air waves were saturated with the ceaseless passing of radar information from better equipped ships to Callaghan on board *San Francisco* and once again this task fell mainly to *Helena*. She reported firm radar contact at a colossal 32,000 yards but the minutes slipped by in chatter back and forth, the telling of radar ranges and bearings and transposing plots. Early opportunities to open fire came and went as the admiral tried to evaluate results. *Helena's* new radar was not yet fully accepted; it was too good to be true.

The TBS circuit could not carry manoeuvring, fire control and radar traffic all at once and when *Cushing*, the leading destroyer, encountered our two Japanese ships, Ben said it degenerated into a babble. *Cushing* turned hard to port to bring her torpedo tubes to bear and there was a pile-up astern, with ships hauling out of the line right and left to avoid collisions.

'You can just hear it,' said Ben. 'Everyone on the air at once:

'What are you doing?'

'Avoiding our own destroyers.'

'Shall I open fire?'

185

'Stand by to – '

'Range 6,000, bearing 300!'

'Corpen 315. Acknowledge, over!'

I had to smile at the theatrical mimicry.

'But that *still* doesn't explain why he charged straight into them.'

'That's the part that nobody knows and we'll never know now. It was a sure-as-hell deliberate course change to 315, the collision course. He must have known where they were, or *Helena* had been wasting her breath for a whole half hour. The last attempt at control was when they ploughed into the Japs and he ordered odd-numbered ships to commence firing to starboard, even-numbered to port. Of course, that didn't last ten seconds. And you know the rest.'

It was even worse than I thought. I had expected a jinx at least, some incalculable X factor such as had dogged the course of battles down through history. 'Oh, God, what a mess. What was he like?'

'Uncle Dan? I'll tell you, he was a good officer. You don't make flag rank in peacetime unless you are. I knew him. He's competent. Sober and fit... no question of aberrations or a heart attack or anything. A moderate, modest guy, a bit religious. So you better watch that mouth of yours or somebody might take a sock at it. Maybe you wouldn't have done any better yourself, Admiral.'

Maybe I wouldn't have. I thought I knew what the trouble could have been, but I didn't dare say so. Savo Island demons; that was the jinx.

'Maybe. But it was still a cocked-up shambles. What about this next battle? All this winning the war and so on?'

'Well, they did bombard the strip.'

'No!'

'The night you left Guadal, at midnight. Mikawa again, with six cruisers and six destroyers. Dumped a thousand 8-inch shells on to it, blew everything to hell. But somehow they kept the strip operational, must have worked right through the night. They flew after him up The Slot at daylight, caught him off Russell Island and sank a cruiser.

'But then the *Enterprise* was coming up from the south and their fliers joined in the strikes. And they found an unhandy thing: a socking great convoy of eleven transports and eleven destroyers boring down The Slot in broad daylight. Tanaka's outfit.'

'Now that rings a bell. Somebody said something about that before I left Guadal. I remember; the planes were flying round trips, smacking them.'

'And they smacked them pretty good... '

It was a terrible story. The transports were destroyed piecemeal by ceaseless air attacks, but there was never a thought of turning back. As the ships sank, Tanaka put his destroyers alongside them, to take off the troops and never wavering, they came straight on down The Slot in a Japanese Charge of the Light Brigade. At dawn on 15th November, the last four transports staggered into the beach at Tassafaronga, to be bombed and sunk as they touched the ground. But those troops did not get off; their killers retched in their cockpits as they cut them down. The water turned red. For the landing of 2,000 men and some bags of rice, 'Tenacious' Tanaka, so-called, drove his whole force to suicide.

'That's butchery for you,' said Ben.

'Butchery is still butchery on whatever scale. And it ... makes... me ...puke! Is there any more?'

'Yes. Sure your stomach can stand it?'

I saw red.

'No, it can't! That's what I'm telling you. You and your bits of paper! Apparently that's all it is to you headquarters sods – '

Shaken with remorse, I wished at once that I hadn't said it. Ben Jones, of all people!

'Get out.' His face flamed as red as his hair.

'I apologise for that – '

'Don't pull that on me, you arrogant English bastard. You better consider your position here. And I'll have you know I've been in combat too. Aleutians.'

187

'I said I'm sorry. Oh, Christ, I can't – bugger it ...'

'Stop the bleeding heart act! You want it to be some kind of croquet game? It's all butchery. And you push your way in here and think you can win the war – where the hell do you get the nerve to criticise the conduct of these operations? You want a voice! Boy, that really eats me out. You had a voice at First Savo, didn't you? What did you say about that?'

It was a hammer blow. I blinked and gulped back my wild emotions. Finally I slumped wearily back in the chair.

'Oh, for God's sake, let's have another drink,' I said. 'Go on.'

But his telephone rang again and after that, he said:

'To hell with it; maybe I asked for it at that. Deadpan Dick, you're not in real good shape. Let's get out of here, I've had enough. Why don't we go down to the club and you can get it from the participants? I'm strictly secondhand news. As you mentioned. There's bull sessions everywhere these days. Get yourself cleaned up and have a shave, for Christ's sake, you can't go around like that on base. Look as if you've been on a three-day drunk.'

'Good idea.' To tell the truth, I was half-drunk, and feeling better. 'I'll see you there, then.'

He stopped me at the door through, and said:

'Are you sure you're okay?'

'What you mean?' I was beginning to slur words 'I'm not going to start a fight, if that's what you mean.'

'Okay, okay, just asking.'

There were excited, ever changing faces at the club, all talking, arguing, telling their own stories of the climactic three days that became known as the Battle of Guadalcanal. I grew tired of telling my story and increasingly incoherent as the drink got my tongue. We reconstructed a track chart in liquor spills on the bar to find out the name of the Japanese destroyer I was in. The *Sterret's* captain thought it was *Yudachi* but someone from *Atlanta* insisted it was *Amatsukaze*. But *Amatsukaze* was not sunk in this battle; the Japanese lost only two destroyers and my ship's track was nothing like the track of the other victim's. *Yudachi* it was.

I grinned, pleased. *Yudachi*; I liked it.

'Gentlemen, charge y'glasses. I give you a toast: the I.J.N. *Yudachi* ! No, serious – seriously. The pilots in the First World War used to toast each other. We'll drink to the *Yudachi*.'

'I'm not drinking to any Japanese.'

'Here's to it, then, and may it rot in hell.'

'That's unchiver – unshovel – not gallant. I insist we drink to a worthy foe. Saturday night and sea room. No. A willing foe and sea room. That Jap captain, now; there's a chap in the tradition. Still wonder why the hell he was driving a destroyer for a living. More like a diplomat or a scholar. Queer type ... in a way I got on pretty well with him.'

'Maybe *we* ought to take him prisoner-of-war. We're on the other side, Limey.'

'Y'know, I suspected it. Embarrassing mistake. I'm captain of the Wahoo Maru.'

Fragmentary, disjointed accounts of the last battle circulated, but there were no participants present, for the ships had not yet got back. The victor, Rear Admiral Willis Lee, had taken the new 16-inch battleships *Washington* and *North Dakota* into the Sound for yet another midnight clash with a Japanese bombardment task force, which included the remaining ships from the force I had left. But Lee knew radar and under his hand in *Washington* he had the best adapted instrument of its kind. At last, the combination worked. The Americans opened fire at a respectable range, sinking *Kirishima* and a Japanese destroyer. But the destroyers *Preston, Walke* and *Benham* all plunged to the iron bottom, victims of the deadly Japanese torpedo.

'Halsey sweated this one out, I can tell you,' said Ben. 'If we'd lost a new battler in one of those dog fights around Savo, his head would have rolled. But we had nothing else to throw in.'

When Ben Jones spoke on the conduct of the war, they listened. He had the ear to inner councils.

'So, now what?' somebody asked.

'Why, that's it. We still own Guadalcanal. Sure, they'll flare back. But they'll never do anything like that again. Those three days were the big one.'

They were shy of it, though, for they had been bitten before.

'No, I'm telling you, they're finished. They just can't mount the scale of thing necessary to retake the place now. It's just been proven. They've lost their best pilots – Tanaka had air coverage and our guys flew rings round them. Their Zeros actually ran from the Wildcats on one strike. Isn't that right?'

He was addressing a wild-eyed young navy pilot down from Henderson Field.

'Flew the ring *off* 'em Commander,' he corrected. 'They had the height on us and they were up sun. It was loaded all their way. My wingman and I were sitting turkeys for three of 'em but they backed off. Just high-tailed it. They all did.'

'And as for the army, those they can't evacuate will starve,' continued Ben. 'They've lost so many transports that they'll never be able to keep the groceries up to 'em. Destroyers can't do it.'

But there was still doubt in the room and an anti-climactic pause that threatened to put a damper on the party. That didn't suit me.

'Good enough for me, Ben,' I said. 'And certainly worth a drink. A whole Ironbottom Sound-ful of drink. Whisky here for Commander Jones!'

'Here's up your kilt. By the way,' he said. 'There was a guy in here looking for you the other day. Australian journalist. The little bastard put one over us; war correspondents are supposed to pass a physical to go on operations and he's only got one arm. He sneaked a ride on the *Washington*.'

'Lachlan!'

'That's him.'

I was overwhelmed with alcoholic love for Lachlan, for

Ben, for everyone in the room. Oh, this was a great day.

'Drinks on me, boys,' I carolled. 'Come on, drink up!'

'Fitz, you're drunk. Good health.'

'Benjo or banzai or whatever.'

The party picked up again and I regressed rapidly to the undergraduate state. When it ended, I wouldn't let them leave, but struggled with them in the doorway. 'Call yourselves Allies? Won't drink with me!' A push of tired abusive bodies swept me aside, until there were four left. I advanced on these and declared that we were going to have a brand new party.

'Commander Jones,' with elaborate civility, 'will you assist me in seeing to the guests?'

'Whose guests? Like hell I will. Somebody help me get this horse's ass to bed.'

With a drunk's cunning, I darted nimbly out of reach.

'Wait! Wait! One for the road, I say! That's American Traditional. Flout your own traditions, would you? Not while 'mable to defend them. What, what else, I *ask* you, do ... you think we are fighting ... for? For Chrissake?'

'Aw, get him a drink, for Pete's sake.'

'No! Five! C'mon ...'

The last drink finished me. They half carried me to the quarters, one on either side and two shoving behind.

'Will you stand up? I can't hold the son-of-a-bitch.'

But I was coming round in the fresh air.

'When this terrible war broke out, war broke out, war broke out,'

I bellowed in song,

'We were the first to go,

'WHERE?'

'Who's that bastard? Pipe down!'

'Down to the wharf to see em off, to see em off, to see em off,

191

'Down to the wharf to see em off,
'But not to fight the foe-oh!'

I roared. 'Here comes the captain of the Wahoo Maru! A bit confused. Drunk as a fiddler's bitch you might say. Honking like a startled goose, what! But triumphant and glorious just the same, aren't we lads? We've won the war!'

'Shut that maniac up! Or I'll come and do it myself.'

At last, they propped me up against my doorway in the bachelor officers' quarters and I beamed at them foggily.

'Now you listen ... this's serious. You've got it *here* ...,' hitting my chest, 'but you're not perf ... not perf ... professional.'

'Can it! Go to bed.'

'No, don't go 'way. Got to pull y'finger out. Farting round with wind and water up your arse. Must train, train, *train*. Night encounters ... flotilla, squadron torpedo attacks ...'

'Oh, of course, the Goddam Limey knows it all. Didn't you know, in SoPac, you get on-the-job-training, that's all. He's past talking to. Come on.'

'Don't move! Give us a cigarette. Using cans like bloody battleships ... won't work, you hear me, gets 'em sunk, you know. At Esperance, we could've – '

'Ah, hit the sack, Fitz, for Jesus' sake. Look out!'

I fell trying to cross my legs and they dumped me on the bed, into oblivion. But still the night was troubled with muttering guns and I dreamt that the Chief of Naval Staff lay badly wounded on the bridge of a ship crying *Chikusho. Baka,* to me in a plaintive martyred tone; and I was too busy firing torpedoes to attend him. My cigarette burnt a round, black hole in the mattress. When I saw it in the morning, I thought it looked like an empty eye socket in a skull.

I was busy at last. There was a committee studying the Japanese torpedo, the sinister 'Long Lance' that had wreaked such havoc and someone who had actually taken part in enemy torpedo attacks was a windfall. I spent days trying to answer the committee's questions and nights trying to recall more detail. I was unable to confirm the rumour that the Japanese could reload their tubes underway but, through my observations, we did work out that they launched the weapon on a hyperbolic track. It was ingenious, for in theory an opposing ship could not correct its gunfire to allow for the curve and could not hit the attacker. But it would not work against radar-controlled gunnery, which still remained a closed book to the Japanese. It was already known that the Long Lance was large, fast, ran on enriched oxygen and was capable of very long ranges, but its accuracy was a puzzle and the committee questioned me extensively on fire control methods. I could only say that these seemed to work on the same principles as our own. The American torpedo of the time was an indifferent performer, being prone to porpoising and to failure of the firing pistol.

I was also questioned by insatiable intelligence officers. It became apparent that they would go on absorbing every facet of my experience as long as I could recount it. I wrote them papers and drew sketches and talked with them for hours. If I protested that, for example, knowledge of the voice pipe layout on a Japanese bridge would hardly be likely to win any battles, they would advance their creed that the whole picture was made up of tiny parts and I would go along willingly. They were professional and convincing.

I was not a celebrity, just a chap who had had a lucky escape and there were plenty of those. It was that kind of war. Stories of downed pilots and shipwrecked sailors slipping through Japanese lines were common. Some castaways became leaders of native guerrillas and some voyaged to safety in canoes.

The Guadalcanal success coincided remarkably with others round the world. One day after our battle, on 16th

November, MacArthur's Navy escorted Australian troops into Buna to mark the end of the gruelling Owen Stanleys campaign and at the same time, the Russians lifted the siege of Stalingrad. El Alamein had been won and the North African landings proceeded unchecked. Roosevelt said, 'It would seem that the turning point in this war has at last been reached' and Churchill proclaimed 'the end of the beginning.'

Russell Lachlan duly returned from his battle, all agog and full of praise for Lee. I heard him out but before he could start pumping me, I forbade any more talk of battles. I was drinking again and on a rather calculated impulse, declared the war over for that night; and while others were just beginning to think of peace, we celebrated it there and then. We triggered a mood; word spread and people joined us. It became known as the 'Great Peace Party'. It was a comparatively subdued affair, however, for the distant vision made them pensive and introspective. There were moments of rare unbending, full of strangers' confidences and drunken grapplings with philosopy.

When the party was breaking up, Ben Jones said that somebody had better start the Goddam war again and as the ranking officer present, he supposed he'd have to do it.

'Young Lochinvar,' he said, 'I can't give you a clearance to go to sea – so if you plan to do that again, you'll have to go over my head, way up the line. As for you,' he said, turning to me, 'I can give you one. You're going up The Slot again.'

CHAPTER THIRTEEN

Out of one eye I could see a brick red slab of Lachlan inert on white sand. He lay flat on his back, trying to balance a can of beer on his stomach. With the other eye, fifty yards further on, I could see some natives, stick-like figures in the heat haze, beaching a canoe. From the water came sounds of shrieks and splashes; two white girls, probably New Zealand nurses, and half a dozen men, all showing off in front of the girls, were skylarking round a rubber raft. The shrieks rose in intensity and we sat up, muzzy in the head with beer and heat, to see one fellow trying to drag a girl off the raft by her foot. Her long slim legs flashed in the sun about his head.

'Oh, the lucky bastard,' Lachlan moaned.

'Anybody'd think you hadn't seen a woman for six months. You haven't been here two weeks and you'll be back in Sydney inside another.'

'It happens any time. Nothing to do with supply and demand.' He drank some beer and flopped back on the sand. 'Schlitz,' he drawled and belched. 'The beer that made Milwaukee famous. Wonder why?'

A puff of wind scurried up from the south, raising whitecaps and blowing fine plumes of sand along the front, then just as suddenly it passed on. I thought these rich blues and the gold and white must make Anse Vata Beach as attractive as any to be found on all the four continents we represented, though its glare made the eyes throb. Today, I found myself observing Noumea sharply, committing its scenes to memory.

'You can have my Schlitz as a parting gift,' I said and stood up. 'I've got to get back and pack, then I'm off. There's a bit of a flap on about this one.'

'Yes, I know. Another convoy interception, isn't it? I'm coming too.'

'You ...'

'Not *with* you. To see you off.'

'Oh. I would have stopped you, you know. And I warn you, I will again.'

I had attacked him over his continuing involvement in the war. I told him he'd had his chance, was pushing his luck and obviously would be badly handicapped if he ever had to swim for it. He refused to admit it. He said it was now his job to observe and record battles, that this was useful and necessary and a missing arm was not going to stop him; he'd be back for the next one. I railed at him that this squalid gutter fighting did not deserve to go down in history. It did not ennoble anybody, it just degraded both sides and was best forgotten. In the end, he stone-walled me with silence, his mouth set in a wry line as if to say, 'You can't argue with a lunatic.' Either that, or he was dodging a full-blooded row with his old captain; attitudes died hard and he still called me 'sir' occasionally.

We left it in the air, with things still unsaid. However, I did allow him to take me over the battles, questioning and making notes for his history, though I found it difficult to concentrate and gave him short, impatient measure. He stuck to it, drawing me out with tact and patience.

'Let's not start that again,' he pleaded now. 'Spoil a good day. Time for a quick swim?'

'All right. But there's no need for you to trail back in with me, why don't you stay, make a day of it? Try your luck with the nurses.'

But he had already sprinted down the beach into the sea. I

followed, noting that he did, indeed, swim well with his one arm.

Then at the jeep we held a ritual exchange of protest and insistence and he got in with me. There were only commonplaces left to say and we drove along the bay in silence. Shadows of palm trees fell on the jeep in a soporific rhythm, cutting across the glitter of sun and sea.

I stopped at the A.P.O. in the dusty Place des Cocotiers, where he said he had some dispatches to file. I disliked being seen off on any journey.

'I think I'm against this book idea of yours because you'll have to make judgements. These battles are flukes, they're almost decided on timing and fortune. But you'll pillory good men for about as much human error as you use every time you park your car. Who has the right to judge? Ex-Temporary Acting Sub-Lieutenant Lachlan, R.A.N.V.R. ? Does he have the right?'

That penetrated, I could see. He looked quite flustered.

'You don't know enough,' I continued. You'll miss the character, the real anatomy of the battles, because you weren't there. History is bunk, didn't somebody say?'

'I was there for two of them. But I'll try to remember that. I think I can make a go of it. As a matter of fact, I can think of only one person who could do it better.'

'Who?'

'You.'

'Good God. No!' This was becoming ridiculous. I changed the subject. 'Don't forget the letters and the packet, there's only a shell necklace in it. She'll be glad to see you and we'll both be grateful. Tell her I'm all right and so forth, the usual things, anything you like and what it's like up here. Only lay off the battles. And don't tell her I'm going on this one.'

'I'll do it first thing. She'll have them in three days.'

'Well, this is it.'

'I guess it is.' A brief handshake and a meeting of eyes.

197

'Young Lochinvar. It's a good name for you.'

'Bloody good luck, sir. Take care.'

It was so hopelessly flat and inarticulate. We both knew why he'd come back. Did he think I was stupid?

'Fascinating,' he'd said it was. 'Couldn't get it off his mind.' 'A feeling of brooding, waiting for something.' Russell Lachlan was a marked man and so, perhaps, was I. But all that had no place in the real world. I kept him in sight, fair head bobbing like a beacon among woolly black ones, until he marched through the doorway and into his own history.

In my room, I got out an old parachute bag I used for travelling and put my things in it. A change of khakis, toilet things, old letters. Something to read; D.H. Lawrence's lugubrious *Kangaroo,* the only book on Australia I could find in Noumea. I tidied up a bit; didn't want them thinking I was a scruffy type when they came to do up my personal effects. As everybody's aunt used to say, you should always have respectable underwear on in case you are in an accident and get taken to hospital.

That was about it. Cupboard light off, fan locked in the desk drawer or somebody would 'liberate' it. I had new snapshots of Beth, so her photograph could stay behind.

I went back to the bed and lifted a corner of the mattress, looking for the burn hole, on the underside now. The chief steward hadn't been able to get me a new mattress yet.

Suddenly, this hot little cubicle of tin and wood was the dearest place on earth to me. I didn't want to go on this one.

In the late afternoon light, the destroyer *Maury*, under command of Lieutenant Commander Carl Gatwick Sumner III, looked a smart ship. Her ensign fluttered close up, halyards taut. No Irish pendants or fenders dangled over the side to blight her washed paintwork. The anchor cable to which she rode was painted white between waterline and hawse hole. Even the trash chute shone. It took a seaman's eye and hard driving work, to keep a ship up to that pitch in wartime. The gangway staff, in fresh pressed dungarees, were on their toes and the OOD's gleaming hat and straight pistol belt could have modelled an illustration for the Watch Officer's Guide. I paused at the top of the gangway and saluted.

'Lieutenant Commander Fitzallen requests permission to come aboard, sir.'

'Permission granted, sir. Welcome aboard. My name's Kelly. This way.'

Lieutenant (Junior Grade) Kelly led me forward and down below to officers' country.

'Hope you won't mind sharing. We're pretty full up,' he said. 'You're in here, in the pit.'

'Of course not. I know very well I'm lucky to get a berth at all. But don't disturb these chaps, I'll just leave my bag here till later.'

Two of the three bunks in the room were occupied by sleeping figures. I had the bottom bunk. The place was cramped and cluttered, but it looked cared for, like the rest of the *Maury*.

'Well, what's the form? When do we sail?'

'We don't know yet, sir. Not for a few hours; we can't until the new task force commander gets here, anyway.'

'But Admiral Kinkaid's here, surely?'

'Admiral Kinkaid's gone. He was reassigned to Pearl and left yesterday. Rear Admiral Wright is the new commander, but he's not here yet. He's on the *Minneapolis* and she's not due in for a couple of hours.'

I sagged against the bulkhead. Kinkaid had just taken up the appointment. He'd held it for exactly four days.

'This is Task Force 67, isn't it?'

'It is,' he said, smiling. 'I'll take you topside to the captain, he'll brief you himself; and if you'll excuse me I'll get back to the gangway.'

'Of course; you lead on.'

I had met Carl Sumner socially. He was a quiet man, not one of the more free-wheeling spirits with whom I had tended, regrettably, to whoop it up at the bar of late. But in the circumstances, that was a definite plus. He had a reputation in the navy as a fireball and an 'unholy son-of-a-bitch', but obviously he got results and that suited me. Nothing like having confidence in your captain!

'Hope I won't be a nuisance to you, Captain,' I said over coffee. 'I did want to see one operation from a destroyer but I know that's a different thing from a flagship, with all its hangers-on. But I'm very good at not getting in the way and not speaking unless spoken to.'

'Oh, come now, I'm delighted you're aboard. I'll be truly glad of some company; this is a lonesome business, as you know. And I'll see to it that the *Maury* shows you a better time than the last destroyer you were on.'

His saturnine manner was magically relieved by the touch of humour. It cleared the formalities away and, I felt, started us on a good footing. Sumner stretched his long legs in a way that invited comfortable relaxation.

'Well, having just said I wouldn't speak out of turn, do I understand from your OOD that Admiral Kinkaid has had a pier-head jump? What's going on?'

'Huh!' He laughed. 'That's old news. The latest is they've detached *Helena* and four cans on something else.'

'Oh. That's not good.'

'Well, it's not all that bad, on paper.'

He stood up and went over to his cabin scuttle, drawing the curtain aside.

'Look at it. Task Force 67: heavy cruisers *Pensacola, Northampton, New Orleans* and, we are led to expect, *Minneapolis*. Light cruiser, *Honolulu*. And four cans. That's still a lot of muscle. That's power, isn't it? At least, for these times.'

I didn't know what to say, so I said nothing.

'Now let's look at some incidentals. One, not one of these

200

ships except the destroyer squadron leader, *Fletcher*, has had any night action experience in The Slot. Two, on the eve of an operation, an experienced, veteran commander, who anyway didn't have time to unpack his bags, is out and a complete greenhorn is in. Three, at the same time, a battle-hardened cruiser, with a great deal of experience in The Slot, is detached, not to mention four destroyers. Four, the ships of this task force have not yet been to sea together.'

'Jesus Christ.'

'Oh, it's the same old piecemeal, patchwork stuff. I don't blame 'em, they can't help it. But, God, it makes it hard. Poor Wright! Those knock-down drag-out Donnybrooks up there are almost specialised warfare, you know.'

'I know what you mean. Look, what *is* this operation exactly? I have only a hazy idea. In Noumea nobody seemed to have really firm intelligence on the convoy and the picture kept changing. Even Ben Jones; he didn't tell me Kinkaid had gone.'

'Understandable. It's a rush job and the deal is still forming up. Ben's got a lot on his plate –'

'I wasn't being critical. Not of Ben.'

'We are intercepting a supply convoy, off the Canal. As soon as Wright anchors there'll be a commanding officers' conference and briefing on board the new flagship. I'll signal now, asking for a berth for you. Should have thought of it before.'

'That will be grand. But I won't be disappointed if they say no. It would be an unusual privilege and it may set a precedent.'

'They won't say no. You're not going to start a riot or leak it to the enemy. You'll just sit there and say nothing.'

'Yes, it's just the principle. Do you know Admiral Wright? Know what he's been doing?'

'That, I don't know.' He took down a Bureau of Personnel publication from his shelf. 'Trade school boy, of course. Annapolis, 1912. Mid-westerner, Iowa. What you would call yeoman stock? Remarkable how many of them go to sea. Escape, perhaps ... well, it doesn't tell us much. By the way, are you all set, your gear aboard and so on? Been shown to your room?'

That was the cue to close the interview.

'Yes, thank you, I'm very comfortable in a three-berther. But I've taken up enough of your time. Thanks, Captain, I'll hope to see you in the boat, later.'

'Okay.' He stood easily, hands behind his back. He did not look like a man worried about a battle.

'Just before you go, can we get names straight? I know everybody calls you Fitz, and that'll suit me. As for what you call me, it will be appropriate and a pleasant change if somebody on this ship calls me by my right name, which is Carl Sumner. Or if you prefer, Gaff, from academy days. Origin obscure.'

Neatly done. 'Gaff, then. Of course, I'll still call you Captain on your bridge and so on.'

'Right. Covers it all ways.'

Back in the stateroom, I crept about unpacking, with an eye on the sleepers. He didn't seem to be such a holy terror. 'Origin obscure'; it could be nautical, but Gaff led to Gaffer, which was old English dialect for grandfather. He did have a rather pontifical air. It would suit a stickler, a stringent, conservative professional.

They did say yes. Sumner and I joined his eight fellow captains in the wardroom of *Minneapolis* soon after dinner. There was tension in the air. While we waited for the admiral they sat smoking, sipping coffee and belly-aching quietly. Task Force 67 was getting off to a shaky start.

Mostly the talk was of 'Bosco' Wright. What was he like? What experience had he had? Could he do it? They were subdued and serious.

'He's an ordnance man. Spent a lot of time on ordnance. He's had sea time too, of course. He had *Augusta* in 1940, I think."

'No, '41 and I was with him, I know him. He's all right. If he gets any of the breaks, he'll pull through. What happens if he doesn't. God knows, but you could say that about anybody.'

'Sit down, gentlemen.' The tall figure of Admiral Wright stood stock-still before us, surveying the assembly. His number two, Rear Admiral Tisdale, who rode in *Honolulu*, stood behind him.

'Hello, Bob, Charlie. Some faces I know and some I don't. Hello, Frank. Well, glad to meet you all. Let's get right down to it. Intelligence first.' My Iowa farm boy image vanished, but it was hard to say what took its place. Fifty-ish, Anglo Saxon, intelligent, experienced. Fatherly; a positively compassionate mouth. Straight shooter, no frills.

He sat down and a ComSoPac staff officer stepped forward, unfolding a large-scale chart.

'You will have seen some of the take on this. A coastwatcher report as of 1000 November twenty eight has eight destroyer masts missing on count at Buin. That is collateral for other indicators that these ships are at sea in a formed state, under Rear Admiral Tanaka. The up-date as of now is that there has been no visual in The Slot and circumstantial precedent points to alternate routing. B-3 evaluation is that they have exited north about and will re-enter The Slot between Florida and Santa Isabel, transiting west of Savo, like other recent Japanese task forces.'

'What's evaluation B-3? What precedent?' asked the admiral.

'B-3 is probably true but unconfirmed, Admiral. Rating three authorises commanders to act at discretion. The precedent is when he took that helluva beating in The Slot last time.'

'Well, say so. We are acting. Just cut all the fandangle, Weisenberg, and deliver so we can understand.'

'Yessir, excuse me. Air search is negative as of this time. The evidence indicates a destroyer supply operation, as that is Tanaka's responsibility. The predict breakdown on that is for a repeat sortie every four days from here on in, to service their garrison. In this mode, forty-four gallon drums of food are lashed topside on board the ships and jettisoned manually close inshore. They are bouyancy-positive.

'Now, some input indicates he has ordinary transports with him and other input says he has not. The ComSoPac view is that this discounts out, pending hard confirmation. Are there any questions so far?'

'Yes. How do we know he's heading for Guadal?'

'Analysis makes known he is not going to Rabaul. Supply-wise, other options are limited by force location.'

'You mean there's nowhere else he could be going?'

'Yes, I guess so.'

'Terrific!' There was a general snigger. The admiral told Weisenberg to speed it up or we'd be there all night.

'Yessir. The subject Rear Admiral Raizo Tanaka is Commander, Second Destroyer Flotilla, a formation which he has led and trained in peace and war. Bio-data profiles a most resolute and skilful leader who will not recognise defeat. However,' – he had been saving the punch line – 'the methodology imposes a severe limitation on him firepower-wise; the food drums on deck will obstruct the ships' torpedo tubes and, until the drop function is complete, the tubes will be inoperative.'

He paused to let it sink in. No one seemed to be particularly stunned.

'That so, son?' said Admiral Wright. 'Go on.'

'ComSoPac assumes that there will be five or six supply ships carrying drums, leaving two or three ships for pickets and fighting escorts. That's all, sir.'

'But what about his ETA? Can't you give us his ETA off Guadal?' another captain asked.

'Oh, pardon me, I overlooked that. We compute a mean speed of advance of 20 knots, leaving – '

'Okay, okay. I'll handle it now,' said the admiral. 'Plus or minus one hour of midnight, November thirtieth. That's tomorrow night. If you are doing your mental arithmetic, you'll know we've got to move it. Twenty-eight knots, all the way.'

There was a stir of concern.

'Admiral, the weather – '

'You have the forecast for the first twelve hours; it's not ideal but we should be able to manage. After that – we will have to wait and see. But we have nothing up our sleeves. We will be going the shortest route, via Indispensable Strait and through Lengo Channel into the Sound.'

'Sir, what formation will you require on passage?'

'It will be a normal screen but you will have some discretion to move around. I don't expect accurate station-keeping at that speed. All I ask is that you stay within fifteen degrees of bearing and a mile or so of distance. But destroyers must not drop back abaft the beam; is that understood?'

There was a murmur of assent from the destroyer captains.

'Any more questions on the passage?'

'Yes, sir. That direct route will be covered by submarines. Is there no alternative?'

'Er, what is your name?'

'Cummins, Admiral. *Perkins.*'

'Well, if the *Perkins* can make forty knots, you can go your own route. I didn't chose this one for preference.'

'No, sir.'

'Now we had better get on to the battle plan.'

This was a surprise; it was good. I heard it unfold with increasing delight. Here at last was a comprehensive doctrine drawing together the bitter lessons of the past. My depression began to lift and something of the old enthusiasm returned.

The use of searchlights was forbidden.

Ships with the new SG radar would be spread in the formation so that no group, or collection of types, would be without one.

A picket destroyer would be stationed ten miles ahead of the force, to provide early warning.

The other destroyers would be stationed thirty degrees on the engaged bow of the main body and would independently carry out a torpedo attack at the initial contact. Hurrah!

Cruisers would endeavour not to close the targets to within 12,000 yards while this was taking place, and in any case would not open fire until the torpedoes had completed their run.

The destroyers would then get out of it, leaving the range clear for heavy gunfire.

Like all good plans, it was simple. The destroyers would be used properly and from that position on the bow, their torpedoes would have a short run. American gun flashes would not give our presence and position away until the torpedoes had struck. There should be no more jamming the TBS with radar information and no more hideous firing of friend on friend. I felt like cheering aloud. The fifth Battle of Savo Island could be taught in tactical schools as a model for the rest of the war.

'I will also be using the cruisers' float planes for illumination. But I don't want to launch them from the ships on the night, so as soon as we get within range, cruisers will launch planes to fly to Tulagi. The planes will operate from there that night.'

'It's good,' I whispered to Sumner. 'He's got it in one.'

'Sure, it's good,' he replied. 'But it's Kinkaid's, not Wright's. He and Tisdale got it out three days ago. We've all had it already.'

Oh. Well, that didn't make it any less sound.

Wright invited questions and comments but there were none.

'That's it then,' he concluded. 'Now you know this is my first operation in the South Pacific and I could have wished for time to settle in and bone up. As it is, I must rely greatly on your collective experience. But if our radar, numbers and fire power can't lick eight destroyers all cluttered up with deck cargo – damn it, I put it to you. What do you honestly think?'

There was another chorus of assent. But it was tepid, a politeness, carrying no conviction. Their hearts were not in it.

'Can do!' said Admiral Wright. 'Tails up, then and let's go.'

As the *Maury's* gig put-putted back to the ship, Sumner was preoccupied and answered my questions in monosyllables. He explained that tonight's briefing was mainly for Wright's benefit and to see whether he wanted to modify the battle plan.

'He's got problems,' I said. 'But the plan's a winner. Every scrap of experience over the past four months has gone into it. I must say, I can't see why all the grief, Gaff.'

Sumner shifted his weight impatiently on the bottom boards.

'Suppose you tell me what this is all about. What difference is it going to make if a few drums of rice get delivered to the Japanese or not? Why does Halsey want this operation? It's not as if they are going to bombard the field again or even land reinforcements.'

I said obviously Halsey's view was that the odds were all ours and it was a chance for an aggressive initiative to clean up. It would have significance, to deny the Japanese control up there at night. And if they did have transports with them, that must mean reinforcements.

'I don't buy that, Fitz. You remember my incidental points? As far as I'm concerned, you can add a conclusion: this operation should never have been mounted.'

Now he was a man worried about a battle.

CHAPTER FOURTEEN

We sailed, feeling our way in the dark through the Segond Channel minefield and setting course for the six hundred mile dash to Guadalcanal at midnight. A destroyer is uncomfortable at high speed even in a flat calm, for the machinery sets up a rough vibration and constant clatter. Everything jiggles; screws work out of fittings and things fall out of racks. Any object not bolted down 'walks'.

But in any sort of sea, it is like riding a wild horse. We were heading into a short, steep swell, badly out of phase with it, so that the *Maury* tended to take off from the crests and crash down into the troughs. The after part rode wildly up and whipped on the take-offs and the bows dropped through nothing but air on the descents, hitting the water with a bone-jarring shock that threw up tons of stinging spray. The ship was riding it, but only just short of structural damage and I didn't see that we could increase speed if we fell behind in the formation. She wouldn't stand another knot.

It always seemed to me that there was a high incidence of knee cartilage damage in destroyer crews, which I put down to the physical exertion of keeping on one's feet. At any rate, as the *Maury* punched and corkscrewed her way through it, there was little we could do but hang on immobilised, for to move about meant to risk losing one's hold and gaining a couple of broken ribs.

Sumner thought we would be unable to keep it up and the formation would have to reduce speed. Otherwise, we could only hope that the swell would flatten out; the forecast suggested it might.

Admiral Wright asked *Fletcher*, the destroyer squadon commander, for a report on conditions. *Fletcher* called for a report from each destroyer in turn and the consensus seemed to be that we could carry on without damage, but the point was made that the ships could not reasonably be expected to increase speed for station-keeping purposes. The *Drayton* suggested that a small alteration of course to starboard, even five or seven degrees, might help.

'Roger, I got all that,' said Wright. 'You seem to be maintaining station quite well, anyway.' The course change followed.

But the swell did begin to moderate slowly, so that after a few hours, I was able to leave Sumner trying to cat-nap in his chair and go below. One sleeper, a man named Chisholm, the engineer officer, was on watch but the other was still prone. I even got some sleep myself, but just before dawn another vicious whip of the stern flung me out of my bunk and that was the end of it. Swearing and trying not to disturb the other fellow – but I saw that now Chisholm was back in and the other one was out. How we chased each other round. I dressed and struggled back to the bridge.

The third man was wide awake, as officer-of-the-deck. As I came up, he was calling Sumner with the first light report.

Dawn at sea can be revitalising, even in miserable weather, for the ship stirs into life again. Men begin to move about the deck. Often there is a change of formation and dawn action stations. The blackout is lifted. A whiff of frying bacon might drift up from the galley where the cooks are starting breakfast and tired watchkeepers send down for fresh coffee.

Some of those things began to happen, though there was not much lift to my sluggish faculties that morning. Seen for the first time in daylight, the grey, racing swells looked horrendous. But undoubtedly the ship was riding better.

Sumner came up and I started a round of salutations.

'Morning Captain. Morning.' Nodding to the OOD.

'Good morning, Commander.'

'Morning, Fitz. How did you sleep?'

'I didn't, did you?'

He made a sound between a snort and a hollow laugh, and rubbed gritty eyes. The *Maury* had no SG radar and she had run blind for most of the night. I had a good idea of the tense, uncomfortable hours he'd spent.

'At least it's flattening out.'

'Hmmm.' We were too groggy for much talk.

A skinny, tow-headed young seaman worked his way up the ladder manhandling a huge pot of coffee from rung to rung.

'Coffee, Captain?'

'No thanks, Snaggle. Call me at half-seven,' he said to the officer. 'Keep proper station now, she'll take it. Use plenty of revs and bold alterations. Tell Mr. Richardson we'd better defer battle drills for two hours ... that anchor gear's talking, isn't it?' His voice crackled suddenly.

'It is loose, Captain, but I didn't believe it was safe to put a detail on the forecastle at night in these conditions –'

'Mr. Bogle, there are lifelines and it's been light for twenty minutes. As a seaman, you'd make a good Condy's boy in a brothel. You are expected to take charge of the ship. Either get the sea detail that secured the forecastle last night to do it again correctly, or put their petty officer on report. Whichever is convenient.'

Apart from the words, the dry, blistering delivery of it was enough to make even a bystander tremble. This man had a cold steel tongue. I began to see what they meant.

'Aye aye, Captain,' said Bogle crisply, but with the faintest hint of resignation. Evidently, you never objected, even if – perhaps, especially if – you had a case. You just bent before the wind.

Sumner went below and I pretended I wasn't there. Mr. Bogle went about his business. Soon, four oilskinned life-jacketed figures came into view on the forecastle, inching their way forward. They were doubled on their haunches, dropping to all fours and clinging to the deck when the roller-coaster motions of the ship tried to suspend them in mid-air. They had been set a strenuous and unreasonable task, but they should be safe if they kept their balance and the ship did not take any green water over the bows.

'More cream or sugar, sir?'

It was the young seaman, still there, watching me drink my coffee.

'No, thank you.'

'Begging the Commander's pardon, but they say you have been in most of the battles.' The forecasted detail had reached the spurnwater now and crouched behind it, ducking from the spray.

'Yes. At, rather than in, though. I was a spectator.'

'This will be my first. I guess it will be quite an experience.'

I was intent on the four men, now right forward on the heaving bows and at their most exposed. They were kneeling between the two anchor chains, working on the lashings and strops that secured the gear from moving about in bad weather. A lashing had worked loose and the heavy chains had been clanking and scraping on the steel deck: 'talking'.

'Did you know there were five brothers killed on the *Juneau?* The Sullivans. And I had a buddy on the *San Francisco*; he said you could scarcely stay on your feet for slipping and sliding in the blood and oil. They were walking in blood! Holy cow!'

Oh, he was one of those. Poor kid. That might explain why he seemed scarcely aware of the little drama being played out up forward. The sailors had nearly finished the job and had suffered little more than a drenching and barked knees. They began to work back towards us, along the forecastle, with ungainly, frog-like gymnastics.

'No, I did not know about those brothers. That's shocking. But one of the worst things is thinking about what could happen; it never does. You can get over that, but you never

211

get used to battle itself and that's just as well. A scared fighter is a good fighter. Gets you into top gear. Whoa!'

With a sudden whip and tilt of the ship, a man lost his footing and shot towards the guardrails in a breakneck slide. But he was brought up short and jerked back to his feet by his lifeline and he dodged acrobatically back to the shelter of the screen door in a second.

'Phew!' Bogle and I said together and looked at each other. Bogle was 'responsible' and the whole thing had been a bane and humiliation to him.

'Well, I dunno, I guess,' whined Snaggle.

Bogle wheeled on him and gave him the full store of his own pent-up feelings.

'Oh, shut your moaning, for God's sake. It'll be the first time for a lot of us on board. We're all scared, that's to start with. Only we don't go blabbing about it. Now let's have some more coffee here.'

The boy shot him a baleful look. 'I just wanted to know what it's like, is all, Lieutenant.' That we had nearly lost a man over the side seemed not to register with him. He went off, trying to appear casual, whistling. He had irregular teeth, with two prominent front ones. 'Snaggle'; I saw the connection. The general effect was fetching.

Bogle and I exchanged another look.

'He's under age,' he said. 'Supposed to be eighteen, but I think he's only sixteen. He's a good kid and he pulls his weight. Become kind of a mascot.'

'Why don't you get him off, then?'

'I can't prove it. Don't worry, I'm trying. Anyway, I could use some advice myself. What would you say?'

'About battles? I think I've just about said it all,' I said. 'Mental preparation helps. The Duke of Wellington said to a young officer who asked him the same thing: "My boy, never neglect an opportunity to pass water". And I tell you, I was in a hell of a jam over that once. It's difficult to improve on.'

He smiled. 'And how was the conference? How do you think we'll go?'

212

'If we stick to the battle plan, we can't lose.' And I had a feeling that the *Maury* would be all right, however it went. Gaff Sumner was as hard a man as any blue-nosed Yankee of the old clipper ships. I was still willing to trust him with my fate.

By noon on 30th November, the swell had dropped away and the going was easy. At dusk, approaching Lengo Channel, we met head-on a friendly eastbound convoy of three transports and five destroyers on their way to Espiritu, and on Halsey's orders the destroyers *Lamson* and *Lardner* were detached to join us. But the newcomers were not briefed on the battle plan and other force procedures such as recognition and communications, and they carried no SG radar. The problem was, where to put them? At this time our ships were in line ahead; four destroyers with *Fletcher* leading, then the flagship, followed by the other four cruisers.

Wright made the new destroyers 'tail-end Charlies', astern of *Northampton* . There was little else he could have done but to me, playing admiral on board the *Maury*, it was like a blow. Back to the old single column again; van destroyers, cruisers and rear destroyers. Eleven ships long. Callaghan's recipe for disaster.

However, sunset was a milestone safely reached. The *Maury's* bridge was crowded as the ships filed up the channel and in spite of the cloud over the operation, an infectious, nervous energy began to build up. People moved more briskly about routine tasks and their voices acquired a brittle quality. Sumner held court in his chair, in withering form. Once, just as Richardson, the exec, reported the ship darkened, our next astern came up on TBS with the information that a chink of light was showing aft. Either the ship was darkened or it was not and as Mr. Richardson evidently did not know the difference, he was to give reasons in writing why he should not be relieved of his duties. Meanwhile, this was a warship, not a carousel and its captain

213

would be pleased if he would get it into a fit state of battle readiness, before it got torpedoed. Next it was a signalman's turn for a roasting, for needing a shave.

How they must hate the man! I fingered my own five o'clock shadow and decided to clear off. Being a visitor had its etiquette and the margin between tolerated on-looker and resented over-looker could become thin.

I filled in the hours with trivia, resisting the claustrophobic urge to get back on the bridge until general quarters sounded at 2200. Then to the urgent clang of the klaxon I joined the *Maury's* crew scurrying along passageways to their stations, like soldier ants defending their nest.

I re-emerged on the bridge into a throng of helmeted, life-jacketed figures milling about amid a flurry of reports and orders. Then sound and movement died away and the muffled, expectant stillness took over. I slipped into my accustomed role; to watch and wait, to keep out of the way, to speak when spoken to, to be a dummy man, afraid, useless and alone. I wondered if I would ever be anything else.

We were on time. By 2225 the formation was through Lengo and had reduced speed to 20 knots. Now the Sound was utterly still. Not a ripple moved on the black water and no breath of air stirred. There was no moon and visibility was down to two miles. It was perfect. Even Japanese eyes could not see us.

We were still in single column. I looked over the radar operators' shoulders at the screen but the *Maury* carried only an air warning set and apart from painting in a few high spots on Guadalcanal, the display tube was blank. Nevertheless, the picture was good enough to see that we were hugging the Guadalcanal shore line and would need to alter course soon, to gain sea room. But this radar was quite useless for tracking targets.

However, both *Fletcher* and *Perkins* ahead had the proven SGs. *Drayton* was next astern ... but that meant there was no picket destroyer, didn't it?

The TBS cut in with orders for a simultaneous turn that took us away from the coast then another turn back westwards that put the ships on a 'line of bearing', very fine and with the lead destroyers deployed on the wrong bow – assuming we would engage to port. But there would be time to fix that, and for the moment, it was good to be out of that single column death march ...

I'd ask Sumner about the picket destroyer. I must have missed a modification to the plan. But he was busy and likely to remain so; he was checking his bearing on the flagship, not easy to do in these conditions for she was the faintest of black smudges through binoculars. I hovered just out of his line of sight, not intruding, but where he could spot me out of the corner of his eye.

'That you, Fitz? There's no picket destroyer.'

'Yes, I know. I was going to ask you, why?'

'Snafu,' he said curtly and bent over the alidade again. He didn't know.

'Small Boys, this is Culprit. Skunk, bearing 285, range 23,000. Multiple echoes. Course south-east.'

God! It was *Minneapolis* and she'd got them. They were almost right ahead, between Savo and Cape Esperance. They were early, too; time, 2306.

There was that agitation that always accompanied an enemy report, but *Maury* could not do much about it yet, except mark the plot. Immediately Admiral Wright ordered a 40 degree turn to starboard, which put the van destroyers 20 degrees on the engaged bow and not 30 as the plan stipulated, but only the literal-minded could quibble with that. Now it was looking good. We needed to stay outside Tanaka, to sandwich him against the coast.

We ran for eight minutes while *Minneapolis* developed her plot and the other ships searched for echoes. *Fletcher* picked them up. *Perkins* got them and *Drayton*. *Minneapolis* reported seven ships in line ahead and an eighth, well out on the port bow of the leader. That would be a picket. Their speed was 12 knots, a slow crawl suitable for dropping the drums overboard. That proved they did not know we were there.

My confidence crept back. Any minute now the destroyers

should be detached for their torpedo attack. It could be a historic moment in the campaign, marking the end of waste and sacrifice. I prayed they wouldn't blow it; it was a straight- forward problem as these things went, though of course they'd had no practice. But all they had to do was steer in, fire and steer out again. If nothing untoward happened, they ought to pull it off.

But poor old *Maury* was still blind and we had no target settings yet. In the radar shack, operators coaxed and cursed the set but the little green scanner swept round and round, showing nothing. Sumner stalked to and fro in a ferment of frustration, tongue-lashing all about him.

'What's the delay on that fouled-up fuel pump?' he crackled down the engineroom phone. 'Mr. Chisholm, is this ship going into battle or must I ask the Japanese for a ten-minute recess? Get it pulled down, then, and fly! The performance of your black gang reflects no credit on you, sir. They couldn't pull down a soldier off their sister.

'Now you radar operators, you are to report any new blips to me personally, you understand? Never mind what you think they are, you get me to that scope and keep hollering till I do get there.

'*Range*, Mr. Kelly, confound you! I want a range and bearing every fifteen seconds, not once a week!'

Oh, Lord, if he was going to keep this up ... Patience, man, patience, with any luck, the float planes from Tulagi will light the targets for you bright as day –

The planes hadn't turned up. Something had gone wrong.

'Small Boys, this is Blackjack. Execute to follow, three zero zero Turn, I say again, three zero zero Turn. Stand by.'

Good grief, that was back to single column! We were committed now, there wasn't time to deploy the destroyers on the bow again. What had happened? Why had they thrown the plan away?

Still, no tactical advantage had been lost and it was a good firing course, nearly reciprocal to the Japanese. We'd do it yet.

Two minutes later, *Fletcher* reported his targets broad on

the port bow at 7,000 yards and requested permission to attack. On the *Maury's* bridge, there was an electric silence as we strained for the answer. Without radar, we were as ready as we could ever be.

'Roger. Wait, out.' From the flagship.

Wait? What for?

Then Admiral Wright came on the air.

'Understand your range is 7,000, but if that is their picket destroyer I think it may be excessive. Their formation goes back another 2,000 yards from that. Your range ought to be 6,000 or less. What is the situation, over?'

We had no way of knowing. We could only listen with growing consternation as time went by and the *Fletcher's* captain and the admiral debated the position of the targets, track angles and torpedo settings. Sumner seemed to have been struck dumb. Now was the time to let the destroyers off the leash, they could close the range themselves if necessary, but – LET THEM LOOSE!

My mind ran like a computer. Mark 15 torpedoes, set for 10,000 yards, speed 34 knots – target closing speed 32 knots – the range would close to about 5,000 on the beam but the bearing would be opening at a rate of – oh, fuck! Forget it! It was too late! The targets would have passed the beam. It would have to be an overtaking shot.

'Very well, then. Fire torpedoes.' said Wright. Four minutes too late.

Fletcher fired two spreads of five. *Perkins* fired eight. Carl Sumner raise his arms in a gesture of despair and said 'I pass.' *Drayton*, astern, was having radar trouble and only fired two. They might as well have fired at the moon. It was a fiasco. We looked miserably after the disappearing wakes.

They were hardly out of sight when the ultimate folly was upon us.

'Small Boys, this is Blackjack. "Roger". I say again, "Roger". And I do mean "Roger".'

I broke my rule. 'He's opening fire!' I yelled.

'What? What's happening?'

'The flagship's opening fire! They must have seen us! We'd have heard! He'd have p-passed that on, wouldn't he?' It was the first time in my life I had ever stuttered.

'Hell, I don't know, he's lost me. Maybe he thinks they're slipping away from him, that four minute delay ... but our column stretches back a full four miles. *This* bad, I never dreamt ...'

It was no use speculating. We could only wait for the sheltering darkness to burst apart. I was always waiting for something to happen in this battle and it was always bad. It had a pattern of action and consequence.

Minneapolis opened fire. *New Orleans, Pensacola... Honolulu* was a bit late, but she made up for it with a spectacular rapid fire technique. Vivid flames lit the long line. Some of them were firing starshell as well as main battery 6-inch and 8-inch. The two tail-enders joined in and then the van destroyers started. There was nothing else they could do now. *Maury* opened up with starshell. I had never seen such intense fire, not even at the height of the Battle of Guadalcanal. The armada squandered light, sound and energy on itself as if too long deprived of its natural state.

And we *still* should win. We should blow every one of them out of the water. We mentally followed the arcing projectiles over the water, ticking off the time of flight and scanning up and down the line for winking red pin-points of shell bursts.

There must have been straddles, near misses and shrapnel nicks, but the gunnery was bad. That hair's breadth adjustment that meant the difference between devastation and a lot of harmless noise was missing. There were no hits.

Another of those moments that reversed the order of things had passed. We had thrown it all away.

Over there, there would be surprise, but no panic; confusion, but no error; disorder, but no loss of control. They would disperse like a nest of surprised snakes. Discipline, training and cool-headedness would get them out of it. I saw no answering gun flashes; of course not. They were too wise to give themselves away like that. But there would be torpedoes. Oh, yes, the Long Lances would be on their way. I pictured them frantically dropping the drums, clearing the tubes ... 'Japanese-uh smart. Work hard.'

Away out on their port bow, their lone picket destroyer seemed to be drawing all the fire. She was swamped and sinking. That was all.

'The destroyers would then get out of it, leaving the range clear for heavy gunfire.' In a last forlorn gesture to the battle plan, *Fletcher* led the four van destroyers off at 25 knots, towards the west coast of Savo. We began to draw away from the belching, bellowing cruisers and there was cowardly comfort in that, but every eye on the *Maury's* bridge was fixed astern.

Minneapolis got the hammer at 2327. Two thick columns of water rose to masthead height and fell on the ship like a tidal wave, swamping fires already started.

New Orleans turned hard to starboard and steered into a warhead abreast the forward magazines. They all exploded together and severed the ship in two. The fore part, with its turret still smoking, squatting grotesquely on top of it, bounced and bumped down the ship's side. I imagined the shriek and rasp of stressed metal breaking up and coloured ship-entrails spilling out.

I could neither bear to see nor turn my eyes away. Oh, let the earth split and the sea run dry. Let these ships fall down into some cavernous cleft and there all dissolve.

'You can stick that up your ass-hole!' shouted a choked, shaking voice. I registered Kelly hurl the operations folder, with the battle plan in it, into a corner and stand making savage thumbs-up gestures at the injured flagship.

'That's enough of that. Tend your deck, Mr. Kelly. Pick that up,' said Carl Sumner, but in the quietest tone I'd heard him use yet. Kelly went after the folder, hiding his working face.

Pensacola turned to port and silhouetted herself between the Japanese and the burning American ships. She took one abreast the mainmast. Showers of flaming oil fuel deluged the whole ship from truck to waterline and stem to stern.

Honolulu scrambled clear on the blind side and skittered

away to the north-west, fishtailing wildly at 30 knots. She was not touched.

'One to go,' somebody said.

It was *Northampton,* trying to run with *Honolulu* but the heavy cruiser hull was sluggish and she lagged behind. She was laid open to the sea. Burning oil fuel sprayed the upperworks and the fuel-soaked mainmast burst into a pillar of fire. She listed over to port.

'And that's the lot.' The voice rose hysterically. 'All the heavy cruisers. Every single one! Oh God, look at the – '

'Be quiet, Lucchetti. It's not the lot.' Again that strangely calm, almost gentle voice. Sumner was still looking astern, waiting for the two tail-enders, *Lamson* and *Lardner.* But we couldn't find them. Shocked and bewildered they might be, but they were also wise and wary and had hauled clear. Then Savo Island loomed up on the starboard quarter and slid across the stern like a dark curtain, cutting off the view.

'Hello Blackjack, this is Fieldmouse One, Fieldmouse One. We will be orbiting you in ten minutes at angels two. Sorry we're late, we have been trying to take off for over an hour but we couldn't raise enough wind, it's a flat calm in there. Used up half our fuel on taxi-ing. What orders for us, over? Blackjack, this is Fieldmouse One, I say again... I see burning ships... three, four... Christ! *Blackjack this is Fieldmouse One. Do you read, over?"*

'Shut that crap off!' barked Sumner, with something like his old form.

After that, nobody spoke or even moved much. Once, *Drayton* claimed to have picked up the retiring Japanese on radar and fired a spread, but if she did have them, it was too long a shot to score. No one took much notice.

We ran right round Savo, less than half a mile off shore at times. The long black slopes stretched overhead into the darkness and vengeful emanations reached out.

And how else should it have ended? It was the final salute, a ritual circling of witches, at midnight. Celebration of the offering, demonology, homage to bloody murder. We bring fresh tribute, more rusting catafalques and new bones. We are only scurrying beetles but we have done well. It's an ancient tithe, something to do with a primordial curse. Lachlan said something like that.

But why here? Why us?

No one had much grip on reality. There was another ship following us, astern of *Drayton*. It was the Japanese, chasing us! They were monsters! We must get away, full speed —

Sumner said it was *Honolulu* and why couldn't they give him a destroyer crew instead of a rabble of Indian squaws on the run from getting raped by the cavalry? It helped.

Then Admiral Tisdale on board *Honolulu* broadcast that Wright had handed over tactical command to him. *Honolulu* was to patrol the Sound for enemy and act as picket while destroyers were to close the torpedoed cruisers for rescue operations. That was practical and down to earth. We came down the east side of Savo ashamed of ourselves and ready to do what we could.

First, the swimmers. We wove in and out among them as if on tiptoe, lowering boats and streaming flotation nets. We heard them before we saw them, calling out with far-away voices. At one time a soft lamentation from many throats, '*Honolulu, Honolulu,*' like the wail of lost souls, was borne over the water as the cruiser moved among them, but she could not stop and threw them flotsam. *Fletcher* and *Perkins* netted these and many more, but *Maury* had less luck and the seabirds overhead seemed to screech reproof at our meagre score. Once, a deep, rich voice called out, 'Any you guys from Alabama?' and we pulled in a black with flashing teeth.

Northampton sank at 0300. She was past help but the others saved themselves with good damage control and crawled into Tulagi Harbour.

The *Maury* stood by *New Orleans* that morning. We circled round her slowly as she laboured from the battlefield at 2 knots, down by the bows to twice her normal draft. As the sun was rising, we shepherded her alongside the land in a high-sided jungle cove, making her fast to palm trees along the shore. Here she must stay for weeks, concealed from Japanese bombers, while her sweltering bluejackets cut down trees from the forest to shore up the bulkheads and fashion the

221

jury bows.

Then the *Maury* nosed in to berth on her in turn and in the early light we looked straight down on the severed bow section. In the centre of the jagged tongues of twisted steel perched a bright, white sailor's cap and nearby was a single shoe. There was a sound of sobbing. Snaggle, a telephone talker on the bridge, bowed his head into his phones and wept.

Richardson went over to him and said something.

'All engines stop,' said Sumner. 'Mr. Richardson?'

'Aye aye, Captain?'

'Leave him.' His voice was cracked but gentle. 'It's just as well somebody can still do that. Let him do it, for all of us.' It may have been the light, but his face against the sun seemed black with a private fury.

I understood then why no one on board the *Maury* hated Gaff Sumner. Snaggle's racking sobs rose on the still air.

CHAPTER FIFTEEN

Beth always said with faultless logic that the one good thing that came out of the Battle of Tassafaronga was that they recalled me straight away. The fact is, that with Guadalcanal secure, they considered my job finished and the timing was incidental. The orders were waiting for me when I got back.

God knows, I was glad enough to go – but not in the way I went, slipping away almost unnoticed. I tried to arrange some farewell calls, but the place was in such turmoil after the battle that no one, from Halsey down, had time for formalities. In the end, I just had a drink with Captain Browning, the chief-of-staff; a quiet, pleasant interlude when we talked about anything but the war and Tassafaronga. Ben Jones saw me off. Carl Sumner somehow heard the news and sent me a warm signal from the *Maury*.

I rang Beth from Townsville. I marvelled that there was a voice at the other end, that she really did exist. But it was a patchy line.

'Dickie! Where are you?'

'Townsville. I'm coming home.'

'Dickie! Is the war over, or something?'

'Hell, no. It just has to get along without me for a while, that's all.'

'Oh, that's wonderful. You sound American.'

'Beth, I want to marry you. Will you marry me?'

I thought she said, 'No.'

'No! Did you say no?'

'No, I said "Oh!" Dickie, hadn't we better see each other first? We might have changed.'

'Might have what?'

'CHANGED. One of us might have changed!'

'Beth, can you hear me? This is hopeless. I'm coming to Sydney by train, it arrives the night after tomorrow. I'll have a bit of time there, just a few hours, then I'm going on, but I'll be back. I'll be back! Check with the R.T.O. about the time – the RAIL TRANSPORT OFFICER, got it? Well, never mind, I'll ring you when I get in. I love you.'

'I can't hear you, it's no use. It doesn't matter, all that matters is you're here... '

But the troop train, containing a draft of exhausted, yellow-faced infantrymen from New Guinea drinking Queensland rum, was half a day late into Sydney. We had to scramble for the south-bound connection and I had no time to telephone her. I rang again in the middle of the night, changing trains once more at a state border, to tell her I would be back for her within forty-eight hours with three weeks' leave and a car.

In Melbourne, I reported to Navy Office still in my travel-stained American uniform. I found myself oddly reluctant to discard it.

The Chief of Naval Staff said he had found my reports useful and the account of my time with the Japanese particularly interesting. He said it was probably unique and I should write a book about it one day. It was a pity I hadn't been able to throw more light on their torpedo technique. But the appointment had been successful and he was glad he'd made it. He added that he had not been prepared for the continuing abysmal state of American training and efficiency.

'They did the best they could, sir.'

'Naturally. What I'm saying is that wasn't very good.'

'From my perspective, it was more that the Japanese were very good indeed... '

I expect he noticed the subtle shift in identification. It was all very well for me to rave at Ben, for that was, well, in the family, but I resented criticism from an outsider. When we got on to Tassafaronga, I defended Wright and sought to minimise the mistakes.

'Hmmm. Well, you'll be writing a report about that in due course. You'll be here, in Navy Office, you know that? In Manning, I think.'

It couldn't have been better. As soon as I decently could, I raised the question of leave. He said testily that he didn't preside over leave entitlements and I'd better see his secretary. But I'd only had the job for three months and I wasn't due for any, surely?

'I was thinking of survivor's leave, sir.'

'What, again? But that's only for our ships. You don't get it for getting sunk in an enemy ship, do you? Oh, hell. Get my secretary in here.'

The paymaster captain said it was a 'curly one'. It was a nice point, but it was certainly not covered by the regulations. Survivor's leave was for our own ships. He was sure there was no precedent.

'How about crashing in one of "our" aircraft? Will that do?' I managed a gruesome facial tic for their benefit.

'Sir, Fitzallen's obviously had a strenuous time and I think we could – '

'Oh, go on, get out. Three weeks.'

I went to the same car-hire firm and insisted on getting the same car. I wanted to close the circle completely. Driving up this time, the road did not seem so endless. The hills were covered in young spring growth and the sun shone.

We were married in a church, but that was one offew concessions to a traditional naval wedding. Beth looked the part, though, in chiffon and silk and her joyful bloom and sparkle told me all I wanted to know: she had no doubts.

I invited the Darlings by letter and card, giving them some brief news of myself, but they declined laboriously, saying they couldn't leave the farm. They would be still vulnerable to grief and perhaps they had an inkling that our experience, intense though it was, owed itself only to abnormal circumstances and should be left at that. Sometimes we should not go back. Sadly, I put aside a notion to visit them, with Beth.

Her father, a country solicitor, led the family contingent. They were a good-humoured lot, though taken by surprise and concerned to take stock of this stray seafaring character the girl had somehow got involved with. I saw in turn that my miraculous beloved was one of a human production line, after all. Russell Lachlan was my only true guest, though I did round up a few thirsty, uniformed acquaintances to do odd jobs and to fill some pews on the port side. The parson, apparently sceptical of my chances of staying alive for long, said at the reception that we were a brave couple to be hastening God's purpose.

We had a long time together though, during which I learnt many things, not all of them flattering to myself. One thing I learned was that I had a buried instinct for the earth. It probably saved my marriage. I had scarcely lived in a house since I was a child and had obscure notions of domesticity. In the beginning, Beth heroically maintained a light touch, but there was a showdown over some prawn remains left nocturnally, unstrategically and alcoholically. A breathless and abrasive parallel was drawn with pigsties. She maintained that we bought enough food for ten people; we were overspending and had to cut down. And the first thing to go was booze. And I could pick up my baggy old navy underpants off the floor...

Reflecting that even the surface froth of a relationship inexorably shapes it, I set about the garden to make amends and found I could dig such troubles into the soil. The plants and I conspired for her delight and we all thrived. Equilibrium was restored. Accepting the bounty of my early celery, she mimed a tableau and remarked that I should have been a farmer. Without thinking, I said 'I will be.' We looked at each other, surprised, but didn't say any more about it then.

One Saturday morning, she came out to where I was happy and muddy among the rhododendrons with a parcel just arrived from Noumea. Inside was some film I had left to be developed, the wretched *Kangaroo,* a few other odds and ends and a note from Ben Jones, evidently smuggled past the censor:

'Hello Limey,

'Some mothers have careless children. How's it going? Plenty of snatch down there? It hasn't been very gay here since you left. That last tangle with the Japs was nothing to what broke out around here afterwards. Wright accepts full responsibility for getting the cruisers torpedoed. But Halsey's really got it in for poor old Bill Cole of *Fletcher*. Says he deserted the cruisers when he took off round Savo. I know what you're saying: It was in that bloody battle plan and what about *Honolulu?* Keep your shirt on, that's what everybody's saying. But I'm afraid it's in the record.

'I'm still up to my ass in it, with no reassignment in sight. I figure on changing my name to Ludovic Katzenjammer. Ben Jones is too easy. You'd think twice about saying "Get Ludovic Katzenjammer to do it," wouldn't you?

'Oh God, I could do with some of your green vegetables and white women. I have this fantasy about you – these lewd women catering to your lusts and dangling asparagus tips and French beans before your mouth.

'Well, keep on truckin'. Take care. Ben.'

It was months old.

'What is it?' Beth asked.

'Oh, it's just my last mess bill from the club in Noumea. I'm sure I paid it.' White lies start early.

The last sad echo from Guadal. Old Ben.

God, what a long time ago it seemed!

At work, in Navy Office, I requisitioned certain files. I

already knew the contents, but reading between the lines of the terse signalese, I could reconstruct the actuality and atmosphere. The desperate night battles had gone on, shifting westwards up The Slot as the ground forces took one island after another. And as I read, I was there, racing through the Sound at night again, but with a new breed of winners: Tip Merrill, Moosbrugger, Pug Ainsworth and Thirty-one Knot Burke. For these had got the measure of it.

Dodging torpedoes at Empress Augusta Bay, Merrill took four cruisers through continuous manoeuvres for over an hour at 30 knots, firing coolly all the time and not one of them was hit or out of station at the end. And that was done on TBS!

Moosbrugger took six destroyers into Vella Gulf on a black midnight and sank three out of four Japanese counterparts – with a squadron torpedo attack! And one of the victors was *Maury*.

But at the Battle of Kolombangara, turning wide astern of *Honolulu*, the New Zealand cruiser *Leander* was torpedoed and Russell Lachlan died. Kolombangara was another massive, circular, cone-shaped island, a larger edition of Savo.

I sent the files away. It was time. Marriage vows... but she knew and she would understand. I'd miss the rhododendrons. Any fool could do my job here, it was a crashing bore, a mere numbers game for bureaucrats... *Oh, God, stop this war!* But first, I had those 180 ghosts to lay.

I telephoned the paymaster captain and asked to see the Chief of Naval Staff. Then one day towards the end of 1943, I rang Beth from the office with some news. There was a new destroyer building in Sydney and I'd got it. Women had a rotten war.

The stink of wet paint was everywhere. They never gave you enough time to finish anything.

The first lieutenant knocked, cap under arm.

'The ship's company's mustered, sir.'

'I think a short pause, George. Timing, you know? Good theatre.'

He thought I was merely being facetious, enjoying the moment. It was theatre; first night nerves.

I went out into the sunlight, and hopped up onto B gun deck. Three hundred patient, nearly bored faces gazed up. At an age when policemen started to look young, these looked absurdly so – a whole crew of Snaggles.

The platitudes were easily said. Glad to see a young ship's company, there was no particular virtue in age. Happy ship, right of the individual, cabin door always open to anyone with a problem. The disciplinary side; leave-breaking, drunkenness, V.D. That required tact, to lay down the law without preaching.

'But mostly, I want to talk about the war.'

How could I get it over to these babies?

'You will know that I lost one of these ships once. We are not going to lose this one and I want to tell you why.'

I had somehow to convince them that they could have confidence in me despite any ignorant scuttlebutt that may have revived about my first ship and also that I had to have confidence in them.

'Think about what a destroyer is. Think about the name. It should be just that; it is fast, small and it packs an enormous wallop. Used properly, these ships are battle-winners and the more properly they are used, the safer they are. I have seen them win and lose battles so I can fairly claim that I know how to win. And we must all know how to win.

'If I make a wrong judgement, it won't work. But I won't, of course.'

Make a half-joke of that. Nobody grins.

'If a gunlayer is not following his pointers properly, it won't work. If the person on the manoeuvring valve in the engineroom is too slow, it won't work. If a look-out is day-dreaming, it won't work. I saw a destroyer blown to pieces because someone neglected to set the depth charges to safe... '

I couldn't seem to get conviction into my voice. It sounded flat.

'... and if it doesn't work, if we lose, we may be killed. We are dependent on each other for our lives. You are going to get tired of hearing me say these things because I'll keep on saying them over and over again, every chance I get. Months and possibly even years may pass, and I'll still say them. Then one day or night it will happen and it could all be over in ten minutes. And it will be too late then.

'Now I want to say something about the other navies you will get to know, the American and Japanese. The U.S. Navy is organised much like ours; it was greatly expanded when the war started, manned with hurriedly trained volunteers and it had to learn by experience. They have learned and they are winning. You can forget every fifth-rate Hollywood film you ever saw, these are *real* Americans. Flesh and blood, and guts! I can tell you about the guts...

'Well, I won't do that now. But if we can hold our own with them, we may be proud.'

'The Japanese Navy is an élite, professional force which was at its peak when the war began. But it is unable to make good its losses and that is the critical factor; they are going down while we are going up. But never underestimate what's left; they simply will not recognise defeat and they fight like hell... '

There was no lack of conviction about that.

'... And I wish you all a happy commission and good luck. That's all I have to say, except that unless the first lieutenant has any other plans, I think we'd better get ashore while the going's good, because we have a lot of work to do.'

George nodded his head and school was out.

'What time will you be bringing your wife on board, sir?' he asked as we walked off. The next event was the wardroom commissioning party.

'We'll aim for six-thirty, but allow us some leeway for traffic. Or laddered stockings. You are getting the dockyard to shift that crane, aren't you? You won't have room for the

230

cars, otherwise.' I was fussing. George set his lips in disapproval and mumbled. It wasn't even my party.

I went ashore and hailed a taxi at the dockyard gates. Home was now a flat on the north side of the city, across the Harbour Bridge. It was too small, but cheerful and served well enough as a transit camp. I shut my ears to the taxi driver's matey, monotonous flow of filth and sat back, musing. It was pretty rum how it had all turned out. How things had changed.

It was a good party. I drove back to the ship with Beth on a still autumn night with just a hint of crispness in the air. My ship gleamed under coloured lights and bright signal flags festooned the quarterdeck, beneath the new awning. It could have been a peacetime affair. George, the host, greeted us at the top of the gangway with:

'Beautiful night, sir, for a beautiful lady.'

'George, you are gallant,' said Beth. 'You mean the ship, of course.'

'I mean both of you. Let me take your wrap.'

They were both beautiful. I felt immense pride. She was like a flower, with her fair hair and glowing skin, contrasting with the blue silk of her dress.

The gunner got us a drink. Everybody stood there, looking at us. The party seemed to be suspended.

'Well, come on, what's the matter? George? Do we go home now?'

'I withheld a signal from you, sir,' said George airily and gave me a piece of paper. I had been promoted to Acting Commander. Somebody came forward with a cap with the gold oak leaves round the peak, a brand new brass hat. Beth kissed me and they started cheering at that and clapped. I couldn't speak. It was well meant, if a little out of place. Promotion is a personal matter. Of course I was pleased and went along with it, shaking all the hands I could reach, and the party started. This wardroom had a bit to learn.

We were talking to Doc Stevens, our young doctor and his fiancée, when I saw the flag, a blue signal flag with a white centre, amidst all the others tied like curtains between the

231

guard rail and the awning. In International Code, it was known as the Blue Peter. It was the flag we had wrapped Able Seaman Kirkwood in and lowered him down the bridge ladder, without his legs, to die, at First Savo. It was a shocking, galling thing, but *it* was not out of place. The more things changed, the more they stayed the same!

Beth was in high spirits, gossiping about the other guests all the way home. She had a sort of party afterglow. After we made love, with her hair spread on my chest, she murmured something about her gold-hatted, bouncing lover.

'Who, me? Your what?'

'It's a poem. I don't remember it all. It says you should wear the gold hat for your girl and...

'If you can bounce... bounce for her too,

Till she cry Gold-hatted, high bouncing lover,

I must have you!'

'It's terrible.'

Later, I said, 'What have you been reading?' She was asleep. It was just lovers' idle murmurings; and that it was only an 'acting' gold hat mattered even less.

CHAPTER SIXTEEN

The spirit of that party prospered in the ship and kept us going for months at sea, in the knockabout drudgery of escorting convoys and ferrying stores around the Pacific. Through wheeling days and nights, we sailed forever on long, monotonous journeys and at every stop the war had always moved on somewhere else. I grew peevish with the strain of battles never fought and laid no ghosts.

Then came the invasion of the Philippines. One soft, black night in October, 1944, MacArthur's Navy was piled up in a log-jam of ships five miles thick across the Surigao Strait, guarding the Sixth Army's transports lying in San Pedro Bay. We had put MacArthur ashore at Leyte on 20th, formed the block and waited for the Japanese.

Six battleships trundled to and fro. Forward of battle line, two score of cruisers and destroyers made up right and left flanks. Along the shallows and to seaward for fifty miles, lurked another two score MTBs. We'd come a long way since Guadal.

On the third night, they came; battleships, cruisers and destroyers, in two separate striking forces, steaming an hour apart. They were beaten already, outnumbered and doomed, but they had one thing still to do – to die for the Emperor. They had not the slightest chance of getting through but there was not the slightest doubt that they would try. It was their *Götterdämmerung*.

At 2235 on the last sticky night Captain MacManes, ComDesRon 24, turned us due south, for the umpteenth time. Unlike the others, our squadron patrolled north-south, hugging the western shore, for there just wasn't room in the narrows for another formation to move east-west.

'Lobo Two, this is Remus Two. Execute to follow... '

Round we went, *Hutchins, Bache, Daly*, another Australian *Arunta, Beale, Killen* and me.

'Lobo's a good name, don't you think, Pilot? Know what it means? It's Spanish for wolf-pack. Hence Remus, I suppose. Someone with a bit of imagination issuing call signs.'

Making cocktail party chatter was one way of pushing down the awful, leaden dread and it was better than snarling at them.

There were three Lobos; Captain Coward's DesRon 54, our own and Captain Smoot's DesRon 56. We were to make squadron torpedo attacks as they came up the strait, before battle line engaged. Everything was made to order; a head-on approach, close range high speed, darkness... I'd waited for it and I'd got it and now if Somebody up there was rather annoyed at my about-face, it was no more than I deserved.

A message came from the plot that we had picked up the MTBs on HF radio and they had made contact with the enemy. It was earlier than expected. I went down.

The voices were vehement and high, like pilots'.

'... Peter Tare one-three-one, closing echoes due north. Section One, closing.

'Enemy in sight! Destroyer, course 065, speed 18 at, ah, three miles. Oh, wow! There's two battleships astern of it. Going for the big ones!'

'By God, that's jaws-of-death stuff.' George bent his head over the radio speaker and his eyes shone with exitement. George, you're still a Boy Scout. You've done a lot of things, but you've never done this. You'll soon sing a different tune.

Peter Tare one-three-one missed. So did one-five-one, four-four-six, one-three-four, four-nine-zero... Thirteen separate

234

sections of them attacked but the enemy ships brushed them off like gnats and came on steadily.

George was desolate.

'It's par for the course,' I told him. 'You can't throw forty MTBs into a show like this and expect them to perform miracles, George. They've had no practice. It's probably the first time most of them have fired a torpedo in anger.'

'Well, it seems so. So, it's still up to us, sir.' His look changed to one of grave determination.

There was another turn. I went up to the bridge and down to the plot again. Coward's ships, the farthest south, reported that the enemy was creeping on to the outer edges of their radar screens.

On the bridge, Midshipman Doubleday, the understudy officer-of-the-watch, had the ship. He was new, just come to us from the cruiser *Shropshire*, our compatriot stationed on the right flank and I wasn't happy about him. He seemed a slow boy, not much use for anything but football. He had to learn, though, and I had to let him.

But he was coping surprisingly well tonight. I'd just seen him do a faultless turn, keeping dead in the wake of the next ahead.

'That's pretty good, Mid. Much better. I should think your next turn will be your last, because we'll probably go to action stations and carry straight on down for our attack. What's your station, by the way?'

'I'm officer-of-the-quarters aft, sir.'

He sounded so proud of that. We had to put him somewhere, but it was really a supernumerary position. We had good gun captains aft; and I didn't want an over-zealous young officer rattling them. I'd speak to George, see if we couldn't fit him in closer to the bridge, where he'd learn something.

'Hmmm. Well, what do you make of it all?'

'Oh, I wouldn't be anywhere else in the world, sir. And my people wanted me to be a *farmer*! They're all on the land.'

I sat down in my chair. Within the hour, the ghosts would

be laid or there could be new ones. It was too momentous to get the mind round.

The last turn was coming up. *Hutchins* gave the order and reversed course. The rest of us would follow in succession. It was simple and routine but it was necessary to be there, to see *Hutchins* loom out of the darkness in the expected place and one's own ship turn the right way, at the right time. Yes, here was *Hutchins*; the black blotch just under that low star, ten degrees on the bow.

But the midshipman had lost it. He was star-gazing on his own, out over the starboard beam, at nothing.

'Oh, Doubleday, what the hell are you doing? Has your girl friend turned up out there, or something? There's a ship coming straight towards you at 20 knots and for all you know, the bloody thing's going to hit you. Get – '

'Sir, there's something out there. Green 70.'

Yes, by Jove, there was; a small, black blob. Could be a Filipino fishing boat or –

'Yeoman, put the ten-inch on it.'

The ten-inch signal projector, a mini-searchlight, flashed on and wavered across the water.

'There! No, back... There! Hold it, now. Get two and four Bofors on to it and open fire. Flat out! Make to Remus Two: There is a floating mine on my starboard beam and directly in your path. Am exploding it with gunfire.'

We were lucky. Sometimes you could plug away at the damned things for hours without hitting a vital spot but it blew up with the second clip of Bofors. There was a flash and a nasty eruption of black and white water.

After that, my legs felt less rubbery. It was only a small thing, but it was satisfying to have brought it off effectively.

'Well, take back what I said, Mid. That was good work.'

The pinnacle of his career, at seventeen. He blushed.

I took a great breath of the soggy air. There would be time for one more visit to the plot, to see Captain Coward lead his ships off for the attack.

The first enemy striking force was trickling on to our own screen now. It looked like a family of bedraggled little bugs, crawling so slowly up from the bottom. Nearer, in between, was a cluster of five brighter, clearer blips; DesRon 24. George and I watched them intently and waited. Silence fell on all the radio circuits. The minutes dragged by and I began to fear that they would leave it too late.

Then up came Coward: 'Hello Round-up, this is Remus One. I am proceeding now.'

The voice of Admiral Wilkinson, in charge of the right flank, rasped:

'Roger. Go get 'em. Good luck.'

'Lobo One, this is Remus One. Hold on to your hats, boys, here we go. Mike speed 30. DesDiv 108, hold back until you get your proper bearing on me, which is... 120.'

Comets' tails began to show on the five echoes as they moved off, picking up speed: *Remey, Melvin, McGowan, McDermut* and a brand new *Monssen*. For all that, it was high drama, an unforgettable thing to see.

Just then a signalman came in with a message from Captain McManes in *Hutchins*. It read:

'Your vigilance and prompt action probably saved many lives tonight.'

'Oh. Good. Show that to Mr. Doubleday.'

Suddenly, the world was a better place.

'George,' I said. 'Action stations now, please.'

'Aye aye, sir.' He passed the word to the bridge.

We turned to the radar screen again for a last look at the speeding comets.

'And we're next,' he murmured. 'Nothing to stop us now. Is there anywhere you feel we may not be on top line? Any situation where we could be lacking?'

'Well, you would certainly have heard from me if there was,' I said. I searched his face for a long moment. Then other faces formed in my mind's eye: Jesse Coward, who had commanded the old *Sterrett* at Guadal. Ben Jones, somewhere out there now, with his own destroyer. Dead ones: Jonathon Darling, Treloar, Barney Forrester, Norman Scott... Commander Tomeshige Nagasawa of *Yudachi*. And the living again, inextricably mixed: Snaggle, Snowy Rhoades, McMorris and Bosco Wright... Halsey, just north of here at this very moment with his Third Fleet, scouring the ocean for still more enemy.

And now, here was George. All the threads drew together at this point. It's up to you now, George, I thought, it's your show now. 'Should mature, given the new horizons he needs.'

Call it 'tempered'; you will be tempered, but left clean and unscarred, because you have a certain chivalry. Like Cy Brubaker. You'll be all right, if you live; and that might begin to make sense of all those deaths, if anything ever could.

'We'll be all right, George,' I said. 'We'll be all right.'

AFTERWORD

WARSHIP LOSSES IN THE GUADALCANAL CAMPAIGN August 1942 to February 1943		
Type of Ship	American Losses	Japanese Losses
Battleships	–	2
Aircraft Carriers	2	1
Heavy Cruisers	5 (1 Australian)	2
Light Cruisers	2	2
Destroyers	15	12
	24	19

The forty-three wrecks are strewn through the clear black depths like stars in the Milky Way... an undersea Pompeii. Of the 15,000 skeletons in and around them, some would be forever frozen in a last act of closing a breech or tending a steam gauge, while others may be free to stir with the vagrant tide, to gesture and to nod unknowing at friend and enemy alike, in stately, silent dumb-show. To the Japanese particularly, with their private and mystical taboos, to disturb them would be a desecration and, in any case, the waters of The Slot are too deep for salvage or photography. The ships are not likely to be seen again.

On the land, Henderson Field remains a jungle clearing as it always was; that does not change. But they dropped the name, cleared a huge bomb dump at one end and converted it into the civil airport. The strip is longer now and slickly sealed. But for many years a blackened Liberator shell lay in the rank grass and strange, clinging lichen that grows there, and fragments of crashed aircraft may, even now, be found. On Beach Red, the ribs of the wrecked landing craft are still visible at low tide.

Otherwise, there is not much to say about the place. When the Americans and the Japanese went away, the British came back and limply saw out two-year postings under the sulphurous sun of this outlandish place. No doubt the islanders themselves, like old Kaspar, hand down some ancestral legend – *"But what good came of it at last?" quoth little Peterkin. "Why, that I cannot tell," said he, "but 'twas a famous victory."* – telling of the mad clash that had seized them, of great battles that raged around their shores and of the ships that lie wrecked at the bottom of the sea.

The years of peace passed and in 1978 the Solomon Islands became independent. The event was reported in the press under the dateline 'Honiara', the new capital built on Point Cruz. The Duke of Gloucester represented the Queen and there were American, Australian and New Zealand warships present, some under captains not yet born in 1942. The newspapers filled sparse copy with accounts of small absurdities, such as the closing of the bars for the ceremony and a public wrangle over the proper time to haul down the flag. The war was little mentioned.

Then in 1982, one hundred veterans from all the nations involved, mostly Americans, returned to observe the 40th anniversary, with low-key ceremony and baffling reflection. *Time* magazine reported that they laid a wreath at sea for the sailors and the old artillerymen, marines and pilots poked about the relics on shore in sombre mood.

They were greeted by Sir Jacob Vouza... the Sergeant Vouza of this story. According to *Time*, Sir Jacob was frail and spoke with difficulty, but he had no need to repeat a message he had sent to the marines two decades before, on the 20th anniversary:

> '...*Me old man now and me no look good no more. But me never forget.'*